THE ANGEL OF BISHOPSGATE

BOOK ONE IN THE DARKER CITIES TRILOGY

ELOISE REUBEN

For my sister,
who read this thing a thousand times.

ABOUT THE AUTHOR

A lover of old cities, history and travelling, Eloise is an Australian living in the United States with her husband and young daughter. She listens to (probably too many) true-crime podcasts, loves cooking, old maps and endless writing snacks.

Join Eloise's mailing list at eloisereuben.com

www.eloisereuben.com

CHAPTER 1

LONDON. MIDNIGHT - NOVEMBER 20TH 1848

The East End stench caught on Arthur's clothes. In a gentleman's frock coat and shiny black shoes, he stood broad and square as a working man. He was waiting, an unsettled rage dancing in his pale blue eyes.

From the abattoir, a sour wind blew hard as moonlight singed the canal waters with ripples of gold and silver. He rolled his large knuckles as a barge moved out of the fog.

The strapping man on board wound the anchor rope to the side, his dark skin glistening in the light rain.

"A man'll lose his wits in this bleedin' stink, Castor." Arthur's gruff cockney accent rolled out, all the more notable in his elegant and groomed attire. "Hurry about it."

Castor spoke politely, though his dress too did not match that of a lighterman. "The Wapping lads were circling. I had to wait and you needed to see this for yourself."

Arthur crouched by the canal edge, scratching his sandy sideburns and goatee, as Castor hoisted his athletic frame across the barge, dragging a long wooden crate from beneath a tarp.

"He came with the shipment from Dublin. She sent him back to us..." Castor continued.

"Who came back?"

"*He* did." He nodded towards the crate.

"Open it then. Go on, man."

Leaning down, Castor cracked the lid and slid it to the side. A bloated corpse stared back at them with greying flesh, flushed with purples and blues. It was the face of a man distorted with moisture, his eyes bulging, ogling them in horror. The foul air blew up at them in a putrid cloud so that Castor took a step back for air, as Arthur leaned towards it.

"Who is it?" Arthur's voice lowered an octave.

"It's Smithfield. You know, with the eye."

"A man who was all blow and no hard. The liquor? The tea?"

"She filled the bottles with piss. And the tea was gone. Who knows where that ended up."

Arthur locked his jaw, staring down at the man in the box with slitted eyes. "She's out of her bloody mind."

"She's gone too far, Artie. We have to respond now." Castor spoke with confidence and familiarity as Arthur stood back, considering his response.

"This is about her bloody cut."

"She wants more," Castor agreed. "She'll always want more."

"She thinks she deserves more is the thick of it, and she don't. If I want the route to go north of her, then it goes north. If I want to use another dock, then I use another dock." Arthur turned his attention to the bloated corpse, a sizeable letter A scorched into the man's forearm, still distinguishable in the decaying flesh. "And he let them do this?" He looked down in disgust. "He bloody begged me for a chance. Let me go, sir, I'll take care of it, sir," he mocked. "And he right fucked it up didn't he?" Arthur lifted his leg and stomped his foot against the dead man's face, ramming the heel of his boot into the skull again and again, until the cracking sound turned to mush and his anger exhausted. Extracting his leg from the pulpy mess, he shook it over the canal waters. Passing Castor his top hat as he propped his foot on the barge, he leant with his handkerchief to clean his boot.

"More promises than he had good bleedin' eyes. That shoulda been the warning right there. What a waste. Get rid of him." He held out the dirty handkerchief to Castor in exchange for his hat and straightened his coat as he leapt back off the barge onto the bank. "I want to see Moses first thing, you hear?"

"I'll get him." Castor nodded. "What are we going to do?"

Arthur strode back to his carriage. "We'll take care of it. Like we always do."

essie had waited all day for a tin of treacle. As merchants pulled in their display trolleys for the evening and workers hurried home for tea, she huddled outside Page and Son's grocers, stomping her feet against the slush on her boots. Bracing against the icy wind, winter's light faded over the Thames, but still she waited.

At home a stick of butter and a cup of milk lay out on the table, the scent of ground ginger hung in the air and the stove grew cold and unattended. Her plans that morning had been thwarted only when she scraped the bottom of the treacle tin. Four days earlier she'd run out of butter, and not a week ago she'd scrounged together a handful of pennies for yet another pint of milk. Having stocked up on one thing, she'd run low on the others. It was the way of it, always striving and never getting ahead.

It was late into November when merchants carefully eyed their unpaid accounts and guarded their generosity. But Tessie wasn't one to wallow. It had been a long day keeping strategically close to Mr Page's window so he did not miss a moment of her lonely frame standing in the cold.

He was a softer old man with watery brown eyes and he had done well to turn her away. She was almost proud of him for doing so, but she was sure his heart would get the better of him. As the bells of St. Mary Le Bow chimed six o'clock, he wrapped his grandpa knuckles on the window and called her inside.

"Alright, love, patience is a virtue," he said, pushing his glasses up his nose.

"Thank yer, sir, though I suspect I'm guilty of necessity and being stubborn, more than patience," she said, an Irish accent lilting through a small but distinctive gap in her front teeth as she dusted rain from her shawl.

Mr Page chuckled as he settled again behind the counter. "Nonetheless, I've had a few customers pay their accounts so I can afford you a couple of things on tick. What do you need, love?"

"Treacle and flour, Mr Page, thank yer." Tessie stood on her tippy toes to scan the shelves.

"Still baking those ginger cakes I see."

"They're sensible cakes, Mr Page. If yer can't have an iced bun or apple tart, yer want a piece of ginger cake and a cup of tea. That's what I say. I'll bring yer one by tomorrow, shall I?" Mr Page plonked a tin of treacle on the counter and Tessie counted out five pennies. "I can put this towards our account."

"You still owe a shilling," he said at the meagre offering. "Have you eaten today?"

"Some oatcakes this morning, sir."

Mr Page took a deep breath as he heaved the sack of flour onto the counter too. "Keep it then, and take some bread from the basket over there."

"Thank yer, sir." Tessie obliged and wrapped some staling slices in paper.

"But you must be paid out by the thirtieth," he reiterated

without malice. "And don't be telling your friends, or more importantly my son, I'm too generous now."

"We'll be paid up. Finn will be in this week. Bless yer too though." Sweeping her auburn curls off her face, she signed the register, and balancing the flour and treacle on her hip, she bid her farewell and moved back into the icy evening streets.

Outside, the city silhouetted against the pale carpet of evening cloud and the rattle of carriages. The smell of fish and manure swelled in the air as vendors emptied wash buckets into the street. Her features flushed with effort and she weaved into the dark warren of alleys and tenements of the Old Nichol slums.

Finn would be home and she was keen to see him and rest a little before starting her evening chores and baking preparation. What a waste of a day, she thought, her body weary and ready to huddle at home by their humble fire.

As she struggled to hold her shawl around her with the flour on her hip, and her mind whirred ahead to what she had to do at home, she ploughed into a figure who suddenly blocked her path. The sack of flour dropped heavily and the treacle tin cracked against the stones as another man shoved her backwards. Her cheek struck the alley wall with a thudding graze and she let out a cry as she stumbled.

"What the hell..." Her heart sank as the treacle tin oozed its dark molasses across the cobbles. *Not the bloody treacle!* "You owe me half a shilling. The both of yer!" she said, holding her cheek and looking up at the men. She recognised one of them, his ginger beard highlighted in the shadow. "God curse yer Billy Brittle. What are yer playing at?"

His expression showed it was not an accidental collision and leaning down close to her ear he said, "The Angel is looking for you." Tessie swatted him away.

He chuckled lightly. "He's looking for you," he repeated in

a sing-song tone. "The Angel has a job for you, Tessie O'Shea." They backed out of the alley as she scrambled to her knees trying to save as much treacle as she could from the stones.

"I'll be telling yer ma!" she called after them, her cold hands fumbling to close the lid and covered in a sticky mess.

The Angel of Bishopsgate was a name that shot fear down the spine of all who heard it. She'd never seen the man himself and knew of no one who had. She didn't even know if he were real, though it hardly mattered. Throughout the Old Nichol and all the East End, stories of the Angel accompanied every body fished from the Thames, every death and scandal or tale of woe. Named for the length of his reach and influence, the Angel was said to see all. His men were everywhere, watching. She saw them daily, wearing his black leather cuff on their wrists, displaying it with pride and brandishing its power. It gave them sanction for all manner of evils.

She and Finn had always kept their heads down, drawing no attention to themselves and crossing no one. Though not everyone was so fortunate. She'd seen those branded with the Angel's mark — a small letter A in a circle, seared on their wrist or their neck or shoulder, branded like livestock with a scorching hot branding iron. A stain they'd never rid themselves of without peeling their own skin from their bodies. They were owned men or women from that moment on. Passed a point of no returned. A mark reserved for those so far gone they'd never get out. They owed too much money, allowed themselves to sink too low and had surrendered any power of their own. Every dollar they earned, every move they made, they made on the Angel's behalf. She'd seen them, and they couldn't be helped.

Struggling across the Old Nichol's courtyard and up the

stairs to her apartment, Tessie slammed the door behind her, breathless and brooding.

"There yer are!" A warm Irish voice called from the shadows. Finn propped himself up on the bed, the scar above his left eye giving him a menacing scowl as his dark hair hung low at his brow. He was fierce looking, with a shine to his eyes and affection in his voice.

"What's happened to yer?" He moved toward her but she shooed him away, dumping her flour on the table and moving to the pail of water to wash herself.

"Billy Brittle and his mate have only gone and knocked me over in the alley. I've lost half the treacle and I'm covered in the stuff." She took a damp cloth to wipe her skirts.

"He did what now?"

"Trying to make a name for himself in the Nichol I suppose. God only knows."

"Not by knocking over women he's not." Finn grabbed his boots but Tessie pressed her hands on his shoulders to stop him.

"He said something to me." She turned serious, widening her eyes at the prospect of speaking the warning out loud. "He said the Angel was looking for me."

"The Angel of Bishopsgate? What do yer mean?" Finn rubbed the scar above his eye.

"Yeah." She put her hands on her hips. "Why would he be saying that then?" She kept her voice light though a sinking feeling tugged at her insides. Finn moved to the window, searching the courtyard below for any sign of Billy.

"To upset yer and be the big man about town, that's why. Someone needs to knock it on the head right quick."

Tessie nodded, trying shake the feeling of dread, though a sour aftertaste lingered.

"Well," she sighed, still wiping sticky scuffs across her skirts. "I ain't got time to worry about it."

Finn took the washrag from her and wiped her brow before wrapping his arms around her from behind and nestling his face into her neck. She closed her eyes briefly, appreciating the warm pause, before moving her attention to the rickety wood stove in front of her.

They lived in a single room with a bed and a small kitchen table. The shelves were lined with old treacle tins Tessie now used for storage of other bits and pieces, and two cake trays she used for the ginger cakes every evening. She'd mix the batter before bed and then, rising early, slide them over the stove so they were warm and fresh for the morning.

It was a humble life, laced with dreams and imaginings of one day having something more. The New World was out there, a buzz on the periphery, promising a life beyond their everyday means. America. They spoke of it like a bedtime story, cocooned in the half-light before sleep. Even if they didn't half believe it was possible, on nights they were weary, beaten down and tired, it wove hope into their bones and gave light to the gloom of the Old Nichol slums.

"Are we out of coal?" she asked, and Finn lifted his head to check.

"Aye, I just used the last of it."

Tessie let out a groan. "I tell yer, this day is going from shite to shitter. After all that I won't even have enough to cook in the morning." Finn let go of her and picked up his boots again.

"I'll head over to the Simms for me Saturday wages and get some coal on the way home."

"From where? Everything is closing."

"The Murphy's will swap me. I'll find somewhere."

"Well just wait a while will yer? Sit with me while I get warm. I've been stood frozen to death the whole day out."

Finn stoked the fire, pushing around what was left of the coal. "Flashing those blue eyes at poor old Mr Page I gather."

"He's been good to us," she sighed. "He let me take some bread. Have yer eaten?" She nodded to the small paper parcel on the table.

"Aye. I got something on tick at the Byrds. Those jellied eels will be the death of me." He held his stomach and feigned sickness.

"Yer were home early?"

"Aye. No dock work today. Potter paid me a threepence to muck out the stables."

She watched his shoulders round as he reached across the table for the bread and it sent a burst of warmth through her chest. How she cherished those shoulders and the man attached to them.

They had not spent a day apart since crossing paths all those years ago. Fresh off the boat from Dublin, and flinging herself into whatever life held, they collided on the streets of Liverpool. They were barely fifteen then and had battled the last eight years together with good times, and worse times.

They had found each other in a similar state, adrift and abandoned, running and roaming because it was the only thing to do. Finn spoke of a brother, and parents long since gone, while she had fled a mother she could barely bring herself to speak of.

At her wrist, she wore the twisted band Finn had made her last Christmas, spun of woven leather scraps, laced together with odd beads and metal bands. Different colours platted over each other in deep rusts and blacks, rough and smooth in a writhing loop. Finn wore another, a simpler version of her own.

Finn handed her the bread and she took a rough bite as if to chew it down without tasting it. "This is rock hard. If only we had an onion for broth," she said listlessly.

"Or a big slab of cheese from the Fosters. We'll go back

there again when we have the dosh. And their sausage. Now yer got me thinking my belly is gonna grumble."

She scoffed down another bite, so dry she could barely swallow it. "Yer will be out there with them kids pressing your face to the windows like a right tosser." She held her hands up to mock him as if pressing herself against the glass.

"Alright woman." He jumped up from his chair. "Now I gotta go if I'm to be tortured."

He threw on his coat and tossed a kiss roughly on her forehead.

"Watch the alleys."

"It's Billy who best be watching. I'm looking for him now."

While Finn was gone, Tessie finished her bread, brooding over the encounter in the alley and the half tin of treacle she had lost. Setting down her wooden mixing bowl, she measured the flour and ginger, and in a small saucepan melted the butter and a measure of treacle over the stove. The spicy sweet aroma radiated through their room, like an added layer of warmth and comfort. It was a delicious torture they'd grown to endure - that while their bellies ached for something more than stale bread or oatcakes, every slice of ginger cake they took for themselves, was a few pennies less in tomorrow's takings.

As she whisked the batter, the door opened. Expecting to see Finn, instead there stood a man with dark eyes and a ragged maroon coat that hung to his boots, almost scraping the floor.

Tessie froze, cradling the mixing bowl in one arm and the wooden spoon in the other. Stepping into the room without invitation, he sat down at the table. Her breath caught in her throat as danger raged through her body. His eyes moved about the room, drinking it all in. He was savouring the moment. She thought to run past him but her legs stuck to the spot.

"You can call me Moses," he said, settling into his chair.

"What the hell do yer want?"

"Listen carefully." He spoke in a whistled tone that sent needles down her spine. "I'll only say it once." Reaching into his oversized coat, he pulled out a knife and rested it on the table, then leaned over as if calling her in close. She didn't move.

"What is it yer want? Who are yer?"

But Moses wouldn't be rushed. Leaning back again, he rubbed his stubbled chin. "The Angel has a job for you." He pulled a folded envelope from his back pocket and placed it on the table beside the knife. "You'll deliver this to a man tomorrow at midnight. You will bring back a pendant. A necklace, like."

"I'll do no such thing."

"I won't repeat it," he said, a half-smile lingering.

"I don't understand what is going on. Why are yer here? Why have yer come to me?"

The man slowly rose from his seat, and grabbing her jaw, jabbed his thumb into her mouth and the small gap in her teeth. Tessie struggled, but he gripped her close. She could smell his breath as he whispered instructions in her ear, then pushing her back, he pulled something else from his pocket, and like an afterthought, tossed it into her cake batter.

"Why? Why is this happening?"

"Let's just say..." He paused as if relishing the words. "Your mother owes a debt." With that, he clicked his tongue loudly, and walked from the room, his long maroon coat whipping against the door.

His footsteps grew faint as he descended the stairs and Tessie dared to look down at her mixing bowl. It was a human ear, grotesque and bloody, sliced with jagged edges.

Dropping the bowl to her lap, she stumbled back on the nearest chair. Her head reeled and her heart raced. It was all too surreal. What did he mean her mother owed a debt? Tessie hung her head in her hands and slumped over the mixing bowl. She hadn't seen her mother since Dublin. No. It could not be true.

WHEN FINN RETURNED, Tessie sat ghostly pale on the edge of the bed. Without a word, she lifted the bowl for him to see.

"They were here?" he asked, anger rumbling in his voice.

"He stood right there in front of me." She pointed to the spot.

"Well whose ear is it?"

Tessie couldn't help but laugh as he stared down at it the bowl and jiggled it.

"I don't bloody know." She threw a rag at him, the sick feeling settling in again like a shroud. "Is this real?" she asked. "I don't understand what's happening."

The envelope rested untouched on the table and Finn scooped it up. It was crisp and clean, sealed with a fancy letter "A" pressed into black wax. That was his mark. That was it.

"It looks real, don't it?" she said, ominously. "That's his mark."

"I don't know."

"It is. Black wax and a letter A. Yer know it is."

"It could be a forgery," Finn insisted. "It could be anything."

"Who is going to forge the Angel's hand? Who would dare?"

"I don't know, Tess. I don't know."

"I want to rip that bloody thing up!" Tessie stepped forward and snatched it, staring down at it before tossing it back on the table. "It's ridiculous..." Her voice faded and her body prickling all over. What could she do? Refuse? Test their resolve? No. She took a deep breath, letting it shudder and ricochet through her belly. It was a simple errand. That was it. A delivery. She could do that, surely, and it would all be over.

"I can't afford to waste more batter," Tessie said, looking down at the ear in the bowl.

"Just scoop it out. No one will know."

Tessie shook her head and set the bowl on the table with a thud. The Angel had already cost her half a tin of treacle and now a bowl of batter.

She lifted her head. "He said my mother owed a debt."

"What does that mean?"

"I have no idea."

"Did your Ma have dealings with the Angel?"

"I was a kid when I left, but anything is possible with her. I should have known she'd be a black mark on me some day."

"Maybe it's just something he said to get to yer. To make yer nervous. To make your mind tick over with worry. That's how they work. It's how they control people."

Pacing, Tessie's mind raced. She had fought to escape her past for all these years. Could Finn be right? Was it just a game of control? So much time had past and she was here, with Finn, in their new life together. A life that was hard and dreary, but it was their's none-the-less.

Though she rarely talked of her mother, she was there, like a shadow she couldn't outrun. In everything she did, every waft of fresh ginger cake, every prayer to St. Brigid, and every flash of temper that flared. The memories dug deep in the pit of her stomach, stirring it up like the bottom of the ocean. Aileen Fisher had left her mark - a stain of which she would never be free.

She had heard stories, even here on the streets of London, of the woman across the Irish Sea called the Black Bonnet.

Though it was never quite clear if she were an associate or rival of the Angel, or simply another figure to weave into late night tales. Tessie knew her mother well. She was wild enough to be involved. Though even if this all fell on her, there was no connection between them. No one could place her as Aileen's daughter. She no longer went by the name Fisher but had taken Finn's surname for her own. She was Tessie O'Shea. Someone far removed from her mother and her past. Though none of her rationalising stopped Moses' parting comment ringing in her ears.

She thought of Billy Brittle's stupid face glaring down at her and wished she'd given him a piece of her mind. Her cheek throbbed now and it tightened as she moved her jaw. She would have a bruise by morning. Just great, she sighed.

Finn stood and, struggling to push open the rickety window frame, scooped the ear out of the cake batter and hurled it like a small catapult into the dark courtyard below. "There."

"Someone's gonna find that."

"Nye. The rats'll get it." He set the bowl on the table, now nothing more than innocent cake batter.

CHAPTER 3

The clattering of children on the stairs woke Tessie sharply from her sleep. After tossing and turning through the night she had knotted herself into a ball, somewhere in the early hours slipping into a restless slumber. By the window, Finn had already fetched water from the courtyard and was splashing his face and drying off.

"Yer didn't wake me," she said, sitting with sudden alertness. He slipped his hand beneath the covers and rubbed her feet.

"I wanted yer to sleep. We've got time."

"I didn't get the cakes in," she chided herself, rubbing her eyes wearily.

"I put them in for yer. Don't worry."

Tessie moved to the table where Finn had set them to cool. "Look at yer. Thank yer," she teased and rested her chin on his shoulder.

Below them in the courtyard, families were up and busy with their daily routines and preparations. The Joyces mended their sacks along the front stoop and the Campbells loaded wares into their wagon, readying for market. It was a picture of perfect normality in the Old Nichol, though, as she joined Finn at the window spying to see if the privy was free, last night's events tumbled back in a black tangle. Were they being watched even now? Was someone spying up at them from the darker corners and alleys? Her body ached with dread, and in every breath she took, she felt it. Something terrible was going to happen.

The white envelope rested on the mantle, the perfect "A" imprint in the wax glaring at them from all vantage points. She couldn't bear to see it and slid it behind an old dusty treacle tin. The delivery wasn't until tonight and in the meantime they both had things to do. They needed money to pay Mr Page's grocer account, and Black Monday would soon see Mr Lawson climbing the stairs in their tenement for the next month in rent. For once, she was grateful for a busy day of distractions.

Dressing quickly, she gently broke her cakes into squares before packing them into the baskets. When Finn returned she had a more organised air about her. "I thought to walk with yer to the docks," she said as if it were any other morning.

"Are yer sure?" He rubbed the scar on his forehead. "I can walk the markets with yer."

"Yer need to work today, yer know that. Please," she strained. "Let's just get on with it."

Finn took a reluctant breath as Tessie bit at her lip, covering the small gap in her teeth. She knew he was watching the tension brewing inside her and had no wish to stir it.

"I'll not quarrel with yer." His warm eyes set on hers and he passed her one of her baskets. "Come on with yer then."

Turning their backs on the envelope on the mantle, Tessie instinctively snatched up a figurine of St. Brigid hanging from a loop of wool and dropped it into her skirts.

Out in the courtyard, the rain from the previous night had given pause and the cobblestones were coated in a silky layer of mud. The usual activity was heightened with urgency as families readied for the half mile journey to Spitalfields. Those with food and goods were usually gone with the first grey light to set up their stalls with fruit and vegetables, cakes and bread. It was the pieceworkers, squeezing in their last stitch and hammer for another penny, who lingered in a panic making voices harsh with hurry and hunger.

"Did yer know the Rowleys have been smoking their kippers in the privy?" Finn eyed them across the courtyard.

"Aye, did you not?"

"I bought a good five of them kippers last week," he said. "No more, mind yer."

Barrelling towards them was a small boy with a huge cabbage, barely able to hold it in his arms. "That's quite a cabbage, Teddie Baker." She found some cheer as he squeezed past them.

"Yes, mam," he gleamed. "It fell off the market truck."

"Let him through, let him through," Finn called after him with a chuckle as they stepped out of the Old Nichol.

As they passed through Spitalfields Market, they had no time to linger, though Tessie called out through the mass of candle makers and tailors, soap makers, coopers, carpenters and smiths, all bartering for the best price with cranky buyers and shrewd homemakers. Tessie joined the call of sellers with trays of walnuts, flowers and boiled cockles, and their bellies stirred with the smell of cinnamon cakes, iced buns and apple tarts as they threaded through the crowd, onward to the docks.

"Get yer ginger cake, still warm, fresh from the oven," she called, flashing a smile at the vendors and handing out paper cones filled with the rich cake, slipping the pennies into her skirt pocket. Despite her smile, the urge to check over her shoulder plagued her every move. Were they here watching her now?

Every customer who approached she expected would make another comment to her about the Angel or whisper beneath their breath about the bruise on her cheek, but no one said anything, except Mrs Spicer who hushed, "Are you right, love?" as she bought a paper cone filled to the brim with cake. Tessie gave an emphatic laugh and said she had tripped in the alley and the portly woman had squeezed her arm as she walked away. They weren't asking because they assumed it was Finn, and though it pained her for them to think that of him, she was powerless to correct it.

She kept an eye out for Billy Brittle and the man called Moses, though she had no inkling of what she might do if she saw them, and knew it would probably make matters worse if she did anything except what she'd been told. So she kept her eyes bright and her smile warm as she called out to the East End. "Mr Brown, yer look famished. Don't be shy now!"

If she was being watched she wanted them to know, Tessie O'Shea was not afraid, though she was all the more convincing herself. "Mrs Cooper, take a few pieces for the little ones! Come on now, Paddy Trader, I know that look of hunger in your eyes, though it's not cake yer want," she teased. "Yer are sweet on a girl? Take her some cake, Paddy!"

"You haven't stopped this morning, Tessie," Mr Sykes called across the way.

"I have me a lot of cakes to sell, Mr Sykes. Yer want to take some off me hands?" She smiled back, straining on tippy toes to see him bent over the table he was sanding.

"She makes a good cake, does our Tess." Finn grinned, striding ahead. "Don't be turning her down now."

"Aye. I'll take two but you best move on. We'll be spending all our wages if you keep that up."

"Oh me cakes are good, Mr Sykes, but they're not worth starving the rest of the week for."

Hurrying to catch up to Finn, they found a lull in pedestrian traffic and a lone pie-seller wheeling his cart. They paid five pence each for a warm meat pastie with crisp and buttery pastry. It was more extravagant than their usual oatcake or porridge, but when Finn suggested it, she knew it was a gesture of reassurance. Their stride slowed as they ate, savouring the moment. Would this all be resolved by morning?

As the tall gates of the West India Docks came into view, they could hear the fray of men gathered at its entrance. Tessie knew she'd slowed him down and he was later than usual. He would have to fight his way to the front now to better his chances of being selected, and if he was overlooked he would wander the market stalls offering his services as a labourer or a stable hand. Though those jobs never paid as well, and he preferred to be near the water, straining with a team of men to get the job done. Tessie thought he liked its all-consuming nature. It was fast-paced with no time for over-thinking or lamenting one's life. And something about the excitement of travel and movement kept him returning.

When he had first taken dock work his back had bled through his shirt and she had sat up nights mending the worn fabric across his shoulders. Now she could feel the leathery surface on his back, worn from the heavy hessian sacks of sugar and flour. He was a seasoned worker and many of the foremen recognised him. With any luck, they would show him favour today.

Tessie watched his broad shoulders pushing their way to the front of the crowd. Something in her chest begged her to stay — she wanted to linger and make sure he faired well — but she could not. She turned to the river, inhaling its briny stink as it lapped at the docks. Brown and soupy, heavy with refuse, a dirty foam laced its edges. It was not a pretty river, but it was the pulse of the city. She would follow its winding curve along Lower Thames Street.

She reached Southwark Bridge and cut through Cheapside, selling the rest of her cakes and walking home with the pennies jingling in her skirt. It was late afternoon when she made it home and the light was fading fast. She was exhausted. Laying on the bed she stared across the room at the letter that held her fate. *What did it say?* she wondered. Who was the man she was supposed to meet? Would she be in danger, or would it be a simple exchange? She fell asleep on the covers, rolling over scenarios over in her head.

WHEN FINN PUSHED OPEN the door, she startled awake, sitting up with her hair in disarray. "There's my shining light of London," he said.

"Leave it out." She managed a weary smile and seeing the fire was barely holding its flame, she rose quickly and added more coal. "Are yer later than usual?" she asked, wrapping her shawl about her and sitting at the table.

"Aye, I stayed back for a few extra."

Tessie placed her day's takings on the table thinking of the rent. "Will we have enough?" Finn spilled out his coins too and counted.

"How much for the grocer?"

"A shilling and a half."

"Two shilling short. I'll have to work tomorrow and Saturday to see us over, but they'll not see us in the dosshouse just yet," he assured, stashing the collection in a small space in the wall beside the bed. Tessie returned to the bed, flopping down as the feeling of dread tingled in her belly. Sleep had helped the hours at least, but she stared at

Finn and let out a sigh. They could see it hanging in the air between them, the angst neither of them wished to speak out loud. The time was coming fast.

"Did yer eat?" Finn asked. She shook her head and rolled onto her side, twisting her leather band at her wrist, tugging it so it grazed warmly against her skin.

"I'm not sure I can stomach it," she said, though Finn stepped forward and put a bruised apple in her hand. She held it up against the shadowed light and took a listless bite.

"Go on," he coaxed, fussing about the fire and taking off his coat. "You'll be back here tonight and this will be over."

She had no wish to argue with his sentiment though the 'what ifs' swirled incessantly. When she didn't get up from the bed, Finn joined her and wrapped himself around her in a solemn ritual of waiting. What else was there to do, but listen to the night around them and wait for the chime of each hour to stir the butterflies.

Finally, it was time to go. Tessie kissed Finn goodbye and rose from the bed in the quiet, padding across the room.

CHAPTER 4

Finn paced the edges of their small room. He would have traded places with her in a heartbeat if she'd let him. Instead, he waited. It went against everything he expected of himself and the worst of images flooded through him. He wanted to protect her. Always. What was she walking into? What would they do to her?

Around the room, her belongings were strewn about. Her emptied cake baskets full of stale crumbs - her treacle tins and stockings, a drying petticoat and a burgundy shawl - one he had given her for a birthday kept only for special occasions. Things that smelled of her, things worn with her touch. In all their years together, he had wanted to give her more. To provide a life that let them flourish and rise above the struggle of the Old Nichol. And yet here they still were.

They had settled here by accident, glad to be anywhere but Dublin, and he'd slogged each day of the last eight years in its work yards and grime. Always striving. Always. Breaking his back and busting his knuckles, fighting back the niggling feeling that a day would come when he couldn't hold on any longer. A day when Tessie too might disappear.

At ten years old his mother had taken her last breath in the street, tossed from their boarding house for fear of spreading her infection. He and his younger brother, Tadhg, only six, had been left to forage alone. They'd survived a year with Finn making sure Tadhg had food in his belly, that he was warm enough, that he was safe. He fought for that little boy as everything he had left in the world. Until Dublin took him too, in a moment of carelessness, of reckless boyish abandon. He carried the weight of it with him always and had barely spoken the details to anyone, even Tessie, only sharing shreds of the truth of it - that he had lost him. That he was gone.

It seemed Dublin wouldn't rest until it had stripped him of everyone and everything he cared for. Until he'd found Tessie and they'd found their way to the Nichol. It only amplified his love for her.

They should have left this place already. If he'd ever been able to get the money together they would have been long gone. It was what they had dreamed about on so many nights, Tessie's head on his chest and his hands tangled in her honey-auburn hair. He told her stories of New York, of Boston, of how their lives would be out on the gold rushes. Stories he'd heard from immigrants or paperboys screaming out the headlines. But he wanted more than stories. He wanted it all to be true.

His shoulders ached and burned from his day lugging crates on the barges, and he felt them straining as he moved their bed to the side and pulled out their stash of rent money. Laying it out on the table he willed there to be more. If only they had enough to run now!

Counting it out in small, meagre piles, the numbers had not changed. Two shilling short for rent, and a full six pound shy of two steerage tickets to the New World.

Finn ran his large hand over the cracks and crevices

inside the wall at the chance a stray coin or two had become lodged. It hadn't, and he packed away the rest of it, a heavy weight burning in this chest.

Whatever happened tonight, they wanted to be the authors of their own lives, not weighed down by class or history or where they had come from. Especially not by the Angel. He wanted to give that to her, for all that she had given him. They just needed to survive. He had to keep her safe.

CHAPTER 5

The bells of St. Mary Le Bow peeled through the Old Nichol, sounding midnight and drowning out the rain. Tessie's heart thudded with every toll as she slipped through the rookery and the rain flushed against the cobblestones of Bethnal Green Road. Despite the late hour, strangers bundled beneath the tenements for shelter and the city's malodour hovered in a damp low-hanging canopy. Her hair darkening in the downpour, she pulled her shawl around her like a cloak, checking behind her in the darkness. She was late, yet couldn't bring herself to run.

Nearing a doorway, Tessie recited the instructions she'd been given. It was marked as described with a white handkerchief waving in the wind. A faint light emanated from beneath the shutters but gave no hint at what waited for her inside. Her instructions were clear. *Deliver the message. Get the necklace.* She hesitated, stilling her breath. Pushing the handle, she went inside.

By a low burning fire, a gentleman turned toward her in a navy frock coat, wringing a top hat in his hands. He was young and pleasant-looking with neat blond hair and intense brown eyes. When he made no move towards her, Tessie stepped closer, letting her water-logged shawl fall away to her shoulders.

"Is it yer I'm here to see?" she asked, aware the purple bruise across her cheek gave her a dramatic appearance.

"Yes." His voice was hushed, as if afraid to break the silence. He didn't belong in this part of town. "Who are you?" There was something unreadable in his expression.

"Our names don't matter. We'll not likely see each other again."

"Perhaps. Though, the future is something I've learned not to g-guess at," he said, with a small stutter that didn't diminish his charm. "It is cold out. Come into the f-fire." Tessie hesitated, reluctant to get too close.

"We have no need of hurrying," he said. "Indeed, you are free to come warm yourself." She dared to step closer, as he motioned at the seat beside him, though she instead stood to the fire, breathless and bold. Tessie's earnest repose held steady as they took a moment to assess each other. He was a few years older than she, though worlds apart in stature. Where Tessie may have usually averted her eyes, she held them now with fearful and serious contemplation.

"Are you..." He seemed to be fishing for words.

"I just want to get this over, sir," she said. Propping her muddy boot on the chair in front of him. She lifted her frayed petticoats, causing him to stiffen and avert his eyes.

"What are you d-doing?"

Tessie paused a moment before rolling her stocking to her ankle. He seemed more nervous than she.

Plucking the Angel's small envelope from her ankle, she held her hand towards him. "I have a message for yer."

"A message?" he whispered, and a flash of panic rippled over his cool expression. He picked it from her fingers and turned his back as he read. His shoulders heaved and stretched. Whatever it said, it was not good news and she watched as he tossed it into the flames.

"Will he never stop!" He cursed under his breath, talking only to himself. He wrestled with something inside him before turning to Tessie and regaining a confident repose.

"Is this some kind of trick?" he asked, his eyes brooding on her.

"A trick?"

"Where did he find you? Where has he pulled you from?"

"I don't know what yer mean."

"What is your name?" He demanded it now, all politeness called away.

"Tessie O'Shea," she said, confused and defiant.

"You're from where in Ireland? Dublin?"

"What difference does it make?"

"Tell me how it happens that you are running errands for the Angel of Bishopsgate?" He spoke with soft authority. A shudder of fear rumbled now in her spine, but she had to hold on. She wasn't finished yet.

"Is that not how he is known?" he persisted.

"I don't run errands for him."

"Well, then w-what is this?" Waving his fist at the note perishing in the fire, his face flushed in anger. "Tell me what he is to you!"

Tessie's mouth gaped open, her chest seized and tight. "I...I must get a pendant from yer. A locket. A...a necklace, that is what I was told."

His gaze froze on her as if searching her eyes for truthfulness. Finally, he gave in, bringing his hands to his brow and dismissing her.

"I need the pendant, sir!" She was urgent now. She could not let him leave. As he pulled on his gloves and moved to the door, Tessie lunged at him, blocking his way and tugging at his coat. He pushed her away and she fell to the floor in front of him.

"I don't know what kind of game this is," he said, straightening his coat. "But I will play no part. Tell him I made up my mind and he'll have to deal with it."

He has to deal with it? As if she could tell him that!

With that, the gentlemen ripped open the door, and setting his top hat in place, stepped out into the night. Tessie's skirts were splayed across the floor as she leaned back on her arms and watched him go. She wanted to chase him and pound his chest. How dare he leave her empty handed!

Instead, she pulled herself to her feet, holding in her hand a fashionable man's wallet. Tucking it into her bodice, she again wrapped her sodden shawl about her head and she too re-joined the rain outside.

It was long after midnight by now and the streets cried out with scuttling footsteps, echoing drunken disputes and late night laughter. Tessie hurried down an alley, and another, past the Bethnal Green stables, and over a canal bridge. Reaching the doorway of her grey tenement, she made her way up the stairs to see Finn anxiously pacing by the stove.

"What happened?" he asked the moment she opened the door. "Are yer alright?"

"Aye," she nodded. "I'm fine. Give me a minute." She moved to warm her hands by the fire and catch her breath, smoothing the rain from her face.

"Yer'll freeze through, Tess. Get this off." He pulled her shawl away as Tessie unbuttoned her jacket and skirt. Wet hair tumbled down her back as she pulled the hairpins and held her long tresses close to the fire. Finn wrapped the blanket from the bed around her shoulders, gently running his fingers over her hair and down her cheeks. "No harm done?"

Tessie gave him a half-smile. "I'm just cold."

Finn pulled his chair close, cupping her hands in his for warmth. "Did yer get the necklace?"

"No."

"Who did yer meet?"

"A gentleman, and whatever the note said, he didn't like it. He said he won't play this game."

"Game?" Finn frowned. "Let him call it a game when it's not his neck on the line."

Tessie rummaged in her cleavage and pulled out the man's wallet. "It'll be alright," she said. "The pendant's not in there, but he has a calling card. Can yer read it?" Finn rummaged through the wallet, and held up the card, though he was only slightly better with his letters than she.

"Albe. Marle. Albemarle Street. I've heard of it. It's in Mayfair. Number 22." He paused in concentration, sounding out the name. "Kyran Luther."

"That's him then. Kyran Luther. I'll go to him tomorrow."

"I'll go, Tess. Tonight was dangerous enough."

"They said me, Finn. I have to do it. It's the only way. And besides," she said. "If I can convince him it isn't a game, perhaps he'll hand it over. And he knows me now. If he sees yer, well, he's got no reason to talk to yer."

Finn slumped back in his chair. "Did he say anything else to yer? Anything that might help us?"

"Nothing." Tessie bit at her lip, bouncing her knees before the fire. Her mind was racing over every detail of the strange encounter.

"Well, how much time do we have? I mean, when are they coming for it?"

"I don't know. Soon. I'll have to go early."

The frustration bit at Finn's features as he rummaged further in the wallet, his brow tweaking above his scar as the man's coins spilled into his hand. He set them out in a line on the table and his brown eyes lighting up, he looked up at her. "Why don't we run, Tess? We should go. Right now. Tonight."

"To America?"

"Aye. Like we've talked about. This is it." He gestured at the coins on the table. "This here is enough for our passage. It's luck smiling on us, mo chara. It's a sign for us to go."

"What if we're being watched? What if there is someone out there right now watching our doorway?"

"We'll find a way to get past them. I don't know, Tess. But this is our chance."

"For all we know they'll follow us all the way to America. And if they catch us trying to run, our fate will be worse than…"

"Worse than what?"

Tessie sat back in her chair, fixing her eyes on the fire. "There's still a chance I can get the necklace tomorrow. Then we can go on our own terms, not in fear and flight. We cannot run. Not as thieves on another man's coins. We'll always be looking behind us, always waiting for them to catch us. Right now that necklace is more valuable to us than any coins."

Finn stood up, pacing before the fire as Tessie felt the truth of it. She wouldn't taint their new life with their old. "I want America. I want all of that for us. But if we take this mess with us, it'll be none of the things we want it to be. We need to see this through with the Angel. I'll not drag it into a new life across the oceans."

"If we do this we will always be under his thumb. We cannot live this way, beholden to this man and whatever ruffians he has patrolling the streets."

Tessie's brow creased. "They said I just have to do this. Just this. Get the bleedin' necklace." Saying it out loud, she knew it sounded feeble and hollow. Not even she believed it, and it hung in the air above them.

Finn swept the coins back into the purse and out of sight, his large shoulders slumped. She knew it was eating him up. That was more money than they'd ever seen at one time. She reached her hand to Finn's arm and squeezed. It was his instinct to resist and fight. He could not bend his will to fall in step with this man. Even if this man was the Angel. It was painful for him. Tessie could see the turmoil, though it only mirrored her own. She was a fighter too, but this, it felt bigger than both of them. Her chest heaved under the weight of it. What choice did they have? What else could she do?

Tessie moved toward him, pressing her icy skin against his warmth, she kissed him, hiking her skirt up to her waist, and wrapping herself around him. Forcing the wretchedness she felt to the back of her mind, they lost themselves in each other's breath and warmth, holding all the rest of it at bay. Whatever else would happen, in this moment they were still together, in this room where they had struggled, laughed and cried. Whatever villain watched on from the dark courtyard below, they were not here now.

Later, laying across the strewn covers, Tessie's wet hair hung over the back of the bed, her cool cheek pressed to Finn's chest. His heart thudded and he squeezed her repeatedly. She could feel the worry in him as they lay quiet and still, their minds ticking over with all that awaited them.

Pulling away from the bed and back to the fire, she lifted the flour tin and treacle from the cupboard.

"Yer should rest," Finn said, rolling onto his side.

Tessie stared at the tin of treacle. "The Angel hasn't caught us yet, mo chara, and we need rent."

～

THEY WOKE BEFORE FIRST LIGHT, moving around quietly in the dark. Tessie's baskets waited by the door, already packed to the brim with ginger cakes as she sat the table with her head in her hands and her stomach in knots. Behind her, Finn dressed and pulled on his boots, the minutes ticking by at an excruciating pace.

As light peeked through their window, the courtyard activity below heralded the hour. It was time to go. Making their way to the street below, the world around them hustled on with all the energy of an ordinary day. It was over an hours walk to the West End, and Tessie needed to keep a fast pace.

"Well, my love," Finn said, taking a few pennies from his pocket and tucking them into her palm. "I know yer have some, but take these too. If yer don't know where yer are just get in a hackney cab without another thought."

"Aye, I will," she nodded.

"Can't I come with yer? I should come with yer."

"I'll be alright. I will. And we need the rent."

"I don't like this, Tess. If they hurt yer, I swear to God..." he trailed away, and she saw his fear momentarily cutting through his cool demeanour. There was nothing she could say, so she waited. Rubbing the scar above his eye, he sighed in surrender.

Leaning in he gently kissed her forehead and whispered, "Mo chroí, mo teas." *My heart, my warmth.* She squeezed his fingers tightly as he stepped away. "I'll see yer at home."

"Yes, on with yer now." Tessie smiled, as casual as possible. "Haven't yer got stuff to do?" Finn followed her lead and backed into the crowd.

"A man such as I always has stuff to do." With a wink, he turned around and walked away.

CHAPTER 6

The mass of tussling bodies at the gates of the West India Docks greeted Finn as they did every morning, and the sound might still have been deafening if his mind hadn't been on Tessie. He had marched his way from the Nichol, barely remembering a moment as he wove through the busy streets and scoffed down a handful of oatcakes he'd bought warm from an old woman's basket.

There was more chaos around the edges as those left out vied desperately for a foothold and Finn braced for the impact of forcing himself into the middle of it all. He'd learned early to hold his own or be pushed aside, and knew how to manoeuvre himself through the crowd and into place near one of the gates.

With each step further into the fray, and further away from her, the feeling of dread tightened in his stomach. He forced it down. He had to believe she was going to be alright - that she would soon to be on her way home with the necklace and it was all going to be fine. They needed the rent money or they would be out on the street. That had to be his focus now.

As time wore closer, the mood around him grew urgent and the men impatient as they pressed in together so tight they could hardly breathe. When two foremen finally appeared, one at each side of the jostling crowd, the men surged at the sight of them and Finn let himself be swept along.

Pointing at faces in the crowd, the foremen called some by name and signalled others randomly. "You. And you. Get back the rest of you, come on. And you over there." The crowd hollered back at the foremen, every man vying for attention, something to make himself stand out. These foremen weren't known to Finn like some of the others, yet he couldn't bring himself to raise his hands and fight for the spot he so dearly needed. Instead, his eyes bore down at his boots and his mind raced.

"You!" The foreman jabbed his finger through the gate at Finn's chest. "You're the last one. That's it. Clear out. Clear out." A collective moan swept through the crowd and the swell fell back in disappointment.

Where Finn's chest usually surged with relief and triumph, his heart sunk, spilling heaviness through his muscles and indecision through his mind. What choice did he really have? He couldn't forgo a day's work, not when there was a possibility all would turn out as it was supposed to.

As Finn's body obeyed the call, a stocky young man beside him lunged at the gate, pulling himself up to get the attention of the last foreman moving away. "Come on. One more!" he called after him. "Please brother, I just need a day's work. Just the one!"

"Get back!" Security men took over the line, shoving the crowd back. "That's it for the day! Move along! Move along!"

"I need the work. Come on!" The young man dropped

from the gate and chased after those selected as Finn too threaded through to join his crew.

"Brother. I have to get out of here. I'll be on a boat by week's end if I can get a shilling more. That's it and I'm gone. I'm begging yer. For my wife and baby." The man's Irish accent rang over the crowd, drawing the attention of the security men who started to move towards him.

Almost every day someone tried to slip through the gate when they hadn't been chosen and it rarely ended well. The other men ignored his pleas lest they too lose their spot, though the young man was not deterred. He darted beneath one security man and as Finn caught his eye, he came towards him, arms outstretched. "The Angel's men have ruined me, brother. I have to leave before they take everything." The mention of the Angel struck Finn in the guts and he looked upon the man's spritely gaze, wringing his hat in his hands in earnest. His pleas were not those of a defeated man, but one determined to get away. How many lives had the Angel's men ruined? Who was Finn to stand in the way of a man trying to get away?

"Are yer being honest?" Finn asked, keeping his head down and moving still toward his crew though a spark of urgency was building within him. Was this a sign? An opportunity?

"Aye. I'll be gone on one of them there boats. I just need this. Can yer get me on the crew, brother? Can yer?"

Finn felt it rile up in him. This was his chance. His reason to turn around and go after her. Even if he'd need to find another way to pay the rent, he wouldn't leave her alone. Not again. "I can do yer one better," he said and slapped the man on the back. "Tell them yer name is Finn O'Shea."

The young man's eyes widened and he thrust his hand forward in a gruff handshake of excitement. "You're a godsend, brother."

"Aye. Yer might be yourself, man. Be on that boat, will yer. Get out of here."

"Aye, I will." And with that, Finn turned his eyes away from the docks, everything in his head screaming he shouldn't be there. He should be with her.

CHAPTER 7

*A*rthur smoothed his white shirt and crisp blue waistcoat as he picked over the breakfast selection. Settling on a piece of toast and a lacklustre slab of ham, he turned back to the table to see his wife's head wobble ever so slightly as she cut her toast into bite-sized pieces. Cynthia Crabbe wore a light mauve dress and sat opposite his father in quiet morning reverence.

Setting his plate down with a thud, Arthur ignored her nod of greeting and instead reached for his empty teacup. Cynthia filled it immediately with strong and steaming tea.

Ten years his senior, and a seven-year marriage of convenience, he could barely stand the sound of her rustling skirts in the hallways, yet alone her expectant gaze in the morning. She wanted from him what most wives wanted - attention. She knew what he was, and she knew he needed her, if only for her family connections. That seemed to be enough.

On his other side, his father, Otis, stabbed aggressively at his eggs, having folded his large frame into the elegant dining chair. Grey and bloated with stale whiskey, he held up the weight of his miserable expression with an elbow on the table.

"Well?" Otis interrupted the silence. "Did it work?"

Arthur bit into his dry toast and gulped back the entire cup of hot tea. Cynthia filled it again.

"No business at the table." Arthur, though cranky, pronounced his words more carefully in this setting, his accent refined and clear to match the shiny silver cutlery and unblemished tablecloth.

"Ha! Should have left Kyran out of it."

Arthur rolled his neck but didn't take the bait.

"He's rogue," Otis persisted. "You've lost control and you'll not get him back now."

"I didn't get where I am by giving up so easily. If I can put up with you, I can take my chances when I have to."

"It's too late. He's gone. He's weak. Always has been."

"He is whatever I say he is," Arthur said with more finality.

Cynthia reached her hand out to Arthur's forearm and he glanced down at her long decorated fingers and shrugged them away.

"You're dropping your H's, husband," she said in the tone of a loving wife which only grated on Arthur's nerves all the more.

Castor appeared in the entrance, holding himself with appropriate poise, and having exchanged his barge clothes for a smartly tailored suit. Tucked beneath his arm, he held a document folder and Arthur signalled for him to approach.

"Get in here, Castor." Arthur let his East End accent return for Cynthia's benefit, letting his pale blue eyes dart in her direction.

"Yes, sir, Mr Crabbe." Castor used a more formal greeting in front of Cynthia and Otis, though he often spent more time in their abode than his own.

"Should have kept it simple." Otis drew the conversation back. "That girl would be shipped off and taken care of by now."

Arthur wiped his mouth with his napkin, glaring at his father though he spoke directly to Castor. "What have I got today?"

"The Home Secretary this afternoon. He'll be by at two o'clock. And this morning, Mr Burke from the Merchant's Association."

Arthur nodded, glad to be re-focused. "Very well."

"This is about that Irish bitch, not him, you know," Otis pressed again. "Sending a message. Protecting your legacy—"

"He knows what it's about," Cynthia cut in, dropping her fork onto her plate.

Arthur put his hand out to silence her. "Since when is this a bleeding family discussion?"

"Where did you get the girl from anyway? You found her quickly." Otis seemed oblivious to the trouble brewing.

Arthur closed his eyes and rubbed his sideburns, his hand straining in aggravation. "I am a man of means, father. Whether you acknowledge it or not."

"That's not stopping Lady Muck across the Irish Sea wreaking havoc, is it?"

Arthur snatched at Castor's document folder to distract himself and strode to the other side of the room. "Must I hear your grumbling from the moment I wake?"

"He's always been weak because you let him play these games...You let him-"

"I let him?" Arthur swung around.

Cynthia and Castor exchanged glances and she stood to block the eye line between Otis and Arthur.

"Come on, Otis, it's time to go," she urged, trying to raise the old man from his seat. "Betty!" She called for some assistance, as Castor too joined her in trying to rouse him.

"Wipe your face, for pity's sake," Arthur said with disgust at the egg lingering on Otis's chin.

"Wipe your own damn face."

Lunging forward, Arthur whipped his arm across the table, clattering his father's plate and showering in him in eggs. "You watch your mouth, old man. Not a man alive speaks to me like that, least of all you."

"I'll bring you down, boy. Come on!" The old man stood, casting Cynthia aside and beating his chest. His eyes were alight with venom and fight as Betty bundled into the room, all but too late.

"Get him out of here, Betty. Get him out. He's having one of his spells. The angry ones." Cynthia moved out of the way.

"Yes, ma'am."

Otis held his fists up, ready to spar. "Come on, boy! Time for another beating from your pa. I made you, remember. I made you."

Arthur gritted his teeth, his fists aching to strike. He could annihilate him. He could beat that old man's bitter, nasty voice from the place it had echoed for all those years. And yet even as it choked up inside him, his veins pumping and stretching with rage, he held it back. If he were any other man he would not have hesitated even a moment. But this old man, so wholly ruined, his flaws sprawled out for all to see in every word and action, this old man was of himself. A part of him. Inseparable. To annihilate him would be to annihilate himself.

"Get him out!" Arthur bellowed as Castor and Betty ushered Otis back from the table and out the door leaving Arthur and Cynthia to the room.

In the quiet that followed, Cynthia held a hand to her chest and dabbed at the pooling tea on the tablecloth with a napkin. "Look at this now." She pointed to the egg and toast on the floor. "Must Betty always clean up after animals?"

"Eat somewhere else then." Arthur's tone was harsh as he tried to calm his beating chest.

"I know he is family-"

"Yes. Family. My family. So we'll eat here together if we stab each other to death." Arthur clenched his fist. It was blood that bound them. Blood.

"He's an old man, Artie. He's not well."

"I know who he is! What he is." He thumped the table. "You, do not. And I'd sooner get rid of you."

Cynthia pressed her thin lips together, placing a hand on her hip, her eyes shining as if the comment cut deeper than she would admit. "But you can't, can you, Artie. Let's not forget…" Cynthia's voice fell away, but Arthur wasn't paying attention.

"When I were a boy that man drank every penny we had and when I dared complain of being hungry, you know what he did?" He jabbed his finger directly in Cynthia's face. "He woke me in the dead of night with a slop bucket he stole from the bloody pigs and rammed it down my throat!"

Something strained in Cynthia's voice. "You know what this is about and it is not a sick and belligerent old man. What's done is done now. Kyran has made his choice. You must let it go."

"Get away from me, woman." He shooed his hand at her.

Cynthia's head wobbled ever so slightly and she moved to exit just as Castor reappeared. She replaced her serious expression with one of refreshed cordiality. "How are Violet and the girls?"

"They are well, Mrs Crabbe, thank you."

"You must bring them by in the spring to pick berries. Our hedge grove in the yard is always more than cook can keep up with."

"Yes, yes," Arthur interjected, his back still turned. "Let the girls pick berries and bake pies to their heart's content. We need to get through the business of winter first."

"Good day, Mr Castor." Cynthia let them alone.

"Have you had any word?" Arthur tugged at his goatee, his chest still beating rapidly beneath his blue waistcoat.

"We ought to let Kyran stew on it some. It's early yet, Artie." Castor spoke in a calm tone as Arthur pulled at his collar and re-filled his own tea.

"Blasted, bleedin', heck and hell." He rolled his knuckles and placed them on the table. "Sod that. Get the girl. Get her now."

CHAPTER 8

Tessie had sold flowers on the steps of St. Paul the previous summer, but that was as far as she'd ventured to the West End - a world of bankers and aristocrats, Buckingham Palace, fashionable shops and expensive townhouses. It was a long walk and she had sold almost half her cakes by the time she reached its edges, the pennies jingling in her hidden skirt pocket.

Passing Temple Gardens, the retailers became more up-market, home to high-quality tailors and jewellery shops, specialty artisans and home goods. It was like a different country. The streets were wider and cleaner with polished surfaces and vibrant colours. As the landscape evolved, so too did the residents, as Tessie passed women in elegant dresses, with matching bonnets and coats. She did not belong here in her faded dress and ratty shawl. With her unkempt hair and dirty nails, she would be taken for a pauper.

Coming to Pall Mall East she walked the stretch finding only merchants and up-market retailers. Albemarle St. must be one of these, she thought to herself, knowing she could be walking in circles for hours. She saw no one likely to oblige her with directions. There were carriages pulled in waiting along Pall Mall, though none were likely to accept her patronage. If she was seen getting out of the cab, no self-respecting gentry would likely get in after her, though she had to at least try for directions. Approaching from a discrete corner of the street where she would not easily be seen, she interrupted the driver reading his paper.

"Excuse me, sir."

"Aye," he said, barely looking up. "I don't drive indigents."

"Sir, I'm just after directions."

"On with you."

"Albemarle Street, sir, which way is it?"

"I said on with you."

"Please sir," she begged, hearing a panicked urgency in her voice.

"It's right at the crossroads up there. Now get away from me carriage or I'll call a bobby."

"Thank you, sir."

"Away now. Away!"

Hurrying to the crossroads ahead she sounded out the letters on the street sign as "Albe..." and had to take the chance. Seeing the number 22 marked on the mailbox and a blue door, she came to a quaint terrace home and paused. She had no idea in what state she would find Kyran Luther, or if he would even see her. Maybe she hadn't thought this through, but what other option did she have? She looked up and down the street, a drowning feeling flooding her chest. What exactly was her alternative? To go home and wait for the man Moses to come? She needed that pendant.

Approaching, she saw the curtains fidget at the window as she hastened to straighten her appearance. The door opened before she had a chance to knock and a broad woman with a stony face held her hand out, "No paupers!"

Tessie was startled. "I'm not a beggar," she said, trying to sound reassuring. The woman pushed the door, leaving Tessie dismayed. She pushed back on the door, determined to keep it from shutting in her face. "I need to see Mr Luther. Please." The woman seemed surprised she knew his name and paused.

"What do you want?" she asked quietly but firmly, eyeing the basket of ginger cakes looped through her arm.

"Tell him Tessie O'Shea is here. He will see me. I'm sure."

The woman looked her up and down with a scornful expression.

"Tell him!"

The woman, who seemed reluctant to leave her on the doorstep for all to see, ushered her inside, her eyes lingering on the mud on her boots. "Wipe your shoes. I don't want to be cleaning up after you when you're gone."

Tessie obediently wiped her feet on the mat as the door closed behind her and the woman disappeared down a corridor. Left alone in the entrance, the smell of wealth flooded Tessie's senses. The décor was simple but elegant with a large artwork looming above the stairwell. The sweet smell of lavender and scones wafted around her. A mirror glistened beside a coat rack and Tessie was stunned by the contrast of her drab appearance in the rich surroundings. Her pale complexion flushed with the brisk morning air, drawing out the life in her blue eyes. She could usually flash a charming smile and it would outshine her crumpled dress and windswept hair, but in these parts, people cared only for refined manners and good breeding. She felt dirty all over, as if she would leave a smudge on anything she touched.

It wasn't the woman who returned to fetch her, but Kyran himself who strode down the corridor. "What are you doing here?" he asked, dressed down in a shirt and waistcoat.

"Listen to me," Tessie started. "Please."

His brown eyes were weary as if he too had not slept, and while his hair was freshly combed, something plagued him so that he looked uncomfortable in his clothes.

"This is not a game," she pleaded in a hushed voice. "I beg yer. I don't know what the necklace is or what this is about. All I know is that I am in danger if I don't get it."

"You stole from me."

"I needed your address." She fumbled in her dress and tossed the wallet towards him. He opened it quickly and checked the contents.

"That there is more money than we make in a month and I've brought it back to yer because I need the necklace more than yer money." Kyran's shoulders tensed as he searched her eyes, though he took on a friendlier demeanour at her words. He was pausing at least, she thought. He had not yet thrust her out the door.

"You do not need to convince me what type of man the Angel is," he said at last, letting out a long sigh and pushing his hands into his trouser pockets. He turned to the window. "What I don't know, is if this stunt is to torture me, or torture you. Probably both."

"He has no reason to torture me."

Kyran considered her answer. "You must tell me then. Are you from Dublin?"

Tessie let out an exasperated sigh. "What can that possibly have to do with anything?"

"Tell me."

"I left Dublin eight years ago, never to return."

"And your mother?" His eyes narrowed as he scrutinised her so that she felt the need to retreat a step back.

"I never knew my mother. I don't know anything about her," she said, though it was a lie. What had her mother to do with anything? And what the hell was he looking at?

"Was there something in the note about my mother?" she

said, turning the questions back on him. "Why do yer care about my mother?"

He didn't answer her, the murky depth in his eyes disconnecting as he turned away again.

"What did the note say?" she pushed. He knew more than he was saying, she was sure of it. Did he know why she'd been thrust into the middle of this mess? He ignored her question and shook his head.

"It took courage for you to come here."

"What did it say?"

"I wish no harm to come to you."

"Then give me the necklace. Any necklace, I don't care!"

"If this is not a joke, then the necklace won't save you."

"Why?" Her voice rose with urgency, a pulsating sickness building in her stomach. "He is going to hurt me. Do yer understand that?"

Kyran's face was shadowed with guilt but she could see his resolve. Who was this man, so defiant to the Angel's demands? He was going to get her killed! She had the urge to run, though her legs held like stones to the floor. Maybe she could find Finn and they would still have time to disappear on a departing ship. Or maybe she could simply tell the Angel's men the truth. If they know Kyran Luther, maybe they expect him to be difficult? But even as she thought through the scenarios, her heart sank into a curdling mess. He was not going to help her.

"If I don't live to see tomorrow, yer will have my blood on yer hands." She opened the door herself and slammed it behind her.

LEAVING the West End behind her, Tessie's mind swirled with guttural panic. She had to find Finn and didn't know whether to run straight to the docks or wait for him as agreed that evening. She had an awful sense they didn't have that much time, but as she fled across Albemarle Street, Finn leapt out from an alley and caught her around the waist.

"Tess!" He grabbed her mid-flight and she caved against him, breathless and panting.

"Yer were right, we've got to go!"

"Did he give it to yer?"

"No," she said, bending over to catch her breath. "He won't do it. Did yer follow me?"

"Aye. I couldn't bear it. Now I'm glad I did."

"Aye. We have to run. Now!"

"Alright then," he said, and giving each other a nod, they both broke into a run.

In the pockets of her skirt, Tessie fumbled for the figurine of St. Brigid and gripped her hands around it, reciting her prayer. "Brigid of the Mantle, encompass us, Lady of the Lambs, protect us, Keeper of the Hearth, kindle us. Beneath your mantle, gather us..." She frowned so hard her head throbbed. "Your hands upon ours, Our hands within yours, To kindle the light, Both day and night..."

As they burst through their door, they moved to separate corners to gather up their belongings. She eyed her treacle tins and the personal effects littered across the room. Most of it would have to be left behind. Finn ripped the bed sheets away to tie into bundles, but they had barely had a chance to stash a thing when they heard a rush of footsteps crashing up the stairwell and three men barged through the door. It was too late.

Pushing his way to the front, Moses gave Tessie a flicker of acknowledgement, relishing his return. "I told yer to be careful, love."

"Stay away from her," Finn urged.

"This has nought to do with you," Moses said, waving his

hand at Finn in dismissal. He nodded to the lads behind him who quickly moved to block Finn's path to either Tessie or himself.

"Have you got it?" he asked, in his slow, sneaking tone. "Have you got the necklace?" Though the look in his eyes told Tessie he already knew the answer, and it didn't matter anyway.

"He wouldn't give it to me."

"Right." He gripped her head and smacked it down hard against the table, the crack sending her reeling as blood streamed over her eyes. Tessie screamed and Finn launched himself forward, instantly pummelled to the ground by the men beside him.

"Get away from her!" he cried, but he couldn't break through.

Gripping her wrists, Moses twisted her to ground as she staggered to see. "No! No!" she repeated, but she hadn't the strength to fight him off.

Finn let out a roar of exertion, twisting and kicking at the men who held him. Tessie couldn't move her head to see him as Moses pinned her to the ground. She wanted to scream but the sound wouldn't move from her lungs. The blood stinging her eyes, she blinked furiously as the man breathed heavily on her face.

"Get the fuck away from her," Finn hollered, blood pouring from his mouth.

One man with tall and lanky limbs said, "Just do it, mate. We ain't got time for this, just get it over with."

Moses bit down hard and angrily on Tessie's neckline and she let out a shrill scream.

"Get off her!" Finn's voice was hoarse with effort and the man behind him launched a kick into the back of Finn's head, the heel of his boot whiplashing Finn with a mighty blow. It knocked the life out of him and his chin slumped to his chest.

Flicking open a switchblade, Moses held it against her skin. "Time to pay that debt," he breathed into her ear. "Say hello to your Mum for me." With his eyes mad and black, he plunged the knife with all his weight into her side. She felt him dig in the pressure as the stabbing heat pierced deeper and deeper beneath her ribs.

She couldn't breathe, but choked and gurgled as the blood seeped out onto her dress. She thought she would drown in it, sticky and hot. As she heaved and coughed she looked to Finn and reached out her hand towards him. She could not help him. His brown eyes were wild moons of fury and panic. He could not help her. She wheezed, feeling cold against her back, and everything went black.

CHAPTER 9

A mixture of pain and thirst dragged Tessie from the fog. Her eyes heavy and laboured, a sleepy crust held them shut as a muffled croak escaped her throat. Clammy sheets clung to her body and freeing one arm from a heavy blanket, she rubbed the sleep from her eyes. Thick wood rafters on a pitched roof loomed over her, and make-shift curtains were pulled around the bed sealing in a small chamber. It was not fancy. The material and bedding were rough to the touch and the mattress lumpy and uneven. She could hear a fire crackling and the smell of hay and earth was in the air. "Finn?" she tried to call, but her voice was powerless, and when there was no reply she thought better of it. Where on earth could she be?

Rolling onto her side, a burst of pain erupted through her abdomen. Under the blankets Tessie was naked and the stab wound at her side glared back at her. Pinched together with crude stitching, she pressed the tender flesh. The memories rushed back as she fell back on the mattress. The attack. The Angel's men. Laying cold on the floorboards with the taste of blood in her mouth. She moved her hand to another wound on her forehead and rough scabbing at her neck where Moses had bitten her. The memory of clamping pain clawed at her throat and she closed her eyes, replaying the waves of panic she had felt over and over and over. And Finn. Her dear Finn. Where was he? Tessie bore down and forced herself to sit up. She didn't yet know if she was safe.

Peeking through a small tear in one of the curtains, she saw a humble cottage, homely, with a well-stocked kitchen, a large rug with two rocking chairs, copper pots and pans, and a kettle and canisters that lined the shelf above the stove. There was a boiling pot on the stove, filling the room with the soupy smell of bacon and vegetables. No one was there.

Daring to pull one of the curtains open, a dark green dress and petticoats hung in the corner and her mind went again to the image of her own dress staining with blood. She shook it away. If she was going to do anything, she needed to be dressed.

Her core twisting and tugging against the wound at her side, shifting her weight to stand was excruciating. Taking one step, then another, her body remembered how to move. Dragging a chair from the table for stability, she made it across the room. Weaker with every burst of exertion, she delicately manoeuvred her way inside the dress. It wasn't new but felt worn-in and comfortable. She looked around for some shoes and when there were none, her mind wandered to the rest of her belongings—the pennies in her pocket and the medallion of St. Brigid, her old woollen shawl and hairpins, and her leather band. Where was the leather band Finn had given her?

Movement sounded outside the cottage and Tessie seized in panic. Snatching a knife from the table she hobbled to the bed. Someone was at the door. Taking a deep breath to slow her heart, she gripped the knife at her side and watched through a gap in the curtain. She waited, and when the door opened, a gasp stuck in her throat. It was Kyran.

Unpacking items above the stove and humming to himself. Tessie watched his figure, calm and amicable. What was he doing here? Everything in Tessie told her to run, and yet she couldn't move. He looked younger than she'd remembered him, unshaven and clothed in farming attire instead of the tailored suit from the Nichol. His hair was tousled and unkempt; his brown eyes were clear and warm. What on earth was going on?

Kyran turned to the kitchen table and, noticing one of the chairs had moved, shifted his gaze to where the green dress had hung. She had been sprung, and before he could check the bed, Tessie threw back the curtains and jabbed her knife into the air. She heard herself hiss at him and though she couldn't move freely from the bed, she stood and leant back on it for support.

"Tessie!" he gasped. She glared at him, her expression surging with adrenaline. "Tessie, please, it's me. Kyran Luther."

"Where is Finn?" She jabbed the knife in front of her.

"Who is Finn?" His voice dropped lower in an effort to calm the situation. "Is he the one who was with you?"

"Where is he?"

"He is not here."

"Tell me where he is!"

"I don't know." He earnestly held out his arms.

"Where am I?"

"Somewhere s-safe," he offered with the same stutter he'd had in the Nichol. He took a step towards her.

"No!" She jabbed the knife in the air again. "Stay there."

Obeying, he sat at the table. "This is confusing. I know. I'll explain what h-happened." His voice was lighter, less deliberate, and he'd lost his educated accent. He sounded nothing more than an English villager.

"I remember what happened," she said. "I want to know where I am. How did I get here?"

"I brought you here."

"Why?"

"We followed you when you left my house. My man and I."

"Why?"

Kyran paused as if unsure how to phrase his next sentence. "Because you were right. I didn't want your blood on my conscience. I don't."

"How did yer get past Moses and the others? Were they still there?"

"We got past them."

"How!"

"We just did."

Tessie's mind whirred. How could he and one other man have possibly stormed in there and taken her? It was three men against two, and they left Finn! It didn't make sense.

"We took you and got you to help. It's been a fever that's kept you out so long." His last words stung.

"So long?"

"You've been here for four days, Tessie." Kyran's shoulders sank with his answer as if knowing it would wound her.

"That can't be right. It's not..." Her voice faded as the reality of it crashed in around her. "Finn was there in the room. Did yer see him?" Her eyes pleaded with him as the possibilities of his absence rose with waves of nausea.

"There was another man there." He shifted uncomfortably.

"What happened to him?"

"I don't know. We were there for you. We only took you."

"And...?"

"I don't know what happened to him. I saw he was hurt. I didn't—" She waved her hand at him as her mind fought its way back to that place where Finn's dark eyes fixed on hers, his head hanging limply from his shoulders, his face swelling from the blows. *How could I leave him there?* The grief plunged through her and she gripped the bedpost for support.

"I have to go back."

"We're miles from London and you're in no state to travel, Tessie."

"Yer brought me here in a worse state didn't yer?"

"Because we had to." Kyran looked exasperated. "The Angel wants you dead. London isn't safe."

"I'm going back for him. Take me back."

Kyran rubbed his forehead, searching for an alternative. "I'm headed back to London in a few days. I'll take you with me, then. Wait till then. Till everything in the city has calmed down."

"It's been four days. I need to go now."

"You need to rest," Kyran said. "At least eat first. Keep the knife if you must but I'm not going to hurt you."

When Tessie didn't argue, he moved to the pantry shelf and placed a loaf of bread onto the table. Tessie let the moment settle, feeling herself weaken, the knife growing heavy on her outstretched arm. As much as she wanted to charge out the door, she could barely hold herself up.

"What kind of gentleman makes his own soup?" she quipped, pulling herself back onto the bed and leaning her forehead against the bedpost. "Will yer be making scones as well?"

Kyran was late to catch her sarcasm and only glanced in her direction. He seemed happy in his element, with an intensity in his eyes that could catch her off guard and a physicality that seemed he could just as easily be outside mending a roof and ploughing a field. She wondered if anything he said was the truth. Who was he here, playing at village life; or had he been playing the gentleman?

"Where are my shoes?" she asked, her bare feet aching with the chilled air.

"If you'll wait for them, you'll have a new pair tomorrow."

"What's wrong with those?" She eyed a pair of his discarded boots in the corner. They looked sturdy enough.

"My man is bringing you some new ones."

"And my other things. I had a leather band on my wrist. I had almost two shillings and a medallion." Kyran nodded and turned to meet her eyes.

"Under your pillow. All of your clothes were ruined. I'm sorry." Tessie felt under the pillow with her hand and found the medallion and Finn's leather bracelet. She quickly slipped the leather band around her wrist and spun it around in her fingers. At least she had that. Her coins had been placed in a small pouch and she stashed that too in her dress.

"I haven't been staying here," Kyran said. "I mean at night. A woman from the village has been staying to watch you and I've stayed with a neighbour." Tessie realised he was trying to assure her modesty had been respected.

"Are yer going to tell me who you really are?" She twisted the leather band.

"You know who I am."

"Do I? The way yer talk, yer accent, yer clothes. Is Kyran Luther a gentleman or a farmer? Is that even your name?" Kyran stayed silent as he stirred the pot of soup. "I met Mr Luther in a fancy suit, talking like a toff. It's like you're..."

"Like I'm what?" He had a glimmer in his eye. Tessie pulled herself upright on the bed as the answer took shape before her.

"You're a bleedin' pretender." She looked him over differently, something rumbling in her spine. "That's it, isn't it?" He was not going to satisfy her with an answer, though she knew it was true. It had to be, and it settled on her uneasily. Was he an associate of the Angel? A colleague fallen from grace? Who was he that he could walk into an attack ordered by the Angel and walk out with her?

The questions danced along her spine. He had been a part of whatever released a shadow into her world, after all. She felt it even now, lurking in the room. She had been with this man for four days; was he truly helping her or was there something else in play? Was she to be a pawn in some kind of tug-of-war between Kyran and the Angel, stuck between the two of them? Tessie's insides tensed. Was she even safe with him? Something rumbled up inside her, and yet, Kyran stood before her, his eyes genuine as he scooped soup into a bowl.

"I suppose a man who pretends must know himself well, or not at all." She flashed her eyes in an effort to draw him out, though Kyran moved back to the stove for his own soup and sat down in front of her.

"Who is to be the judge of that, I wonder?" He turned his spoon over in his hand. "Most of us spend our lives pretending something or other."

"Maybe. Or maybe pretending is not a luxury all of us have." Tessie thought on it, leaning back in her seat as he ate.

"We've all got something to hide, don't we, Tessie O'Shea?"

She felt the challenge in his statement. She had lied to him about knowing her mother, that was true enough.

"How did you come to be there that night?" he asked, taking on a conversational tone. Tessie mulled the question over. If she wanted information from him, she would have to share something too.

"They said my ma owed a debt."

"Who said?"

"The horrible one with the slitty eyes. Moses. When he brought me that letter I was to take to yer in exchange for that necklace yer wouldn't give me. Because my mother owes a debt to the Angel."

Kyran scratched his brow. "A lot of people owe the Angel money. And you said you never knew your mother."

"That's right," she said. "Though I believe she were a princess, covered in gold and silver and glistening in jewels."

Kyran smiled wryly. "You're an orphan?" he asked, again prodding at her parentage. She lifted the bowl to her face and drank the salty broth. It was soothing and she felt it lending strength to her bones.

"To be an orphan I'd have to know if my father were dead or alive."

"You didn't know either of your parents?"

She set her empty bowl on the table with a thud and held her gaze on Kyran, her eyes both wild and calm. She had no interest in resurrecting her mother's memory, and definitely not with this stranger.

"What did the note say really?"

Kyran inhaled, averting his eyes to his soup. "It said to take a good look at you. That he would use you…"

"To get to yer?"

"Yes."

"But how…"

"That's what I want to know."

"Perhaps it's a case of mistaken identity," Tessie offered. "I'm a baker. I bake cakes for pity's sake. Not even fancy ones, and sell them in the market. I scrounge for every penny. Every day. I'm a nobody."

"The Angel doesn't keep track of nobodies."

"From what I've seen he keeps track of all manner of nobodies. I've seen them, branded and marked, wandering around as if their life ain't their own."

"That's how his men earn their keep to pay up to him. The

Angel doesn't care about them. He doesn't know their names. But he cares about you. And he knows your name."

"Then he's made a mistake." She said it with conviction, though the more times she said it to herself, the more forced it felt. There was no truth to her mother's involvement. How would anyone make the connection between them? It was too long ago, and too far away. She looked over at Kyran and pushed her bowl away. "Who is this man who hides behind his legend?"

"No one knows who he is. That's how it works."

"I could make up stories about myself if I wanted to, to make me people do as I choose. But they'd just be stories."

"They're not stories if you go through with your threats."

"So it's all true then. He's as terrifying as they say?"

"I don't know what they say. But you're the one sitting here with a knife wound in your side."

"Yer know who he is don't yer? Yer have to know."

Kyran's eyes flickered to his bowl. "I will not burden you with it."

"I'm already burdened. Am I to be a bargaining chip? A piece in a game between yer?"

"No, that isn't it at all."

"He's like yer isn't he? A villain by night and gentleman by day. Dressed like a toff and with money to spare. He must be someone important. Untouchable. Not like the rest of us." Kyran held her eyes but neither confirmed or denied. Tessie took a deep breath. She wasn't sure if it was all the questions, or the talk of her mother, that soured her belly. She'd said enough.

"Thank yer for the soup. I'm going to go now." She stood up, grimacing as she did. "I have to find Finn."

"Wait a few days more. Please."

"I can't. He'll think I'm dead. And if he is alive I must go to him."

"It isn't safe in London."

"Is it ever safe anywhere?" She shuffled to the end of the table, reaching out for the old pair of boots waiting by the door. There was a walking cane leant against the wall too and she took it without asking.

"He'll not stop, Tessie. The Angel will keep after you until the job is finished. And if Finn managed to survive they'll be after him too."

"So what am I do to then? Hide? Leave him out there? I'll not do that."

"If you want Finn to be safe, you need to find out why this is happening. You need to stop the Angel coming after you."

"Stop him?" Tessie almost laughed. "Now I do question yer thinking. How on God's earth am I to do that? I told yer. I bake ginger cakes for the market. I'm a nobody. This has been a mistake, and Finn and I are paying the price for it."

"Find out what your mother has to do with this. Perhaps she can call it off."

"I told yer. I don't know her. If yer care about her so much, why don't yer find her for me?"

"You can't fight what you don't understand. Finding out what this is about is the only way to end it."

"I don't know her, alright. I can't make up stories about that now just to please yer."

Kyran put his hands up in surrender and Tessie fell back on the bench by the door as she bent over to pull on the boots. It took time but she persisted. The boots were well worn, smooth and comfortable inside and rough on the outside, but they would do just fine. She didn't know how far she would have to walk.

Kyran paced back and forth by the stove but did not interfere. "Take the satchel too then if you insist on going." He looped it off the back of the door and handed it to her, with a large heavy cloak to go with it. "Take it. It's cold out."

Tessie looked inside the leather satchel, stashing her coins inside and seeing there was also some tallow candles, with matches and a small pocket knife, and a few other odds and ends that may come in handy.

"Thank you," she said, bidding her farewell to this strange man.

"I'll be back in London soon enough. If you make it, you know where to find me."

CHAPTER 10

*H*er heart tensed as the train glided into Bishopsgate station. She was back in the Angel's territory, having lumbered to a station outside Kyran's village. The journey had been a laboured mix of turmoil with every mile that passed. While Kyran's words plagued her thoughts, she hoped he was wrong. She didn't want to search for her mother, she didn't want to stop the Angel and she didn't care for the truth. She just wanted to find Finn and for everything to be as it was, though the images that rushed up from her imagination would not stop. What had happened in that room? Would he be there? Did he think her dead? She prayed he'd left her something. A little thread she could hold in her fingers and tug at. Something precious to help her find a way to make all of this right again.

Alighting quickly, she pulled the cloak's hood over her head as she turned onto Bethnal Green Road and drew to a stop outside the Old Nichol. She could barely contain herself from sprinting across the courtyard to her tenement. Finn could this very moment be a few feet away, but it was going to be near impossible not to be seen. Leaning on her walking cane, she approached a line of cranky women waiting at Mr Rawlin's pawnshop.

It was Black Monday, and the courtyard echoed in a tizzy of rent collectors and arguing tenants. Beside her a woman bounced a screaming child on her hip as her husband argued with the collector, waving his hands about as he scribbled in his book. Further down another door was being boarded up, the family standing amongst their strewn belongings as the stray children of the Nichol rifled through.

Using the spectacle to scuttle across the courtyard and up the staircase, she didn't wait to knock before bursting through the door. A young woman stood out of a chair where she'd been making boots as Tessie's eyes adjusted to the dark room.

"Who are yer?"

"Lucy Lambert."

"What are yer doing here?"

"I live here."

"No yer don't."

Lucy's mouth was stuck open. "Yes. Three days now. I paid Mr Lawson ten shillings and all for the rest of the month." Tessie's insides churned as she scanned the room. Most of their belongings were gone though a number of her treacle tins still lined the shelves. The blankets on the bed had been theirs only days earlier. It sent stinging waves through her. Where could Finn be? Lacing her fingers behind her head, knotting them in her messy hair, she looked down at the floorboards where she had lain. Darkened blood stains remained, and moving her gaze to where Finn had been, there were more marks and splatters. A blood map only she could recognise.

Was this their story? She tried to read the smudges. There were drag marks where she had been and she imagined Kyran or his man tugging her toward the door. Where Finn had lain there were only splatters and drops, nothing to suggest he was dragged like a dead weight or stabbed as she had been. Was that enough to count as hope?

Lucy's eyes were wide and nervous. "Are you the ones who lived here?" she asked.

"That's my blood on the floor." Tessie softened her stance, leaning on her walking stick. None of this was Lucy's fault. "What do yer know about it?"

Lucy bit her lip as if nervous to speak it out.

"What did yer hear? What are they saying?"

"You don't know?"

"I wouldn't be here if I knew."

Lucy shifted uncomfortably and picked up a boot from the table, fidgeting with its laces. "They said you wronged the Angel. The both of you did. And that you got what was coming to you."

"What of my husband? Please, if yer heard anything about him, please tell me." Tessie braced herself for the news.

"I only heard the rumours." Lucy's eyes shied away. "My husband heard down at the docks that he killed one of the Angel's men. They were looking for both of you at first. But it didn't make sense to me because they said you were dead. So why were they looking for you?" Lucy paused as if Tessie may answer the question, but she didn't.

"I don't know what happened to your man, but..." Lucy's voice hushed to a whisper, hesitant to say the next line. "A body was fished out of the river on Tuesday and we were wondering if it were him."

Tessie's heart plunged with such force she thought she might be sick. Was that him? Was that Finn? Of course, Lucy could not answer.

"I'm sorry, sweet, I can't tell you any more. But they are still looking for you. You shouldn't have come back here. They're still out there."

Tessie pressed her fists to her eyes. What had happened in this room after she blacked out? Had there been a struggle? She said he'd killed one of his men? Had Finn tried to follow her? *A body in the river. Fished out of the Thames.* Tessie's head swilled with the image of Finn's strong body being pulled limply from that brown water. It can't of been him. It mustn't be. Tessie started to sway.

"You need to sit." Lucy slid a chair towards her and she gripped the backrest but shook her head.

"No." She lifted her head to look at the back corner of the room. Remembering their stash of money hidden in the wall behind the bed, she moved quickly and knocked a small crate aside. Tugging at the loose board, it came away revealing an empty cavity in the wall space. The money was gone. But how? She and Finn were the only ones who knew of it.

"Have yer been in here?" Tessie asked, standing and returning to face poor Lucy.

"No, ma'am."

"Are yer sure? Where is it?"

"I had no idea that was even there. I promise you."

Tessie could see she was telling the truth, and the idea lifted her chest. Finn was the only one who could have removed it. He had been alive. He had to have been, at least he was alive enough to take their rent money with him. Surely that was the case. Please, let it be true.

"Yer mustn't tell anyone I was here." Tessie scrambled to take a few coins from her bag and shoved them towards Lucy, scanning the room for remnants of her life before the attack. Without Finn, it meant nothing. She didn't want any of it.

TESSIE PRESSED her back against the cold alley wall and

looked toward the courtyard. She had to get out of the Nichol. Standing in a stranger's boots and her home commandeered, her chest sank with the pressure of it all as the rumblings of voices wafted down the alley.

Slipping in behind a family and walking in step towards Bethnal Green Road, Tessie's mind wandered to where she might find refuge as a hand gripped her shoulder and spun her around. It was Moses. His dark eyes shot through her.

"There you are!" He dug his fingers into her arm and dragged her to him. She could smell the alcohol on him again. "I seen ya come out of the stairwell, thought that couldn't possibly be you. What a gift!"

Tessie struggled as his hand gripped harder, yanking her toward the back of the building.

"Let me go!"

"You'll be wishing we finished the job last time." He hugged her to him, a vice grip around the back of her neck. "Gotta pay for my Johnny now too."

"What are yer talking about? Tell me what happened to Finn? Where is he?"

"What happened to him? I'll tell ya what's gonna happen to him."

Tessie kicked her boots to trip him but his stride was strong, his maroon coat whipping with each step.

"Let me go!"

Moses came to the corner and looked around, moving his grip to Tessie's jaw. "Need just the right spot," he said. "Gonna take my time, I am. Do this right. Do this for Johnny."

Seeing the dark alley corner awaiting her, she bit down on Moses' hand, clenching her teeth against the meat of his thumb. It crunched, blood flooding her mouth and ripping his hand back in anger, he punched her in the cheek. She tumbled against the stones and rolled onto her stomach, desperately crawling away.

"You fucking bitch! Take my Johnny and bite my fucking thumb off!!"

Flailing her arms for anything to fight with she felt something round and heavy, and struggling to lift it with one arm, she let it come down hard on his head.

"Fuck!" Moses faltered, releasing his grip just enough for her to scramble out, though he wasn't unconscious. He staggered back as Tessie found her feet and sprinted away from him.

"Oh no you don't," Moses yelled after her. "The Angel wants you. I want you. So you'll be got! You hear me! You'll be got!"

Tessie ran, limped and staggered, one leg after the other, pelting against the cobblestones. Bolting up a staircase she followed it higher as it linked to the next building, threading each to the next.

Moses ploughed after her, thunking his heavy limbs, as his head struggled to stay upright.

"You'll be got!" he hollered.

Tessie kept on, heaving her breath in painful huffs. Reaching a steep rooftop, she hiked her leg up, pushing her body to its peak. Flipping over the top, she skated along the tiles toward the edge, reaching for grip. The brittle shingles rippled under her weight, breaking away and cascading to the cobblestones below. Seeing the gutter approaching, Tessie grabbed it. Her body jolted to a stop and with splintered hands she pulled herself upright, seeing a lower roof a short jump across the alley. Could she make it? She looked down at her bleeding hands as her side throbbed, her face swelling from the blow to her cheek.

"Bloody hell, woman," she cursed. "You're gonna break your bleedin' neck."

The thunder of steps approached as Moses clambered up the rooftop behind her, and sucking in her insides, she launched into the blackness. Scrambling in mid-air, she hit hard against the lower roof. She slid again, faster and faster, smashing against the building wall as she flipped over the side and hung on to the last shingle. Her wound tore open, a burst of pain erupting, but there was no time. She let go, landing heavily on her ankles with a crash.

She buckled over trying to stand, and looking behind her she saw Moses peering into the dark from the highest roof. He couldn't see her. She heard him cursing as she hobbled away from him and into the night.

CHAPTER 11

Behind her horses nuzzled their stall doors and shook out their manes. She had passed these stables every day on her way to the markets, and here and now, they were her only refuge. Pulling off her boots, her ankles were swollen grey, and she stretched out her aching frame over the stable floor for a few moments of respite. It had been a long day filled with blow after blow, and seeing blood had soaked through her dress where her stitches had torn, she pressed her cold hands to her cheek to calm the flush rising from her chest. She didn't have long to rest.

A small sliver of sky shone through the rafters as she listened to the voices pass by the stable entrance waiting patiently for the voice she wanted. She had barely escaped Moses' attack and she knew this very moment there were more men out there stirred up by his sighting of her, and the fresh wound to his thumb and pride. She had to get far away from the Nichol, but she had one last visit to make. Pressing her eye socket to a knotted gap in the wood, she kept watch, stilling her breath and ready to pounce.

When she saw the glint of a red beard, she threw her

walking stick across the alleyway and the man passing tripped heavily, landing on his stomach. Launching herself at his back, she pressed her small pocketknife to his neck as he turned over. Its blade was only as long as her little finger, but she would make it count.

"Remember me, Billy?"

Billy's face contorted and he riled up as Tessie pressed the blade hard against his neck. He was stronger than her and could easily push her away, but she would get her cut across his neck first. She'd make sure of that. Gritting down hard so he could see the venom in her, she felt like a wild woman.

"Aye, yer do!" she said.

"Get off me." He was barely eighteen years of age and his voice squeaked with exertion.

"Yer have some beans to spill."

"I don't know anything," he said, and wriggled again. She held fast, ignoring the excruciating pain in her side as she pressed herself against him. She could not let this chance go.

"If yer had let me be that day in the alley I'd have no idea to come for yer. But yer had to crow about it, be the man about town. Be the man now, Billy, and tell me what yer know."

"I don't know anything." His voice took on a pleading tone.

"Yer knew they were coming for me. Well they came, Billy! How did yer know?"

"I heard them talking is all."

"Who talking?"

"Some of the lads. Moses's lad, Johnny."

"Tell me about Finn. What happened to him that night?"

"Are you mad? You were there. How would I know if you don't?"

"What of him?"

"He's gone!"

"What happened?"

"Because." He struggled to pull his neck away from the blade as his voice screeched. "He killed Johnny. Moses' son. He killed him. Some kind of struggle happened. I don't even know how you got away."

"And...keep going."

"I don't know if it happened in your place but they were raiding the Nichol all the next day and I heard..."

"He got out? Finn got out?"

"I don't know! They were looking for both of you so he must have. What are you even doing here?"

"I've come back for him."

"Well if he's still around here he is as good as dead. Same as you are. They've got him or they'll get him."

Tessie searched his face, as she pushed the blade into his neck just enough to pinch the skin, a small trickle of blood leaking out.

"Why did this happen?" She strained, earnest emotion crowding her face now.

"As if I know," he insisted. She let out a frustrated scream towards him.

"What else did they say?" She pressed it further, her eyes wide with adrenaline. He squirmed again.

"Sending you home in a box. That's what they said. I don't know what it means."

"Why?" Tessie asked.

"I don't know!"

"Why did they keep looking for me if they thought I was dead?"

"I told yer. The box!"

Tessie's eyes drifted up the alley, his words circling in her head as she tried to make sense of them. What box? A coffin? Were they sending her home to her mother in a coffin?

Tessie shook her head. Is that why they wanted her body? *Say hello to your mum for me.*

Oh my God. Tessie's head spun. Her mother. It was true. It was all to do with her mother.

Taking his chance to push her away, Billy launched himself to his feet and Tessie rolled to the side of him, a scream escaping her lips as her wound twisted and she doubled over.

"You cut me," Billy said, wiping the small amount of blood from his neck.

Tessie couldn't get up and cut her eyes at him as she lay on her back, catching her breath. "Yer lucky that's all I did."

"You shouldn't have come back. Should have taken your chances and run. Finn's dead. Or gone, and you will be too if you don't get out of here."

"And yer should choose your friends more wisely," she scoffed, both of them now bereft of venom. The tension had passed and he was just a stupid boy.

"Go on. Get out of here," Tessie said, staring down at her boots.

Billy turned to leave, but paused. "Are you going to tell my ma?"

"If yer don't sod off now, Billy Brittle, I just might."

He turned and obeyed, leaving Tessie slumped on her knees.

THE EVENING VOICES died down as the chestnut mare beside her rustled her hooves in the straw. Holding herself against the wall, she pressed the throbbing stitches beneath her dress, steadying herself by inhaling the musty dampness of mud and manure. It was dark and quiet in the alleys outside, the Nichol cocooned in a hibernating fold. She was a stranger here now.

Looping the satchel Kyran had given her over her neck, she ran her fingers over its surface, wondering if the man who'd given it to her could be trusted after all. She'd barely paid attention to the satchel's quality. It was far too expensive for her to be carrying around. Summoning the last of her energy, she braced her side and leant heavily on her walking cane. She pushed away from the stables and out into the night.

Out on Bethnal Green Road where the street lamps were lit and public houses hung lanterns by their doors, she kept to the darkness away from the main road and thought of Finn. She held hope of running into him with every turning corner. This city was where they found their freedom together. Or at least found their own version of it.

The path beneath her chose itself. She was headed to the river - to the docks where Finn had worked almost every day. Her wound throbbed as the gas lanterns along the docks came into view. It was the only place she knew to find a sense of him.

A dull moon cast light over the murky river water, its briny swill prickling her face. Kneeling beneath the lamplight, she looked down into the Thames, the dim light fading quickly in its depths. It was dark and lifeless, and she thought of Finn's warmth and life and energy swallowed beneath its watery skin - held captive and out of reach. She thought of Lucy's story, about the bloated body being pulled from its depths, lungs full of riverbed and sewage. No, that was not her Finn. That was not his story. It wouldn't end in those murky waters.

"Are yer here?" She cried out over the water and the empty docks. "Are yer here?"

The silence rolled back off the river and a scream burned

in her chest, hot, black tar as hot tears choked in her throat.

Behind her, something clattered. Was somebody there? She thought she saw movement in the shadows and focused on a stack of crates beside a warehouse, just missing the stream of moonlight. She almost called out but swallowed it back. She waited, but the noise carried away on the wind and she saw nothing move.

Removing a small tallow candle from the satchel, she set it on the ground and, fumbling with a small tin of matches, struck the flint. The wick flickered into life. Sizzling and sputtering, it claimed a small ring of light against the cold. She held her hands up to seal in its struggling heat and it bloomed in her hands. "That's it," she coaxed. She imagined the heat reaching out into the night, high above the smog and across the city. "Where are yer?" she prayed. "Help me find yer."

She guarded the flame, its spitting black smoke and greasy odour catching every flurry of wind. She willed it to hold. To reach out and shine bright. To bring him home. If only she could hear his call across the city, across the river water. *Tell me where you are!*

Her shoulders sunk under the weight of heartbreak as she pressed her fists to her eyes. The unknown expanse between them overwhelmed her so she breathed it out. "I know yer are out there," she said, resolved, and longing for a sign to stretch out of the water. A sign to speak to her from the last place she knew he had been. A thread she could tug on, and pull across the ocean. From her pocket she gripped the St. Brigid medallion and, kissing its surface, she bent beneath the dock and dropped it into the water.

Finally, she left the candle to beam her heartbreak out into the world. She walked away and the candle shrank against the backdrop of black night. It was the only beacon she had to offer.

CHAPTER 12

*A*rthur's carriage rolled through the late night streets under the cover of darkness. Inside, Arthur's eyes darted back and forth and his fists pounded his knees. "What the bloody hell was he thinking?" he demanded.

Castor's brow was flexed in thought. "Maybe he believed the note."

"Believed the note," Arthur spat back. "He was supposed to believe the note. And if he believed it he certainly didn't follow it. He's lucky Moses didn't slice him to bits."

"Maybe he's up to something? Has something else planned."

"He ain't up to shite but getting in my way and making things worse. And in the meantime, another shipment wasted. Another line of creditors unhappy. And this business drags on. The hell is he playing at?"

Caster sat back and listened.

"I should have sent you. He might have listened to you. He certainly doesn't listen to me." Arthur was talking to himself now, his cheeks flushed with bluster.

"We'll get it back under control, Artie. It'll just take time."

"I want it under control now. He can't...why won't he…?" Arthur thumped the side of the seat beside him.

The carriage rumbled along the side of the canal and settled beneath the bridge. Moses and his men emerged from the shadow and gathered around it in wait, though it was Castor who stepped out first, and, fixing his suit, indicated for Moses to approach.

"Only you," he said, "The rest of you, back ten paces. Now!"

Arthur waited as the men moved back, forming a healthy semi-circle around the carriage, and Moses stepped toward Castor.

"Don't order me, black man. When it's just you and me. It's just you and me."

Arthur watched as Castor gritted his jaw and squared his shoulders. "I'm sorry for your boy, but it is never *just you and me*. I speak for him, you understand. And you will hear me."

Moses squinted his eyes. "Should have been you in that room. Not me. And not my boy."

"Enough! In here." Arthur kicked the door open and Moses quickly turned away from Castor and pulled himself into the carriage opposite Arthur.

"What happened?" Arthur clenched his teeth. "What bloody happened?"

Moses rubbed his hands together in his lap, snivelling from the cold. "Haven't found the bloke yet. Nor her."

"Well it's one thing to rant about revenge for your Johnny, but unless you find him you won't have it, will you?"

"I will find him. Don't worry about that."

"I'm not worried about it. I don't care about him. I care about her. She was the goal, remember. What of her?"

Moses ran his fingers over his greasy beard and looked out the carriage window. "I don't have her neither."

Arthur thumped the side of the carriage with his fist. Glaring at Moses, he did it again. "It wasn't a complicated task."

"It got complicated when Kyran showed up, didn't it?"

Arthur's piercing eyes flared and he locked his jaw. "This has turned into a bleedin' debacle, and I don't do debacles, do I, Moses? I get you to take care of debacles because when I see one, I fucking lose my wits."

"I have men stretched from here to St Paul's. Watching the River. Riding the canals—"

"They don't even know who they're looking for."

'They do. I've given them all a good description. She has auburn hair and a gap in her teeth, right here." He pointed to his own. "A pretty thing. And he has a scar above his left eye. We'll find them. We will."

"And Kyran?"

"You'd know better than I where he might be. Or where he might hide her."

Arthur's nostrils flared in distaste. "You'd be surprised the things he kept to himself."

"One of my men found him coming back into London."

"Who?"

"Right there." Moses pointed to a man a few yards back waiting with the others.

"You," Arthur called and opened the cab door.

A man waiting near the front of the pack raised his head, jutting his chin out in a well-practiced defensive position.

"You!"

"Sir?" he swallowed.

"Come here."

Cautiously approaching, he paused a step or two from the door as Moses's expression offered nothing of reassurance or warning.

"You saw Kyran?"

"I did, sir." His shoulders were relaxed, comfortable, even proud of the topic at hand.

"Tell me."

"I saw him cross the bridge just north of us, sir. Making his way from up South into the city by the looks. So I stopped him."

"You stopped him?" Arthur gave nothing away. His eyes deadpan as he rubbed his goatee in consideration.

"Yes, sir. I knew he'd interrupted the attack of that girl and you wanted her. It was the least I could do. So's I jumped in front I did and he stopped. He had to, I was in his way."

'Masterful." Arthur widened his eyes. "Was the girl with him?"

"No, she weren't, sir. But I did ask him."

"And what did he say?"

"He said she absconded, sir. Ran away."

"And did he give you any other details?"

"No, sir. But he seemed to be telling the truth. She weren't anywhere I could see. And I didn't see any, you know, any girl's stuff. Women's stuff in the carriage, sir."

"So what happened then?"

"Well, I wasn't sure what to do to be honest. It's Kyran, you know. But I thoughts he's betrayed us he has. He's left us and he's working against us now. I couldn't let that pass without a, you know, a bit of roughing up."

Arthur squinted his eyes. "A roughing up?"

"Yes, sir. I walloped him, sir. A blow right to the side of his head. I don't think he expected it neither because I got a few more in before he even reacted, sir. Fell off his wagon and then I got the boots in."

"Did you hurt him?"

The man paused at the question, unsure how to answer. "He was cut up a bit, sir, yes."

Arthur froze in position, pursing his lips, his eyes glazing over. "Castor...?"

Castor stood only a few feet away and approached.

"Do you recall my exact words when it comes to matters of Kyran?"

"He is not to be touched." Castor pursed his lips, narrowing his gaze at the unsuspecting man. It was an accusation, and the man started to jitter.

"He's betrayed us, sir." He glanced back at the other men, but there was no one there who could help him.

Arthur took a step closer. "He is not to be touched. He is not to be touched." Lunging at him, Arthur locked his hands around his throat as behind him the other men looked on helplessly. The man's strangled cries escaped as Arthur's broad frame dragged him down to the canal edge, pushing his head beneath the freezing water with his strong forearms. There was splashing as his arms floundered and Arthur positioned himself back to avoid getting wet. He held him down, longer, and longer till the kicking and splashing died down. Then it was quiet.

Arthur stood up, the man's limp body draped over his foot and lilted into the canal. Kicking his foot free, he rolled the body over, letting it sink into the water and below the surface. Turning back around, he adjusted his hat and re-buttoned his coat without so much as a glance at his shocked onlookers.

"Get the word out," he said to Moses. "I want more men. I want an army, you hear me?"

Moses turned back to greet him. "Yes, sir. An Army."

"We'll flood them out of their own city. I want them arriving there in droves. I want this war over. "

"And what of the girl?"

"Find her, dammit. Find her! She'll strike a blow mightier than anything else this rabble can muster."

"And Kyran?"

"Leave him. He is my problem." Arthur turned to address the men waiting in the shadow. "Kyran is not to be touched!"

CHAPTER 13

Finn huddled behind a shipping crate just out of the moonlight. Dark bruising swelled around his eye, complimenting the old scar above it, and the stoop in his shoulders gave away his exhaustion. His body was fighting to carry on, though his mind felt numb with days of being chased, each hour blurring into the next. He couldn't even be sure how long it had been. Days. Too many days. And the Angel's men were out there still.

He hadn't known the true number of them until he'd had to hide, and every time he'd tried to break free, they were quick on his tail. Every corner, every shopfront it seemed, there stood a man with a black cuff on his wrist, eyes scanning for him.

But it was the image of Tessie's blue eyes, wide with terror, that beckoned him through the fog every time he stopped - every time he thought he could not go on any longer. Where was she this very moment? Lost and wounded, dying in a dark place where he could never reach her?

When he'd woken in that room she was already gone. Her

blood fresh on the floor, with men standing where her body had been. He'd fought his way out of there in a fever of anger and desperation. It happened in a blur of fists and twisting bodies. He'd run with screaming threats at his back and disappeared into the dark Nichol. They'd said she wouldn't last long, and every moment that passed Finn felt the ache. He had to keep going. He had to find her.

He sprinted all the way to Kyran Luther's home in Albemarle Street, to the man who had left Tessie open and vulnerable. Though thump as he did on the door, it was not a gentleman who greeted him, but a pistol and a young woman with golden hair and wild green eyes. She'd given no answer to his demands for Tessie and he could see she had no part in any of it. So he'd retreated to the Docks, a place that even in the dark he knew like his own home.

Around him the night sky swelled up, enveloping him in darkness while all around him the city moved and slept and stirred. She was under the same sky as he, somewhere in this damned city. Clenching his fists, and raising his weary eyes to the stars a wordless prayer escaped with his breath.

It was not the first time he had lost someone. It was not the first time he had failed to protect someone he was supposed to keep safe. It burned in him now, deep in his belly, thrusting him all the way back to his memories of Dublin and young Tadhg. It was the hot coal he carried in his chest. This time it would be different. This time he would get her back.

HE JERKED awake with the sounds around him. Daylight had already gathered strength and the docks bustled. Oh god! He had slept too late.

Pulling his collar around his neck, his head low and his

shoulders hunched to his ears, he walked with the crowd, trying to blend in with the fresh workers of the day. He was known here. This was the last place he should be. Pushing through the familiar street-sellers, rolling their carts with steaming pea soup, eel pies and mash, he pulled his cap down low, his long fringe flipped over his face. His cracked ribs caught with each inhale. He had to get out of here!

"Hey!" a man called out. There it was, like a jolt through his chest. How could he be so bloody stupid! He strode faster toward the exit gates, his body still awkward from sleep and his boots tangling in undone laces. He had to move faster.

"Get out of my way," he strained, weaving through the mass of people before crashing headlong into a man. They met eyes before he lurched in the opposite direction. But he saw the recognition.

"Over here!" The man's gruff voice rang out over the crowd. "He's over here!"

How long could he run from these people? How long could he fend them off? His body was so weary and numb with running, he could hardly control it. His limbs clumsily striving towards the passenger ships and loading bays. Waiting travellers lingered in rag-tangle groups while rich commuters were escorted aboard, their expensive luggage trailing behind them. Finn circled the crowds trying to find a way in. He could hear the chorus of men behind him, their heads bobbing up and down as they too navigated a path and kept an eye on him. Try as he might, he was backing himself into a corner.

He moved behind a waiting passenger group, ducking low and trying to look as if he was inspecting a trunk to be loaded.

The Angel's men ran past and he stood up briefly to survey the outlook but ducked down again as the first one circled back towards him.

"Stay down," a man beside him said without looking down at him. "Or the bastards will see yer." Finn obeyed without argument.

The man kept an eye out, starting to whistle casually as Finn crouched by his feet.

"Are yer wanting to get on this boat?" the young man added in an Irish accent fit to challenge Finn's.

"Not if I can help it. Where are they?"

"Not 20 yards up that away. The rotten pieces of shite. Can smell them from here." The man spat on the ground in front of Finn. "Every last one of them."

Finn cursed too, peeking up high enough to see them gathered in a group surveying the passengers.

"Yer don't remember me?" The young man turned to face him, dipping his hat in a hurried introduction. Glancing up, Finn saw it was the stocky young man from the West India gates - the man he'd given his shift to.

"Aye," Finn said. "Catching that boat outta here I take it."

"That's the plan."

The crowd shuffled forward as the first of the steerage passengers were allowed aboard, dragging their own luggage and herding children up the boarding plank. Finn shuffled with them, rising to a slumped standing position behind the young man to better assess his situation.

To the other side of them, workers were loading the cargo hold, moving back and forward from another gangplank at the rear of the ship. "Aye. They're gonna get yer if yer don't do something. Wait here," the young man said, seeming to get an idea and set off towards the line of workmen.

"I'm not going anywhere," Finn mused under his breath as he ducked lower again and ushered a cluster of passengers to pass him. As he was considering a run for a warehouse diagonal from his position, the man returned with a wheelbarrow stacked with sacks of sugar.

"Duck behind these and I'll walk yer back to the warehouse." He pointed and without waiting to see if Finn agreed, he pushed away into the crowd. Finn dived behind the sacks of sugar and walked quickly in a crouched down position.

"Hey!" A voice called after the wheelbarrow. "That sugar goes in here."

"Walk faster, brother," the young man urged.

"Hey!"

"He's gonna make them look at us. Are they looking?"

"I'm not gonna waste time checking. Just walk."

They ignored the dockworker's calls to come back and, almost breaking into a run as they pushed the wheelbarrow to the other side of the warehouse, they were sprung.

"There! Grab him. Get them." Men ran towards them.

"This way," Finn yelled behind him, and cutting across the yard, Finn darted into a laneway weaving in and out of the row of warehouses. Here at least he had the advantage. He knew these yards well. Darting to change direction at every turn, Finn led the young man sprinting to the edge of the last warehouse. Peering out they saw the Angel's men had lost them and gathered again in front of the boarding ships waiting intently for them to resurface.

"What's yer name then?" Finn extended his hand but the young man's spritely eyes were fixed on the dockyard.

"What?"

"I'm Finn."

"I know. I'm Mickey. Mickey Bell." He gave Finn's hand a quick shake though he was focussed ahead.

Finn observed the workers preparing to pull in the gangplank on his ship. "If yer run yer can make it. You're going to miss your boat if yer don't."

"They'll see me."

"They're not looking for yer," Finn offered. "They might let yer pass."

"They're no friends of mine either, and they've seen me with yer now. If I go they'll know you're over here." Finn watched his face wrestle with the decision, his eyes intense and brow creased beneath his thick dark hair.

"Where is it going?" Finn asked.

"Boston." Mickey took a long deep breath. "It's going to Boston." Staring at the ship he had been set to board only moments earlier he stood up, his expression changing. "Sod it. Sod those bastards. Let's go this way." Finn followed as Mickey slung his bag over his shoulder and pointed further up the river. As they approached, Finn saw a barge preparing to push away. Mickey pulled change from his pocket. "Are yer heading to the south bank, brother?"

The grey-haired lighterman chewed on his tongue and looked him over without answering.

"Half a shilling for the pass?" The lighterman held out his hand without a word as Finn found a place between the hay bales. The mainsail dropped and his young son ogled them, his face pruned up and disapproving as they pulled away.

Finn's heart thudded and his head whirred as Mickey sat beside him, his arms folded. He was staring out at the murky river, his eyes held steadfast on the ship they were leaving behind in the harbour. As they drew away, he pulled a paper ticket from his pocket and held it up to the wind, watching as it flew away, fluttering across the surface of the water. Finn watched with just as much regret, a pang of guilt stabbing him in the chest. He and Tessie had dreamed of a ticket such as that for as long as he could remember, and here he had foiled a fellow Irishmen's dreams. It could take another lifetime to save for that ticket.

"What's in Boston?" Finn asked with a sombre tone.

Mickey glanced back at him with a glint in his eye. "Nothing but dreams now, brother. Nothing but dreams."

Finn heard the pain in his voice and looked down at his hands. "I owe yer, Mickey Bell. Yer saved me back there and yer have paid dearly for it. I'm sorry."

Mickey rubbed his face and shook his head. "Argh. It obviously wasn't meant to be. The New World isn't ready for me yet. And truth be told I was half loathed to leave before knocking the teeth outta a good number of them Angel's boys anyway."

Finn managed a half-smile. The soupy smell of the river bubbled up around them and the icy wind whipped their faces as they moved further away from the West End Docks. They were leaving the East End and Finn watched over his shoulder, scanning the landscape. Was he moving further away from Tessie with every second?

The lighterman steered the barge around the river's bend, past Wapping and towards St. Saviour's Dock where Finn noted he was pulling in to dock.

"You're dropping us at Jacob's Island?"

"You wanted to go across," the lighterman said. "This is it."

"You're not serious, man."

The lighterman shrugged as the barge bumped against the pylons of the narrow inlet dock, shadowed by the overhanging galleries of decaying apartments. "Out," he said. Finn cursed under his breath as he leapt onto the docks.

"Yer paid him how much?" Finn shook his head at Mickey as he too followed suit. The lighterman wasn't interested and scrambled to pull away as soon as Mickey's feet left the deck.

"Hope yer choke on it," Finn called and picking up a stone from the decking, he threw at the withdrawing barge. The lighterman's son picked it up and threw it back. It ricocheted off the side the rickety building and lopped back into the water with an ominous plop.

"Where are we?" Mickey asked looking towards their only exit - a dark alley weaving through a menacing warren of rotting galleries and apartments.

"Jacob's Island." Finn rubbed his face and closed his eyes. Of all the places to end up this morning, it was a rookery dark and notorious for its murder and thievery; a cesspit of open sewage and rats. The stench of carcasses rose up through the sea of shacks before them, each one ready to topple into the mud at any moment. Not here. He had to get back to Tessie. His chest screamed with it.

"I'd cross yourself if you're into that sort of thing," Finn suggested and did so himself before taking the coins from his coat and pushing them into his boots. "And keep yer hands in yer pockets unless yer want someone else's in there."

Mickey nodded. "I know the drill, brother. Let's move fast eh?"

Finn took another deep breath. Battered and bruised, his body moved heavily, twisted and achey from sleeping on the ground in the cold. He was so bloody tired.

"I can run with a target on my back, how about yer?" Mickey winked as if roused by the challenge.

"Let's hope we don't have to." Finn edged closer to the alley and peered down its long tunnel. Then, giving Mickey a hopeful nod, they headed in.

essie had paid her last pennies to the Whitechapel dosshouse. It was all she could do to stop the frost devouring her from the feet up. Though it offered no hearth or fire, no food to share, it was more like a stable, herding the poor in to shelter on hard benches and straw, and paying all they had for the privilege.

Church-like pews had lined the walls, a single rope threaded across them to lean forward and sleep upon. She had lain in a wooden box on the floor with two dozen others, feeling nailed into place with her knees curled up in front of her. The blood had dried hard to her dress and every movement yanked at the swollen stitches as the hard edges of the box dug into her hip. All night she had been restless with the sound of boots scraping on the wood.

It was barely first light when the stewards roused the quiet mass, eager to turn them back out into the street. Tessie snapped her limbs out straight and uncreased her neck as she moved with the herd, limping her stockingless feet through the white snow across town to Mayfair.

The morning streets had barely stirred to life as the blue

door at Number 22 Albemarle Street came into view. The affluent suburb was still quiet enough for her to pass by unnoticed, though this time, she didn't care who saw her.

Clubbing her fist on the door, she collapsed her weight against the frame and waited. Her brow sweaty with sickness, she thumped again, and again. The woman who opened was the same as before, but this time Tessie had a different look in her eyes.

"Let me in."

"Who are you?"

"Yer remember me. I know yer do. Is he here?"

"Mr Luther is not home."

"Then I will wait for him." Barely able hold herself upright a moment longer, Tessie pushed into the warmth of the house and the woman ran down the hallway in a panic.

"Miss Ruby...Miss Ruby..." the woman called. Turning back to Tessie, she pointed at a room just off the hall. "Wait in there. Don't touch anything."

Tessie obeyed and moved quickly towards the fire inside, gripping the mantle to hold herself up. The ache in her side spread a fuzzy burn through her body and she felt the colour draining from her face. She had to hold on just a little longer.

Shifting her wet boots on the lavish rug beneath her, she had never before stood in a room so grand. An impressive bookcase formed the far wall, heavy with leather bound books in greens and reds and gold leaf imprint. Looking up at it she felt dizzy. Cross-stitch artworks and miniature portraits decorated the side tables with delicately crafted ornaments in silver and glassworks. Above the mantle, a large mirror loomed in a striking silver frame, her reflection pale and ragged in contrast to the splendid room about her. Above, a rather modest glass chandelier hung with its lamps unlit, and at the window billowing velvet curtains were pulled to the side, allowing the dull morning light into the room. This was where Kyran spent his time, reading the newspaper, relaxing in his gentleman's attire.

"Hello?" a woman's voice spoke from the doorway. Spinning around, Tessie stood face to face with a young woman of similar age and height. With bouncy blonde curls and an easy air of luxury, she was perfectly put together, her green eyes alight with caution.

"I need to see Mr Luther." Tessie gritted the words through clenched teeth, aware her own hair hung down her back in wild disarray, while her face was scratched and bruised. Below her skirts, her boots were caked in mud and the cloak itself littered with hay and refuse. She was a frightful sight.

"Who are you?" the woman pressed.

"I must see him. Where is he?" She doubled over in a stab of pain. "Are yer his wife? Or his sister?"

"Neither. What's happened to you? Are you injured?"

Tessie brushed her cloak aside, exposing the large bloodstain on her dress.

The woman circled around her, her eyes darting astutely over Tessie from head to toe. "Do you have weapons on you?"

Tessie shot her eyes as she doubled over again in pain. "I'm not here to hurt anyone." She could feel herself losing her wits. *No. Not here, not now.* "Here." Looping the satchel from around her neck she threw it towards the woman. "Take it. See for yourself. I just need to see him. I need to go to Dublin..." she grimaced again, her words disappearing.

The woman snatched up the satchel and looked inside before daring to step closer, touching her hand to Tessie's brow and then squeezing her fingers. "Martha?" She marched toward the door. It promptly opened and the women who had greeted Tessie poked her head in. "Have them draw a bath in the guest room at once. And send for the doctor."

"That isn't necessary." Tessie stumbled in protest and gripped the mantle.

"You have a fever and are fit to freeze. It's the least we can do. Let's go," she insisted. "Martha? Come help me please."

Martha rushed back into the room and, moving to the other side of Tessie, they walked her across the room to the entrance, helping her to lean heavily on the polished banister and up the imperial staircase.

Inside the guest room, a screen was set up behind which a steaming bath seemed to magically appear out of nowhere. Strange hands unlaced her, twisting and turning her around, until finally she was lowered into the tub, the hot water rushing over her in a wave, her skin tingling and her head swilling in a steamy haze. She had barely eaten or slept since leaving Kyran's cottage and, leaning her head back against the porcelain tub, she thought she might sink beneath the water, feeling so heavy. So incredibly heavy. She couldn't imagine where Finn might be at this moment. She did not recognise her life anymore at all.

～

A SMALL SLITHER of light caught Tessie's eye and hearing movement by the bed she lurched upright. It was the blonde woman standing beside her.

"What day is it?" Tessie spoke quickly, afraid she had again slept away three or four days.

"The same day you arrived," she answered. "Wednesday."

"Did yer tell me your name?"

"You did not tell me yours, my dear."

"Tessie. Tessie O'Shea."

The woman seemed to startle, flashing her green eyes but recovering quickly. "I am Ruby St. Claire. And it is time for your medicine." She spoke in a hushed voice as she poured a small thimble full of liquid into a glass and handed it to Tessie. "This here is laudanum for the pain. And there is willow bark tea here to help your fever."

Tessie took it without argument. "The doctor?"

"He's been and gone. He cleaned your wound and gave you three new stitches. You barely moved a muscle. You need bed rest now, that is all."

Tessie stared up at the ornate ceiling, intricate patterns woven into the cornices, framing the room in subtle grandeur. Her side ached and burned, though she felt clean and the rest had cleared her head. Though more bed rest when there was so much to do? The thought of it triggered pressure in her chest.

"I've brought you some food and you must eat. I'm sure you haven't eaten much in the last few days. Can you sit up?"

Tessie struggled to pull herself up against her pillows as Ruby set a tray of food on her lap and poured her tea. "This is the willow bark. Drink all of it if you can."

Tessie looked down at the plate of hardboiled eggs, halved and arranged with thick slices of ham, and a warm bread roll with neat cubes of butter in a serving bowl. She lifted her dainty teacup, sipped from it, and set it down again in its matching saucer, enjoying the satisfying sound it made as it slid into place. Next, she picked up the shiny silver cutlery, chinking the heavy handles against the plate. Never had she seen such a breakfast feast and, feeling self-conscious and clumsy, she didn't quite know how to eat it.

"Eat," Ruby implored when she saw her hesitation. So, ignoring the cutlery, Tessie ripped open the bread roll and layered it with all the ham and as many eggs as would fit. There were six cubes of butter, more than enough to cater one bread roll, though she stacked them all in, not willing to waste an ounce of freely provided food. The salty creaminess flooded her mouth as she took a giant bite. How good life must be, she thought, with a breakfast such as this each morning.

The room stayed quiet as she ate. Tessie felt conscious of the noise her every movement made, while Ruby sat almost entirely statuesque by the window.

"Kyran and I do not have secrets from each other," Ruby said finally. There was a warning in her tone that was not lost on Tessie.

"I'm not about secrets or anything of the like. I just need to speak with him."

"Speak with him about what?"

"I told yer. I must go to..." Tessie trailed away unsure how much of her story to tell. Could she speak to this woman of Dublin...of her mother and the Angel...of everything that had happened? "Is Kyran really not here?"

Ruby shook her head, her eyes creased with concern and seeming to search Tessie for more. "I'm concerned for him. Do you know something?"

The answer stuck in Tessie's throat and she took another bite of her bread roll, taking time to finish her mouthful. "He said he was to return. I believed he'd be here by now."

"Where did you last see him?" Ruby pressed her hands together, her tone strained and difficult.

"In his cottage," Tessie admitted. "Days ago now."

Ruby sat upright, leaning forward in a pleading position. "You must tell me if something has happened to him."

"If I knew that I wouldn't have come looking for him here, would I? I need his help."

"Help with what?" Ruby was more forceful now, stamping her foot beneath her billowing skirts.

"I've lost someone. And he can help me find them."

"Why would you think that?"

"He helped me before. I know nothing about him. Him or his life, but I know that."

Ruby turned her gaze back to the window and wrang her hands in front of her. "You don't trust me," she said matter-of-factly. "Let me tell you something then. I've been in Paris and Kyran was scheduled to join me last week. I received a note in his stead saying he had been delayed. That something had happened. And then nothing. Now I return home to be told he rushed out of here a week ago without warning and has not yet returned. And now you..."

Tessie cleared her throat and shifted on her pillows. She was supposed to add to the story here and explain herself, though she didn't.

"The trip to Paris was important to us," Ruby pressed. "To myself and Kyran. If he did not come it was for a very good reason. Or a very bad one."

"What were yer doing in Paris?" Tessie asked the question if only to stall the moment she'd have to tell her own story. Ruby lightly smiled as if understanding the predicament and paced back and forth in front of Tessie's bed with her arms folded.

"Business. I was there doing the groundwork for something important. Being charming Ruby St. Claire for three months of wining and dining, and fostering mutually beneficial friendships. It may sound like fun and splendour to you, but I assure you it was more than that." She stopped to look again out the window at the street below, always keeping an eye out for Kyran. "I'm sure you know that while men with money enjoy the intelligent conversation of women, and can be indelibly swayed in subtle ways, when it comes to the essentials of business, actually signing on the dotted line, they want a man to be serious with." Tessie heard a sourness encroach upon her tone. "They want to smoke their cigars and chuckle about their business prowess. And so Kyran was due to arrive," she said. "I had the financial workings in place but they wanted Kyran to put their mind at ease, and of course, sign the contract. When he didn't arrive it lost momentum immediately, and while I struggled to keep it going, it would no longer be discussed with me." Ruby gave a rye smile. "And there you have it. I have returned with no investment deal. And now no Kyran."

"Are yer like him?" Tessie tested the water. "Are yer a pretender?"

Ruby squeezed her eyes, any shock at the question well hidden. "That deal was important to us, you understand. Very important. Kyran would not abandon it so easily. So now it is your turn." She said with a challenge in her tone.

Tessie stared down at the last of her willow bark tea having gone cold in its cup. "We were thrown into an ordeal together. I have no connection to Kyran outside of that." She formulated her thoughts. "Over a week ago I was forced to deliver a message to him. A note in an envelope. In the middle of the night."

"What note? What did it say?" Ruby moved closer, gripping the bedpost.

"I couldn't tell yer that. I didn't read it. But it did not go to plan."

"Who was the note from? Who forced you to deliver it?"

Tessie stumbled over the interruption, reluctant to say his name.

"Who forced you!"

"The Angel of Bishopsgate."

Ruby froze, the colour draining from her face. "You work for the Angel?"

"No..." Tessie shook her head, but the panic in Ruby's eyes filled the room. Grabbing Tessie's wrist she checked for a brand mark of the Angel and when there was none she pulled her forward, yanking at her collar to see her neck and shoulders. Still no mark, though Ruby started to back out of the room.

"I don't work for him!' Tessie protested, thrusting her tray aside. She rushed at the door but it slammed before she could reach the handle. "No, please! Yer don't understand." Tessie banged on the door as the key in the lock started to turn. She was locking her in!

"No!" Tessie implored. "Don't leave me here. I was forced to do it. I was forced to!" Tessie could hear Ruby on the other side. "Please. He tried to kill me. He did this to me. Please." Tessie quietened to listen. Was she still out there? Was she listening?

"I'm sorry," Ruby said finally. "I cannot take the risk. Not until I know Kyran is safe. You must pray he returns sooner rather than later." And with that, she walked away.

CHAPTER 15

Finn had heard it called the "Venice of drains" and now he knew why. Winding their way over haphazard bridges, the drain waters below were stained red from the tanneries, and all manner of slime exuded from the cracks and crevices, freezing like stalactites hanging from the rotting structures around them. Finn understood poverty, and even squalor. The Old Nichol too was dark with hunger and hopelessness, but this place sent chills down his spine. Claustrophobic and suffocating in every dread-filled step, soot-covered and sallow faces stared at them through gaps in the flooring and broken windows. An icy wind blustered down the alley's tunnels and rats ran with them as they chose their footing carefully on the iced plank-ways, looking for any sign that they were making their way out and not simply moving in circles.

Prostitutes lingered in the darker corners, flicking their skirts for Finn and Mickey to brush past, but they did not stop, nor did they linger to draw the attention of men emptying sacks to show off their nights of thievery, or worse.

"What's got yer tangled with the Angel then?" Mickey asked with his voice low and his eyes alert.

Finn took a deep breath, knowing he owed him an explanation, some meagre consolation that missing his boat had been for something worthwhile. "My wife," was all he could muster. "They hurt my wife." The words stuck in his throat so that he pointed at a crossroads ahead of them letting Mickey choose the direction. "And yer?" Finn studied the man's face. "Yer said they cheated yer?"

Mickey nodded, his brown eyes darting ahead of them. "That's right. They did me wrong. Thieves. Every last one of them." Mickey raised his eyebrows and shrugged his shoulders as if to change the subject and led the way ahead, moving into a makeshift courtyard.

A small figure crouched in the corner caught Finn's eye. Her brown skin flushed rosy with cold, the young girl wiped her nose with the back of her hand as fizzy tufts of hair peeked out from beneath a green woollen beanie. With one eye the darkest colour brown, and the other a pearly white, she looked at Finn without seeing him, surveying him as if he was simply part of the view. In her hands she cradled a large green apple, holding it as a prized possession. Finn kept his eyes on her as they moved past. She was so small and so young to be all alone in a place such as this.

"Ain't nothing down there boys," a man's voice intruded on his thoughts, and Finn looked to see him perched on a bottom step with a dirty face and one bulging eye. "You must be lost."

Mickey and Finn ignored him, but sure enough, it was a tall blank wall stretching up three levels, with no turn left or right. It was a dead end.

"Fuck," Finn cursed under his breath and threw Mickey a worried look as they were forced to turn around.

"Told ya. Told ya, didn't I? What or who you looking for?" The man purred with a slow, gravelly drawl.

"We aren't looking for anyone," Mickey said.

"Then you're in the wrong place ain't yer." He laughed. As he did, other strange fellows emerged from the shadows, curling out into the light like disturbed insects. Intentional or not, they blocked the alley entrance and Finn and Mickey had nowhere to turn without pushing back through them.

"We are just trying to get out." Finn held his voice calm. "Can yer show us the way?"

"There is no way out," a voice said, and as Finn looked up, a man swooped down and landed crouched in front of them like a gorilla. "You're stuck here." Standing up, he was blonde and agile with his shirt half ripped open despite the cold. It exposed a chiselled chest with grimy skin and a blurry tattoo clawing up his neck. There Finn saw it. The mark of the Angel seared into his skin. What was he doing this far south if he was the branded property of the Angel?

"Says who?" Finn kept his eyes on that mark. Surely they weren't looking for him down here too.

The blonde man grinned a beaming smile of stained teeth and held out his arms to the crowd.

"We don't want any trouble," Mickey urged. "We just want to be on our way."

"Well, we don't like strangers wandering abouts in here like they own the place. Come for a look, did you? Sticking your nose in places like this it'll get bitten off. We bite, don't we lads?"

A few of the onlookers banged their fists on the walls while others watched with only vague curiosity. "This here is Ryder's territory. If you ain't with Ryder, you got no business here. And that there is a tax you have to pay."

"We ain't paying for nothing," Finn said, and Mickey moved up beside him.

"Look. Point us towards the main road and we'll be out of your way."

"That's not how it works, boys. Seems something should come of this. What do you think lads?" The blonde man clicked his fingers, signalling a growing chorus behind him.

"Yes! Yes, Lance," several cried. "Give us a show."

"Hear that?" Lance flashed his large yellow teeth and stepped to Finn. Finn was just as tall, his shoulders broad and strong from years of dock work, and he was used to being singled out for a fight. He'd had his share of them though rarely of his choosing. He could usually talk his way around it, but he could see Lance wasn't a man of reason.

"You'll let us go." Finn gritted his teeth and clenched his fists, preparing himself for the worst. "Get out of our way now."

"This here is Lance Tanner." The man on the stairs cut in again, taking it upon himself to do the man's boasting. "He's Ryder's boxer. The champion boxer. Ryder's best boxer, that is."

Finn cut his eyes. Who the hell was Ryder? And if this is Ryder's territory, why were there men with the Angel's mark swaggering around like they own the place? North of the river these men were as good as slaves.

"If all that's true then yer have nothing to prove. Let us pass." Finn tried to sound nonchalant.

"I need some practice for tomorrow night, boys. You've come along at just the right time. Help me get warmed up." Lance rolled up his sleeves, his large forearms flexing and ready.

Finn's heart pounded, his tolerance stretched to breaking. *Get out of the way, dammit!* But Lance seemed to want this show more than anyone.

The crowd started to chant in small throaty grunts,

egging Lance on and Finn darted his eyes at Mickey. There was no way out of this now. Not without a fight.

Lance turned toward him, swinging his fist to taunt them and Finn surged with adrenaline. Taking his chance to get in first, he gripped Lance's head, yanking it down hard against his knee. The cracking sound echoed off the alley walls and the onlookers fell silent as his body slid to the ground. Lance didn't move.

"Woooooo!" Mickey exclaimed, clapping his hands loudly and mocking the crowd's previous cheers. "Careful lads, this one has the rage in him, so he does."

Finn's eyes scanned the crowd, unsure which way they would turn, but while the loudest supporters of the fight stared blankly at Lance's body, the ones in the back seemed to watch on with no real attachment. "Have you just killed him?" the man on the stairs asked. "Did you just kill Lance Tanner?"

"Ah." Finn crouched down and looked at him, his chest was rising and blood gushing from his nose. He was knocked out, but alive. *Thank god!*

"What's going on?" a commanding voice spoke over the rabble and the crowd immediately parted to let him through. With pointy features and a long narrow coat that emphasised his height and leanness, the man was a mix of scrappiness and authority. He charged the ripple of fear that moved through the crowd.

"It's Ryder. It's Ryder," the crowd whispered in an ominous warning. Beside Ryder, men of girth and ugly jaws gathered close and Finn saw it again. The Angel's mark burned into the forearm of the man beside him. Faded and misshapen, but there it was none-the-less. What was this place? A gathering of the Angel's leftovers. A refuge for the riff-raff of London and those escaping the Angel's wrath?

"No, no, no. Who's done this?" Ryder clenched his fist

over Lance's body, his voice shaking. "My goddamn boxer." He pronounced his words deliberately as if he liked the way they rolled off his tongue. "Not my goddamn boxer! Who's messing with my coin now, lads. Who's been done this?" He scanned his pointy finger across the crowd.

"He started with us." Mickey held his hands up. "We wanted nothing and no trouble."

Mr Ryder's eyes shot back and forth over Mickey and Finn. What kind of man was this? Lanky with grease, and an imperceptible glean to his eyes. He stroked his beard as he stared down at Lance. "If I don't have a guaranteed winner tomorrow night, what I needs is a guaranteed loser." An accusation vibrated in his tone.

"That's no affair of ours," Finn said. "He got himself walloped good and fair. Now let us be on our way."

Ryder jabbed his skinny finger into Finn's chest and clenched his jaw, exposing a row of strong skinny teeth. "You've messed with my coin, lad. That makes it your affair. I needs a boxer now. A punching bag at that." He dipped his beady eyes over Finn's tall frame and moved to Mickey's shorter stature.

"This ain't our fight." Finn stepped forward, trying to wean the man's preying eyes from Mickey.

"It's just about coin, my friend." He rubbed his fingers together and pursed his lips. "Take the stocky one, Charley." He gestured to the gruff man beside him who moved immediately to grab him.

"No yer bleeding don't!" Mickey grappled with him, but Charley was too strong.

"Wait a minute," Finn protested as Charley wrapped his large arm around Mickey's neck and squeezed hard till his face flushed red though he struggled and kicked.

Finn flooded with panic. Mickey had just saved him, he

couldn't leave him to these animals! Mickey's eyes bulged at the pressure. He had to do something. He had to help him.

"Wait! Wait!" Finn held his hands out towards Ryder. "Don't hurt him. Wait just a minute."

"Relax, man." Ryder seemed amused. "If he does what he's told, he'll be back tomorrow. The shit beaten of out of him, sure, but he'll be back." And Charley grinned, squeezing his grip again as Mickey tried to holler.

"Wait!" Finn yelled louder to get Ryder's attention. "Why do your men wear the mark of the Angel?" He held his arms out as if holding back the tension with sheer force. "Why are they marked as the Angel's men?"

Ryder's expression fell, and jutting his chin in the air he glared at Finn. He had his attention now. He had hit a nerve.

"What?" he said, slowly. "What did you say to me?"

"The mark of the Angel?" Finn cleared his throat, fighting for confidence and pointing to the faded marks on Lance's chest and then to Charley's forearm.

"You're the boss here, right? This place is full of the Angel's leftovers. Don't yer want to stop being the Angel's scrapper?"

"The Angel's scrapper?" Ryder repeated slowly. "Did you just call me the Angel's scrapper?"

Finn gulped. He had no idea what kind of man this was. Could he appeal to his ambition? He was guessing, and he had to talk quickly. "You gotta be paying up to him like everyone else."

"What's it to you, boy?" Ryder pressed his face close to his. He was on thin ice.

"If you want more than his scraps, I can help yer."

"What makes yer think I need help from the likes of you."

"He's after me. And if you're paying up to him then you're in no better shape than anyone else. We can help each other." Finn heard the words falling from his mouth, but cocking his head to the side, he nodded towards Mickey. "Let him go and I can do that for yer. We can do it together."

Ryder's tongue snaked through his skinny teeth as he mulled it over. "I've heard crazier things from men in worse situations."

"It's the truth."

Ryder flashed his eyes, looking Finn up and down. "You. You want to take on the Angel..." And he started to laugh, looking to Charley who also started to chuckle.

Finn wasn't sure if it was a question or a joke. But bloody oath he did. If he had to take the Angel down, one man at a time to get to Tessie, then he would. "Aye, I do."

"Why?" Ryder composed himself, stroking his long beard.

"I have more reason than any man. Believe me," Finn said, squaring his shoulders and feeling the truth of it swell his conviction.

"Convince me."

"They hurt my wife. The Angel did. Came after her for no reason."

"He hurt your wife." Ryder stared into his eyes, his foul breath wafting over Finn. "Yessssss." He nodded, seeming to find what he was looking for. "Alright." He clicked his fingers. "This is what I'm talking about, Charley. Initiative. Ideas." Turning back to Finn, he pointed his finger. "Bring me proof and then we'll talk. Until then you're nothing but piss and wind." He spun around to leave and Charley wrangled Mickey along with them.

"Wait! Let him go," Finn hollered after them. "That's part of the deal. Let him go and I can..."

"Piss and wind, lad. Piss and wind." Ryder waved his arm in dismissal and strode away, Charley dragging Mickey with them and the crowd of onlookers disappeared back into the shadows. Finn was alone in the dead end courtyard, with no idea how to get out.

CHAPTER 16

Tessie hollered to be released until her throat was hoarse, though Ruby did not answer.

In her hours alone she had tried to rest, though inspecting the window and the long drop below, she imagined plunging into the snow to make her escape. She had wrangled with the lock with no success, losing hairpins through the keyhole and having no idea what she was really doing. She couldn't blame Ruby for her caution, though the agony of being stuck was exhausting and endless. She needed Kyran's help and they were wasting so much precious time.

That evening as the afternoon's dark shadow fell over the room, she heard Ruby's voice exclaim from the entrance. "Kyran! Dear God!" And Tessie's chest burst with relief.

Pressing against the door, the low rumble of Kyran's calm voice floated up the staircase. "I'm fine. I'm fine, really." His voice echoed through the luxurious hallway, weary though firm.

Was she telling him about her? Would he clear up her story and let her out? Tessie stomped her foot in anticipation.

"She is here?" he asked and she heard them approaching up the staircase, Ruby's voice trailing behind him.

"She is fine, Kyran. Let us see to you first. Please, she is resting—"

Taking her chance, Tessie pounded on the door with all her might. "Let me out! Kyran! Let me out, please!"

"Open it," his voice commanded just outside the door. She heard the rustling of skirts and the jingling of keys. As the handle turned Tessie ripped it open and there he stood, returned to his gentleman's attire, though his cheek was bruised and his hair dishevelled. Behind him Ruby bit her lip, her eyes wide and anxious.

"Are you alright?" he asked with purpose and haste.

"Yes," Tessie said, taken back by his appearance. "What's happened to yer?"

He ignored the question and turned to go back down the stairs showing the fullness of bruising along his jawline. "Let her out. She is fine. Martha?" he called, and her face too appeared in the doorframe. "Fetch her some clothes. I'm sure Ruby can spare some."

"Yes," Ruby agreed, going after him as he turned back to take her hand, squeezing it tightly.

"You will join us for supper," Kyran called to Tessie, leaving her standing in the open doorway in her nightgown. What had happened to his face? Tessie's mind raced. Had it to do with the Angel? Was there more to this yet? Ruby had been right. Something had happened to him after all.

Before long Martha and her young companion maid returned with a simple yet elegant skirt and blouse for her to change into. Tessie supposed it was one of Ruby's more plain outfits, though its quality and detail were far above anything she had worn before.

While still feeling weak, the dull ache of her wound tender and fresh, her heart thudded with renewed energy as they directed her to step into the petticoats and lift her arms as they tightened her bodice. Where her long auburn hair had splayed out wild past her shoulders, they swept it into a tidy bun at the nape of her neck. Tessie did as she was told, paying little attention to her appearance, though glancing at her reflection, it momentarily caught her breath. She was almost unrecognisable with her styled hair and tailored outfit clinging to her differently than her well-worn work dress. It changed her posture; holding her in a way that made her move differently, stand differently, like she was somebody else entirely. Moving her hand to her face and hair, it cast a shadow in her expression. This was the game, she thought, thinking of Kyran the pretender. This was how it was done.

When she was ready, the youngest maid looked at her appreciatively. "You look a picture, Miss."

Tessie ignored the strange and self-conscious feeling in her new persona. "Where to?" she asked. Surely she couldn't wait a moment longer to see Kyran.

"Follow me." The young maid gestured for her to descend the staircase leading her to the ground floor parlour.

Kyran and Ruby spoke quietly by the fire, Kyran on the sofa, his tie slightly askew, and Ruby posed before him, drink in hand. "But she can't be. How would that be possible?" she urged in a hushed voice, and Tessie held back from entering, waiting just behind the door. They were talking about her. She could feel it.

Ruby reached her hand to Kyran's forehead inspecting the bruises on his face. As Tessie stepped out of the dark entrance and into the light, Ruby quickly pulled back her hand and stepped away, replacing her expression with one of a reluctant hostess.

"Tessie." Kyran stood to greet her. Having had a moment

to settle in, his tone and expression were calmer than before despite his swollen jaw.

"Aye. I am fine." Tessie managed a gracious smile, drawn into a more polite engagement than she had imagined. "What happened to yer face? Who did that to yer?"

"It's nothing," he dismissed, dusting his blonde hair to the side to cover it, though it was dreadfully ineffective.

"He was attacked by the Angel's thugs returning from the cottage," Ruby cut in, barely hiding an accusatory tone. "He was lucky to get away, thank heavens." Ruby passed Tessie a glass of wine. "I do hope you'll forgive me your confinement." She dipped her green eyes graciously, perhaps only for Kyran's benefit. "Kyran has vouched for your honesty and told me what happened. Please don't begrudge my caution."

"Of course, there is no need," Tessie accepted, though there was still something heavy in the air.

"Sit. Please." Ruby gestured to the lounge chair behind her. Tessie obliged and sipped the wine, letting its sweetness fizz in her belly. Despite the cordiality, tension brimmed in the room as everything yet to be said braced in the silence.

"Why did they attack yer?" Tessie pressed about the Angel's men. "Do yer know anything more?"

"They were looking for you," Ruby answered before Kyran could.

Kyran nodded, though was obviously reluctant to go on. "Yes, they are still looking for you. They could see for themselves you were no longer in my company and that is a good thing given you have shown up here. I told them you had absconded and I knew not where. Which was the truth. But I do not know how much they believed."

"And they let yer go? I don't understand. If they used me to get to yer, why are they after me and letting yer go?"

"Yes, there is something about you, Tessie O'Shea." Ruby's tone was ominous though she held a light smile.

"I need to speak with yer," Tessie urged Kyran, suddenly leaning forward. "Please. I must. Can we speak alone?"

"There is no need for that." Kyran looked back and forth between the two women. "You two have met under the strangest circumstances, I understand that, but we are on the same side. Anything you can say to me, you can say to Ruby."

Tessie was not convinced.

"Please." He held up his hand. "I am weary from travelling and everything to do with the Angel. My head hurts. Let's at least get through a meal. There will be time." He touched his hand to her shoulder and Tessie slumped, releasing her breath. Time. Always more time.

Mildly satisfied, Ruby seemed too restless to sit still and glided about the room in an elegant mauve skirt. Despite her bubbly exterior, Tessie could see she was still seething, her pretty cheeks flushed with rage. Was it Tessie's presence that vexed her? The Angel? Or the failed trip to Paris? Kyran was watching her and could surely see it too, though no one spoke of it.

"I'm sorry to intrude Mr Luther," Kyran's butler announced from the doorway. "Dinner is served." The man promptly turned on his heel and left the room.

"Thank God!" Ruby gasped. "I'm famished."

Ushered into the dining room, Tessie took a seat opposite Ruby, the high-backed chairs carved intricately and varnished to shining. She diverted her attention to the serving table filling the room with all sorts of delectable aromas. A glorious display of roasted meats and steaming vegetables spread out before her. The sight of it sent her spinning and pangs of guilt rippled through her at all the families at home in the Old Nichol this very night who would never see such a feast.

Through the window, the street was knee deep in snow and the cold shuddered through her just looking at it. She remembered the winters she and Finn had struggled through, foraging for lumps of coal and huddling together in their bare room. Her fingers and joints ached with the memories. How different life was in these two worlds.

Their plates loaded with generous portions of roast pork, potatoes, beans and gravy, Ruby and Kyran descended into their own back and forth, and Tessie looked down at her hands resting in her lap. They were covered in small scars from her stove, her years of sliding hot ginger cakes over the coals, her nails chipped and broken. They were working hands. Despite the tailored cuffs on her blouse, unblemished and clean, she didn't belong here.

As they ate, Ruby quelled the tension with free-flowing stories about her trip. Despite feeling on the outer, Tessie was drawn in by the tales of parties and the characters, a world so different from her own. She could see Ruby's ability to command an audience and orchestrate its mood. She was an effortless storyteller and she and Kyran had an easy affection for each other, one that had history and familiarity. They were likeable and despite the urgency still rumbling inside her, her shoulders relaxed and she was temporarily whisked into a world completely unknown to her.

As their meal finished Ruby signalled to the footman. "I had a crate of wine brought in with my luggage when I arrived last week. Could you fetch a bottle for us?" He left promptly and Ruby gleamed as she turned back to them. "This was the reason for my whole trip after all."

"You've always had a drinking problem," Kyran teased.

"Well, sadly, it wasn't as profitable as it might have been," she said, her tone turning serious in his direction. Kyran accepted the slight and they waited as the footman returned and filled their glasses.

Ruby raised her glass and proposed a toast. "To freedom."

She flashed her eyes between Kyran and Tessie. "In whatever form it takes."

"Ruby..." Kyran paused.

"Is it really safe for us to talk in front of her?" Her bright eyes shot in Tessie's direction.

Kyran took a deep breath and dipped his eyes.

"I have been waiting for three days, Kyran. You must allow me some time to vent. That was our chance! I am filled with grief about it."

"I know it was. I know. I wanted it too. I still do. And we shall have it."

Ruby hushed her voice, reaching her hand for his. "We worked so hard for it. So hard. Can our plans be so easily dashed by a note full of nonsense?" Kyran squeezed her fingers tenderly, their eyes locked on each other with sadness and warmth so that Tessie turned away to give them privacy.

"We will find another way," Kyran assured, his brown eyes creased with earnest regard.

"Will we? How? For heaven's sake." She pulled her hand from his and quickly stood from the table. "Must this man have his claws in everything we do?"

"We will find a way," he repeated confidently and watched as she circled the table, taking deep breaths to calm herself.

"That trip was months in the making, Kyran."

"There will be more opportunities for us. Other connections. Just give it time."

Ruby tapped her glass loudly as she paced, though pausing, she turned to Tessie. "Why did he really send you? Are we to really believe you know nothing? Nothing at all?"

"I've asked her all these questions," Kyran cut in before Tessie could answer.

"And you were truly satisfied with the answers? She is sitting at our table, Kyran. Perhaps the Angel has her right where he wants her. Did you think of that? Did you wonder if she was his little spy?" She angrily re-filled her glass, splashing wine over the table.

"You've seen her injuries," he calmed. "There was, is, nothing fraudulent about that. He wanted her dead. That much I believe."

"Yes." Ruby nodded, her green eyes flashing at Tessie, searching her out. "That was real enough. But he used her to wrangle you back into God-knows-what. And now she is here. With us. Innocent as can be."

Ruby's cheeks were flushed but it was Tessie who felt the accusation.

"I want those answers just as much as yer do," Tessie said. "I have lost everything. I have nothing left."

"My first day returning to London," Ruby pressed. "A man in a rage hammered on the door demanding to see a Tessie O'Shea. Ferocious and rabid, I had to point my pistol at him to make him leave. And not but a few days later, here you miraculously appear. Dishevelled and close to death, out of nowhere! There is a game here somewhere. It doesn't feel right."

"A man came here looking for me?" Tessie's chest rose at the declaration. "Who? Who was it?"

"He gave no name." Ruby turned away again, retreating to her thoughts, but Tessie thudded her palm to the table.

"Who! Was it Finn? Did he say his name was Finn?"

Ruby startled at her tone. "He gave no name."

"A scar? Did he have a scar? Right here?" Tessie gestured over her left eye and the table fell quiet waiting for Ruby's response.

"Yes." Ruby lifted her own hand to her brow. "Yes, I think he did."

Tessie let out a gasp, hugging her arms to her chest. "I knew it! He made it out of that room." She turned to Kyran. "He's out there somewhere. He's alive."

"That was your man? You are sure?" Kyran asked.

"It had to be. No one else would come looking for me here."

"What does that mean?" Ruby frantically searched their expressions.

"Dublin. Yer must take me to Dublin." Tessie leant across the table to Kyran, forgetting Ruby and all else.

"Dublin?"

"That's why I came here. My mother. She has to stop this. If Finn is out there, they're after him, they're after me. If she is the reason for this, she must call it off. Take me to Dublin."

Ruby touched her hand to her neck at the declaration. "Your mother?"

"If yer want to know why he chose me, that's where I have to go."

"You said you didn't know her," Kyran added cautiously. "You said you knew nothing about her, alive or dead."

Tessie sat down again, filled with hope that Finn was still out there. She gulped back the rest of her wine. "I lied."

Finn's heart pounded. It was getting dark and the walls of the alley were closing in around him. He couldn't leave Mickey to those brutes and maybe, just maybe, Ryder was his ticket to the Angel and to Tessie. If there was even the smallest chance, he would make an ally of him yet. He had an idea by the name of Billy Brittle. But first, he had to get out of Jacob's Island.

Straightening his coat and cap, he moved back the way they had come and the girl with the apple crouched still in her corner. She didn't shrink away as he moved towards her, though shifting her feet, she looked beyond him.

Waving his hand in front of her face, she jolted and Finn stepped back. "Can yer show me how to get out of here?"

The young girl sprung to her feet. Pelting away from him, her boots smacked against the wobbling wooden gangplanks. Over the slime-filled ditches beneath, he watched her run, startled by the speed of her reaction.

Her green beanie darted along the narrow walkway, though just before she disappeared from sight, a group of children emerged from a side alley. Finn strained to see them swarm around her. Her apple. They were after apple! Without thinking, Finn hurried towards them as they clustered together in a mass of pushing and shoving. By the time he reached her, it was too late. The apple bounced between their legs and rolled across the muddy slush, and giving chase, they left the girl slumped against the building empty-handed. She paid Finn no heed though he stood only a few yards away, and dusting off her trousers, she turned to trail behind them.

"Wait," Finn said, scrambling to pull a dry oatcake from his pocket. "Here."

The girl looked down at her boots as if speaking to her had frozen her to the spot.

"Here." He gestured again. "It's alright. Can yer talk?"

She raised her peculiar eyes, before dropping them again and shifting her boots in the icy mud. Seeing she was not going to move, he lowered the small offering to the ground and backed away. She darted forward to pick it up, cupping it in her hands.

"Can yer show me how to get out of here?" he asked again.

"I am invisible," she said in a thick Haitian-Creole accent, waving her fingers in front of her face as if creating magic.

Finn smiled. "I can see yer. Those kids could see yer."

"They saw my apple," she corrected, and shoving the whole oatcake in her mouth, she turned and ran away.

"Wait!" he called after her. Was he supposed to follow?

He trailed behind her green beanie as she darted down the alley, swung under a rafter and crawled through a gap in the wall. Finally spilling out onto an open street, the icy air filled with the smell of crisping chicken on hot coals and street vendors gave call.

They were in Bermondsey, rough and busy with immigrants from the trade and spice routes of South East

Asia, pushed out of inner London with the stink and clatter of new industry. It was home to tannery workers and labourers for the Wool Exchange and Leather Markets brought together in over-crowded apartments.

Lost in the bustle, Finn saw the girl watching from the other side of the street and waved his thanks.

"Which way to the river?" he called across to her.

He didn't know what it was about this girl that tugged at his chest so. He had seen many street children in his time. He had been one, in fact, and knew what it was to be cold and hungry and to have no one. She was barely seven years old, the same age as Tadgh when he'd lost him in Dublin. So small. Too small to be alone in such a place.

"The river. Which way?" he repeated. He couldn't waste time getting lost again or worse, accidentally stumbling back into Jacob's Island. He pulled his last oakcake from his pocket and held it for her to see, coaxing her to help him.

The girl looked to her right and started walking.

THREADING a path back towards the Thames, they crossed busy streets of wagons and workers as the afternoon light faded. They reached the river's edge and she followed it onward to London Bridge, every now and then turning to see if Finn was still behind her. He didn't try and catch up, but kept her in eyesight as her small frame silhouetted against the river. They moved past the dark shadowy vessels where men continued to load and unload cargo on the barges, preparing vessels for launch in the morning.

As they walked a man rushed from a loading bay with a stern voice. "Get away from here, thieving little scrapper. You stay back! I warned you, didn't I?"

"Ou se chen an, msye!" the little girl yelled back, waving her fist at him from a distance.

"Get back from here!" He shooed her away, rushing at her and pushing her back from their path.

"Hey!" Finn hurried to intercept him. "Leave her alone."

"I've told her to stay away from here. Always sneaking on the barges. Getting on the boats. All along here. Ask anyone."

"She's just hungry."

"There ain't no food on there. She's a stowaway. Turn your back for bleeding second and she'll be in there hiding. I'll call the sergeant."

"Leave her be," Finn scolded. "She's just a child."

"Just see she don't get on here if you care so much." The man turned back to his barge and she threw Finn a glance and shrugged her shoulders.

"Thought you said yer were invisible?" Finn asked.

"Doesn't always work," she said, the pearly hue in her left eye catching the light.

"Figures." Finn looked around. London Bridge was just ahead of them, but it wasn't yet dark enough to risk venturing back into the East End. He took a deep breath and moved out of the thoroughfare into a small alcove off a laneway. The girl followed him and sat on a crate in the corner. Remembering their unspoken contract, he pulled the remaining oatcake from his pocket and handed it to her. "Why do yer sneak on their barges and boats then?"

"To go."

"Go where?"

She took a breath and shrugged, kicking her legs against the crate.

"Where are your people?"

"Disparu." She flicked her hand up in the air. "Gone."

"Where did they go? On a boat?"

"Wi."

"How long ago?"

She shook her head and rubbed her eyes. "A long time."

"Well." Finn took a breath, feeling the emptiness of it. "Where did they go? Did yer arrive on a boat too?"

"My mama came with Mr Bernard on the boat. Then they go."

"What happened to them?"

The girl put her arms up in dramatic fashion. "We came to leave on the boat. To go. New place. New America. My mama looked for me but could not see me. So I know I am invisible. I wait and I wait."

"Who is Mr Bernard?"

"A French man."

"From France?"

"From all over. From all the boats."

"So you were in America with your Ma and yer came here looking for her?"

"No! Came here on way to New America. But I pa jwenn. Never find them."

Finn frowned into his hands. "Was your mother a slave?"

"Haitians are not slaves. My Mama said so. There are no slaves in Haiti."

"Alright," he nodded. "What's yer name then?"

"Madochée."

"Madochée," Finn repeated.

"Yes. You don't have people?" She looked around as if they should be right beside him.

"My people are gone too."

"Oh."

Finn looked back out at the river, anxious to get going. "I have to go now," he said, feeling a pang of regret as the girl looked up at him. "Thank you for yer help." He placed his hand on her beanie as he walked away though she turned to trail behind him. "Yer must stay here."

Madochée didn't speak, but when he walked again, she walked too.

"Yer can't come with me. Yer have to stay."

Again she didn't respond though he could see she understood. He crouched in front of her, taking her hands in his. "I'm going to find a man..."

"I show you the way. Direksyon."

"Yer don't know the way..." Finn hung his head as his voice trailed away. It was true she didn't know the way right now, but she did know Jacob's Island, and probably Bermondsey. He may need her help again.

Finn searched for words, trying to explain it and asking her to wait, but instead, he stood again. "Just come on." He strode away. "But when I say get down, yer get down."

"Get down," she repeated, her little feet moving fast to keep pace with his.

FINN CROUCHED BY THE STABLES. He knew Billy's evening routine. After closing up the gates he would fill up the animal's water, and walking the wheelbarrow across to the hay yards, return to fill the feeding troughs for the night. Across the alley, Finn had watched him push the wheelbarrow out and he'd be returning any moment.

He jumped out as the red-haired boy lumbered towards him. "Billy!"

Billy dropped the wheelbarrow. "No, not you too..." He took off running and Finn sprung up and over the hay bails giving chase.

"Stop! Stop!" His boots hit hard on the alley floor as he came down hard on his back, crashing them both to the ground.

"Bloody Hell! I told her already. I told her. I don't bloody know anymore."

"Yer told her? Tessie? Yer saw Tessie."

"Yes, get off me!" Billy shrugged angrily, struggling to get to his feet. Finn let him up, but held his shoulder firmly, shaking him urgently and calming his breath.

"Yer saw Tessie?"

"Yes! Bloody hell! I said I saw her didn't I?"

"When?"

"A few days ago."

"She was alive?"

"No, I seen her dead. Of course she were alive. Alive enough to hold a blooming knife to my throat. Look what she did." Billy pulled out his collar to show the minor scrape along his collarbone.

"Oh my god. She's alive." Finn hung his head in relief, hunching over with his hands on his knees. "She's alive."

"She was. I don't know if she is now. She didn't look too good."

"What happened to her?"

"I don't know."

"Yer didn't help her?"

"Help her? She held a knife at my throat and she yelled at me to get out of here. Said she was gonna tell my ma."

"What was she going to do?"

"How should I know?"

"What did she ask yer? What did yer tell her?"

"She wanted to know happened to you, and why they was gonna kill her. That stuff. I told her they was sending her home in a box. That's all I heard. It's all I know about it."

"And her mother?"

"I don't know anything about her mother. And you. You're in worse trouble than her. You killed Johnny. I heard about what you did. Everyone has."

"What else did yer hear then? I need details. Everything you've got. Names."

"What names?" Billy pushed at Finn's hand gripping him at the neck, but Finn's grip didn't budge.

"Yer heard."

"Names of who?"

"Anyone and everyone involved."

"Are you crazy? That's how you get yourself killed."

"Yer have to help her, Billy! Help me get her back! That's the price of trying to benefit from someone else's misfortune."

"I wasn't benefiting."

"What were yer doing then?"

"It's only a relief when it ain't you, alright? That's all. When their attention is on someone else. You think I wanna be wrapped up with that lot? I ain't got a choice around here do I?"

"There's always a choice."

"What? What choice? I can't fight back. No one can."

"Well maybe they should bloody try! Maybe we all should. How are we supposed to live like this? How are we supposed to live if we don't fight back?"

"How are we supposed to live if we do?" Billy's brow creased with genuine stress, and Finn stalled at the question. He was right. It was a question written at the back of all of their minds, every time they walked past the Angel's men. Every time they turned a blind eye to the terror they instilled in the streets, every time they saw them shaking down a street seller or ironmonger or storefront owner. Finn was as guilty for turning a blind eye as anyone else. As long as the Angel was reaching for someone else, they had all turned a blind eye. How were they ever supposed to resist?

"It starts with us, Billy. I need yer help. Tessie needs yer help. Come with me."

"What? No. My ma is expecting me home for supper."

"Are yer a man or a boy, Billy. She'll have to miss yer."

"I'm a man but yer don't wanna to see her cross."

"Yer can tell her yer were doing some good in this damn world."

"She won't care if Mr Simms fires me now, will she?"

"If yer don't, I'll make sure everyone knows yer had a part in Tessie's fate. That yer knocked her down in the alley to gloat and when yer had a chance to help her, yer turned away. Do it, Billy. Be a better man. Come with me. If yer tired of living in fear then it's time to stand up. Stand up with me. Make a name for yerself that means something."

CHAPTER 18

Finn and his two companions weaved through the festive carollers and decorations. Christmas was nearing and Finn felt splintered and separated from it all. The whole world was carrying on around him as if nothing had changed, and yet it had for him in every way.

Madochée led them through the dark shadowy vessels over the bridge and back towards Bermondsey.

"What do I have to do again?" Billy sulked, lingering behind. "If I go home with so much as a scratch on me—"

"What? Your pa will knock me senseless?"

"My pa died last winter."

"I'm sorry." Finn rubbed his forehead and paused with his hands on his hips.

"But my ma's tougher than him any hows. It's her you should be worried about. My pa was soft as butter. Wouldn't hurt a fly."

"I'll not let any harm befall yer, alright. But I need yer to tell them what yer know."

"Why?"

"Argh." Finn waved his hand at him. "Because it's how we

get Tessie back, that's why. I told yer. At least that's what I hope."

"I'm hungry."

"I'm hungry too," Madochée agreed.

Finn looked around for the closest shopfront or street seller as Billy pulled at his sweaty mass of hair in protest.

"I haven't had any supper and you just made me walk for an hour. I'm tired and hungry and—"

"Alright. Alright," Finn relented, softening on the lad. He really was a big goofy oaf. "Get yourself some bread and cheese. Over there." He pointed across the road. "Get her some too. Oh." He rummaged in his boot for another of his precious rent coins. "Get us three then."

Billy took them and Finn stood watch with Madochée. Returning, Billy handed out the crusty hunks of bread and they ate in silence, the street moving around them.

"What happened to yer pa then?" Finn broached.

"Kicked by a horse. Right here." Billy pointed to his temple with his mouth already full.

"And yer still work at the stables?"

"What else am I gonna do?"

Finn took a deep breath, understanding the truth of it. Dusting the last of the breadcrumbs from his hands, he nudged Madochée to continue leading the way.

They wove around the backside of a single tenement. "In there." Madochée stopped and pointed at an open door.

"Is this his house?" Finn frowned, not liking the idea of barging into his private residence.

"In there," she repeated.

Finn took a deep breath and stepped forward, urging Billy to come with him as Madochée darted back into the street, leaving them unguided and in unknown territory. Finn called after her but she was already gone.

Knocking loudly on the wood, a man appeared from the shadow with wide eyes.

"Ryder," Finn said, with more confidence than he felt. "I've come to see him." The man nodded to the side and Finn passed under the threshold. The room opened out as if the walls to the lower floor of the tenement had been knocked out. In the far corner, there he was, reclining in a barber's chair, with no barber, but a small gathering of men standing around him.

"Who is it?" he asked, spinning around. "Is that my barber?"

"It's Finn."

"Finn who? Oh. The man who called me a scrapper."

Finn cleared his throat. "It's O'Shea. Finn O'Shea."

"O'Shea. I'm preparing for my fight night haircut. It's a good luck ritual. Never lets me down, see." He tugged on his beard. "But this here, beauty, she'll only get a trim. Haven't cut it since I last lost a bet...when was that, Charley?"

"1842," Charley answered from the dark corner where he'd been watching.

"That's a six-year streak, lad. Six years." He wagged his finger at Finn. "I'm interested in the bet. Not the fight."

"Where's Mickey?"

"I'm here," a flat voice called from beside Charley, and Finn saw him slumped on the floor as if he'd been trying to sleep. Lifting his bound wrists, he waved a weary hello.

"Yes, yes. He's there. Getting his rest. Don't worry, we haven't laid a hand on him. Can't put a lame duck up to fight."

"Yer asked for proof and I've brought it." Finn cut to the chase, gesturing towards Billy whose eyes darted nervously back and forth from Charley and Ryder.

Ryder stood from his chair to look him over.

"He has information," Finn continued. "Or can get it.

Information that can be useful in getting the upper hand on the Angel."

Ryder tugged on his beard as he sidestepped to directly stare into Billy's frightened face. "He doesn't look useful."

"He knows things. And he can get closer on the inside than we can."

"Is that true, boy? Speak up."

Billy stuttered and swallowed trying to speak. "I know a few of them, sir. Mr, sir. They talk to me. Think I'm harmless. I am harmless...but they talks, sir. They do...I knew they was coming for his wife. For Tessie. They told me."

Ryder waved his arm for him to be quiet, returning to his chair and rocking back so far it looked like it might tip over. Finn held his breath and waited. What would Ryder make of all this?

"I don't publicly bet against my own man, you understand," Ryder started. "No. I place one publicly, and one not so publicly..." Ryder leapt to his feet again coming face to face with Finn. "So, what I'm wondering is if you are doing the same." Ryder narrowed his eyes. "Are you playing one against the other? Playing me for a fool?"

"No. I told yer," Finn spoke strongly. "The Angel hurt my wife. He has her. Killed her. I don't even know, but I'm going to find out. And I'll do whatever I need to. For me, it's that simple."

Ryder squinted his eyes. "So what's your proposition?"

Finn felt a surge of confidence. "Mickey doesn't fight. He'll be no good to yer anyway. I've only known the man five minutes and I know he'll not lay down for anyone. He'll fight to the death and that'll put yer winning streak at risk."

Ryder turned to look at Mickey, mulling over the information.

"Yer best to put forward someone loyal to yer. Someone

who's willing to take one for the team and make it look convincing." They both knew he was referring to Charley and his eyes narrowed.

"You're loyal aren't you Charley?" Ryder tested. "Perhaps there is something to this..."

Charley stepped forward as if to argue but uttered no words, standing stiffly with his arms folded.

"So, if I let your man stand down...?"

"We send Billy back home to get amongst it and bring us back something that can hurt the Angel."

Ryder stroked his long beard, running his eyes over Finn and Billy, taking his time to answer. Finn's stomach tightened and he held his breath. If this fell through he was back out on the street empty handed. Ryder's expression stayed stoney, with flickers of light in his eyes that Finn couldn't read.

Finally, Ryder nodded. "Charley. You have a fight to prepare for. And you, my friend." Ryder pointed his long finger at Billy, standing frozen in the middle of the room. "You had better get busy."

"He will," Finn answered, wrapping his hand on Billy's back.

Ryder waved his arm at them in dismissal and Charley thrust Mickey towards them and quickly ushered them back out into the cold.

On the street, Finn took a deep breath, trying to quell the angst balling up in his belly. He'd gotten Mickey free of the fight, but was he any closer to finding Tessie? He glanced sidelong at the gangly red-head starting out on his long walk home. Of all places to hang his hopes, he sighed, but it would have to be enough.

~

INSIDE A BUSY PUBLIC house with the name of Cora's Place, Finn and Mickey were greeted by a collection of misfits and workers lingering in the warmth before heading home for the evening. It was dark and cosy, and the perfect place to sink into oblivion and catch his breath for just a moment.

"What'll it be lads?" a voice called before they reached the bar. A broad-shouldered woman who must have been Cora was ready and waiting, her chin jutted forward and a dish rag flicked over her shoulder. "I say what'll it be?"

"Two beers," Finn said. "And two bowls of soup or whatever it is you're cooking back there." He turned to his companion. "Yer must be hungry?"

Mickey patted his belly. "I never turn down a meal."

"Ham sandwiches or a fourpenny plate?"

"What's a plate?"

"Whatever the Finch throws on it." She nodded to a tall skinny man moving in the kitchen behind her. "Bread and dripping. Whelk. Some cheese if yer lucky."

"Sandwich is fine." Mickey nodded and Finn agreed. The woman turned to pour their drinks as Finn took the weight off and perched on a stool, letting his head fall heavily into his hands. "Are yer alright then?"

Mickey rubbed his wrists where the ropes had been. "Aye, brother. Wasn't sure yer would be coming back for me though."

"I could hardly leave yer to them after this morning."

"Another man might have."

The woman set the drinks down and there was a moment of silence as they both drank thirstily. "Sláinte," Finn offered after the fact.

"Sláinte, my friend." There was still an undercurrent of amusement in Mickey's expression making it difficult for Finn to guess at his sincerity. He was supposed to be on a ship for the New World and instead he had ended up here.

"Do yer have somewhere to be?" Finn asked. "Some people somewhere seeing as yer missed your boat and all?"

Mickey shook his head. "Seeing as I missed my boat, no. I don't. Free as a bird."

"And yer wife and baby? Or was that just a story to get work?" Finn referred back to that morning on the docks, though his tone was without malice. Mickey's eyes dulled for the first time and he looked to his boots.

"Hey, I wouldn't blame yer," Finn added. "I've said crazier things to get a day's work. How long have yer been in London?" Finn asked, noting Mickey's Dublin accent. Cora expertly slid two plates with sandwiches across the bar so that both Mickey and Finn had to stop them hitting the floor.

"A month."

"Yer made your acquaintance with the Angel's men quickly."

"They made themselves known, shall we say. Thieving scoundrels. Every last one of them."

Finn agreed, taking his first mouthful. The food fell heavy in his belly, and the beer swirled, reminding him how tough the last few days had been on his body. He'd been looking over his shoulder for what seemed like forever and there were no guarantees the Angel's men hadn't seen them crossing the river. It wasn't over yet. Not even close.

"I killed one of them," he said, putting his sandwich down and looking at his hands. "They hurt my wife and I..." His voice trailed away for a moment and he cleared his throat. "I killed him. I didn't mean to. We fought and he hit his head and...well...he was someone important. Now I can barely set foot in the East End to look for her." His head fell forward, and reaching for his glass of beer, he skulled it down.

"I'm sorry, brother." Mickey bit his lip and stared out through the foggy window. He looked back at Finn with wide eyes.

"I did have a wife and baby. Not 12 months ago." He clenched his fist and released it, the expression on his face more intense than before.

"Did have?" Finn prompted.

"He were a finicky baby at first. My Ciara was struggling on her own so she took the lad up to be with her ma for a little while. Just to settle in, yer know. She weren't there a month when the influenza came through, and it all happened so quickly. By the time they got word to me on the farm and I got there, it was too late. It had taken her." He paused, hanging his head in his hands. "After that, I didn't care for the farm."

"Yer baby?"

Mickey rubbed his eyes. "With Ciara gone, there was no way in hell they were handing him over to me. Not with the farm dried up and in foreclosure. They paid me out and I had nothing to offer him then."

"What do yer mean?"

"They have him."

"That's rough. I'm sorry."

"Only way to get him back is to make my fortune. I made a promise to him, so I did. Kissed his sweet bald head and made a promise right into those baby eyes." He banged his fist on his knee. "And I've already lost my way."

Finn gritted his jaw. "No. I got in yer way."

"Brother, missing that boat was just the last thing in a whole string of things. And them Angel fellas had their bleeding claws in every damn piece of it."

"What happened?"

Mickey rubbed his knuckles against his glass. "I needed something to get me started. And I shouldn't have done it, but I did. She probably don't even know they're missing yet. But she will. Ciara's mother. I stole, no, borrowed, her silver spoons. Idiot that I am, I showed one of them in a card game, praying that lady luck might shine on me hand. I won the round, that much is true, but before the night was out the Angel's men shook me down in the alley, knowing full well I carried the full set of 10 of them silver spoons in the lining of my coat. They took the lot."

"They're not known for their scruples."

"Learned that the hard way. And now the only way I'll ever be able to go home is with her spoons and a tonne of cash to make up for everything I done. Or didn't do. In the meantime, I'll hurt those blighters any bleedin' way I can. I'll do what I can to help yer get your wife back. That I swear to yer."

Finn took a deep breath, staring into the bottom of his empty glass, and chinked it against Mickey's.

"It's bad luck to cheers on an empty glass, brother. Let's go another."

CHAPTER 19

*L*eaving Liverpool that morning, Tessie glanced overhead, seeing the dark clouds had followed them over the Irish Sea. Smoothing her navy travelling coat and twisting the leather wristband peeking from her sleeve, Tessie exhaled. The thunder mirrored the foreboding in her belly.

"There's a storm coming," she said, leaning forward in their small first class cabin on the ferry.

"Let's hope we make it to the hotel before it pours." Ruby crowded her face close to Tessie's to scan the horizon.

The journey had been a long one, first on the early train from London, and now hours on the ferry. They were all three, tired and weary. It had taken little convincing for Kyran to agree to the trip, though he had been in a rush to return before Christmas and the days prior had been busy with preparations. They had garnished her with a selection of new and pretty outfits, and Ruby had schooled her in the basics of etiquette, encouraging her not to show her accent too loud in public places.

Trying on garment after garment, she had allowed herself

to admire her reflection as organised fittings adorned her in luscious fabrics, smooth and shiny, accessories and jewellery, and boots that had never been worn. Things she had never imagined would be in her possession had been lavished on her. Her hair and skin felt different to the touch, as did her smell, mixed with scented soaps and perfumed fabrics, her body absorbing a new experience of comfort. As she sat with them now in their cabin, she looked every bit the part, though she wondered if she could ever really get used to it. In every move she made she was reminded that it was foreign to her. The dresses and corsets, even her boots and stockings, gripped her tightly where her previous garments had not been so rigid. The lace at her collar scratched at her neck and she rubbed at the lining.

"You'll get used to it," Ruby said, seeing her shifting constantly in her seat. Tessie offered a mild smile, not knowing if that could ever be true.

"I don't feel myself."

Kyran had been reading the newspaper and stood passing it to Ruby. "I'm going to take a turn about the deck before the rain starts. Would you like to join?"

Ruby shook her head. "Go ahead." She looked to Tessie as if answering for them both.

"Very well. We'll be docking soon. I'll see if I can get an estimate."

The cabin door closed behind him as thunder again clattered in the background. Tessie felt an awkward pause fill the room. In the days past, she and Ruby had navigated a tenuous alliance, one mixed with politeness and caution. Ruby offered kind words and gestures, only to withdraw them a moment later in trepidation, and Tessie too was unsure how much to let her guard down. It was the unknown answers snaking between them, forcing a wary distance, though they each made attempts at peace. Ruby was protective of Kyran in every way, and Tessie was sure there was much more to their story with the Angel than she might ever know or understand. And yet there was something in Ruby's eyes that Tessie felt she recognised, whether it be loss, sadness or the need to be guarded. Those were things she understood well.

"This is where it started." Tessie absorbed the harbour scene as Dublin came into view. "I can feel its shadow."

"How long has it been?" Ruby took interest in the city rising from the sea.

"Many years."

"Are you worried about seeing your mother?"

Tessie smoothed her skirt and shifted her boots again. "She is not a woman yer can imagine." And her insides fluttered at the prospect of Ruby and Kyran beholding the ugly truth of her past. She had invited them here, though as they drew closer to the harbour, the gravity of it built in her like a slow beating drum. She didn't want them here. She didn't want anyone here, but how could she possibly contain this now?

"She won't be happy to see you?" Ruby offered a hopeful smile.

Tessie shook her head. "I'm not sure she'll even recognise me."

"Surely a mother always recognises her child."

"A mother. Perhaps. But that can be a strong word. The last time I saw her she were dragging me to a workhouse."

"A workhouse?"

"Never a more miserable place, let me tell yer."

"I'm sorry."

"I ran away the first chance I got. Yer won't catch me in one of those places again. Not ever again. But I've not set eyes on her, nor she on me, since that day."

Ruby reached to the side table and drained the last of her

tea, setting it down carefully as the ferry shifted. "We cannot choose our parentage, Tessie O'Shea. That is true for all of us."

Tessie leant back against her seat as another rumble of thunder rolled out across the deck. She hoped Dublin's greeting was not a show of things to come. As the River Anna Liffey guided them into the quay, Kyran returned and sat down, followed closely by a steward tapping on their door.

"Sir and madams, you are free to disembark via the observation deck."

"Thank you, sir."

"Here we go." Ruby raised her eyebrows at Tessie as she moved past her to the hallway.

Outside, the city embraced them with a familiar smog. The storm was ready to break and the air hung low and heavy. She could feel her mother close by in the salty sea air and the gloomy brownstones surrounding the quay. It wasn't a city so changed to the one in her memory. It cloaked around her with a feeling of dread.

She'd been twelve when she'd left this city. The workhouse had hacked off her hair for fear of lice and she had been wearing only the plain work dress she'd been given. Seeing an opening for the laundry carriage, she had run like the wind through its closing gates. Nobody screamed or shouted after her and she did not know if they even missed her. She'd hidden for two days in the city, starving and cold, and finally, picking the pockets of the wealthy churchgoers as they exited mass on Sunday morning, she paid her passage to Liverpool.

She was looking upon this city now with different eyes, but still her heart lurched. She'd never thought to find herself here again. Could she really go through with this?

As the rain came down in large splashes, they hurried to

the hotel where the storm had patrons retiring early for the night. The three of them ate a quick supper in the dining room and before long Tessie was alone with Ruby in their room, preparing for bed.

"Why does travel makes us weary so?" Ruby sighed as they pulled dresses from their trunks to air out for tomorrow. "All we've done is sit and I could sleep a hundred days."

"I'm not sure I can sleep at all."

"When I arrived in Paris I'm sure Mrs Fayette thought I'd grown ill, I slept so long." She smiled. "It's all that rocking. Too'ing and fro'ing. I feel like I've been beaten."

The talk of Paris stirred something in Tessie. "Can I ask yer about Paris?"

"What about it?"

"Yer kept saying how important it was."

"Yes. It was important."

"Why? Was it the money, or was it something else?"

Ruby looked at her reflection in the blurry mirror, biting her bottom lip as she rolled her hair up in rags in preparation for bed. "We have our own reasons to fear the Angel. And there are things we need to do if we're ever to be free of him."

"What reason do yer have to fear him? What things do yer need?" Tessie's eyes searched Ruby's trying to understand the woman in front of her. Why were they drawn on this journey with her? They had each other. They had the means to go anywhere they wanted in the world. What was the hold the Angel had over them?

"I'm tired," she said, dropping her shoulders and not answering the question. "And being Ruby St. Claire and Kyran Luther comes with many expectations. I make the people laugh and smile and forget their worries for a night or two. That's why they want me at their parties. I make them feel good and they make me feel empty." Ruby trailed away looking at her reflection.

"So..." Tessie didn't understand. "Yer want to be a different person?"

"No. But sometimes the gap between who we are and who we are allowed to be is very wide indeed. We must play the roles we are given to play."

Tessie was only growing more confused. What had that to do with fearing the Angel? What had it to do with Paris?

"We need to get away, to make our break elsewhere." Ruby nodded as if it was clear enough and Tessie understood the conversation was over.

Turning back to unpack the last of her garments, Tessie slipped to her bed and pulled the blankets over her. Without another word, Ruby blew out the lantern, plunging the room in a dim shadow as the rain splattered at the window.

In the quiet, Tessie waited. The fire crackled low and soft, its glow slowly dulling as time moved deeper into the night. She could hear Ruby breathing, slow and steady, and when she was sure she was asleep, she swung her feet from the bed and pressed them to the floorboards.

If she could find her mother tonight, perhaps she could keep Ruby and Kyran away after all. Wrapping a cloak about her head and shoulders, she padded silently from the room.

Every moment of her last eight years, she'd had Finn with her, to hear her, to hold her and to warm her on a cold day, but she gathered her strength to move out into the storm. She had to do this on her own.

CHAPTER 20

essie hurried across a footbridge heading north over the River Anna Liffey. The wind and rain battered down and she held close to the buildings as she ran, ducking through an alleyway and periodically stopping to look about. Coming to the end of another alley, a small sign batted wildly against the wall so that its picture could barely be seen.

"The Cleary" it read, marking a bright red door in a rundown building. Tessie paused at the window, seeing light gleaming from the corners; though, boarded up for the storm, she could see little inside. She braced herself and burst through the door, the storm pushing her through in a dramatic gust of wind.

Inside the dimly lit room, the bartender and a few riffraff drinkers looked up. Other customers scattered at lonely tables, some in deep conversation, hunched over with voices muted. Every now and then laughter erupted, only to be quieted again. It was the rabble of Dublin's darkest characters, the underbelly exposed.

The bartender set down a drink for her and she slid a coin across. "Is she here tonight?"

"Who?"

"Yer know who."

The bartender studied her expensive dress. She didn't belong in this kind of establishment, not dressed like that, but he nodded toward the back of the room and quickly moved away.

It wasn't long before she heard a voice rise above the pack and her body stiffened. Scanning the back tables she saw her, commanding the attention of a few men. Aileen.

Leaving her drink, Tessie stood a little shaky on her feet, and pushed herself forward. When she was close enough to see their faces, she waited. Aileen was facing her but had her head bowed to keep her words hidden. With Tessie hovering, she glanced upward and her weathered features flickered with recognition. Tessie held her breath.

"Move over, Reg." Aileen flicked her wild black hair and puffed out her chest. "Find another table." The men hesitated, looking towards Tessie. "Find another table!" she repeated. They scattered, leaving a void for Tessie to step into. Aileen's sturdy frame shifted, dark eyes drawing Tessie in.

"Woooooo-eeeee," she said, finally. "Look at the flash lady in her flash clothes." Tessie's heart thudded, but she stepped closer to her mother.

"Must be flicking those skirts for the fancy gents to be getting about like that," Aileen taunted. "Look fellas, it's a sad day when a lady thinks she's too good for yer." There was a small ripple of laughter, but Tessie held her footing. "Take a seat then," Aileen cooed.

Tessie sat down. "Hello, Aileen."

"Hello indeed." Aileen rolled and lit a cigarette. They each let the other's presence settle on them. It had been a long time. How strange it was to look into her mother's face. She was handsome, though older, and mean-looking, with sturdy shoulders, her face puffy with drink. But that's how she was. How she had always been. Tough, with a laugh like a cracking whip, her eyes always guarded, always calculating, sometimes filled with humour or cruelty, but always alive. Aileen Fisher's eyes never rested.

Tessie recognised herself somewhere in there. She had her mother's mouth, down to the jawline, small gap in her teeth, and her broad smile when she laughed. She shared the wildness of her hair, though Tessie's was lighter. Where she had blue eyes, Aileen's were a piercing dark brown.

"What's brought yer out of the mire?" Aileen asked.

"I need information."

Aileen stood and reached across the table, revealing a hatchet tucked into her waistband and hanging about her skirt. Taking Tessie's chin with her rough fingers she inspected the scar on her forehead. Her eyes softened slightly. Only slightly. "All these years, no word from me daughter and now all she wants is information. That right there ought to cut a mother up on the inside. Get me right in the guts, so it should."

"Is that what we're going to pretend? That yer were worried about me? Yer wanted to hear from me?"

"I was never the sentimental type, was I Tessie-muck." She sighed slowly and drew on her cigarette, her sharp eyes narrowing, assessing the daughter before her. "Information about what then?"

"About the Angel of Bishopsgate." Tessie waited to see Aileen's reaction at the mention of his name, but she offered none and settled back in her chair.

"What about him?"

"He tried to kill me. He is trying to kill me."

Aileen went to laugh and instead set off a raspy smokers

cough. "Is he now? Shame, shame." She shook her head, mockingly. "And what have I to do with it?"

"What do yer know about it?"

Aileen rolled her jaw in consideration. She looked hard at Tessie, her dark eyes mulling it over. "What have yer got for me then? If this is just a business conversation me and yer are having, then that's how it works. Ain't nothing in this life for free, my love, yer know that by now."

Tessie's heart sunk. Nothing for free? That's how Aileen lived and Tessie had nothing to offer.

Aileen looked around at those watching and Tessie realised it was going to be a show for the onlookers. "Got a room full of men here. Yer could earn a pretty penny right here and now if yer wanted." Aileen winked.

Tessie felt her face burn, but she bore down hard.

"Oh, she blushes," Aileen teased. "How the years have softened yer, love. There was a time my Tess would have come back at me with a tongue lashing. Where is that Tessie I wonder?"

"You're drunk."

"Too bleeding right I am."

"And yer owe me."

"Owes yer do I?"

"Yer sold me to a bloody workhouse, which was not the worst of it."

"Aye, I did. For much less than I should have so I'm sure they got their money's worth."

"Is there nothing of a mother in yer?"

The insult disappeared without so much of a chink in Aileen's armour. "That's a lot of grumbling for a girl in a fancy dress." A chuckle danced on her lips.

"I couldn't give a shite about my dress!" Tessie knocked her chair over as she stood up. The room braced awaiting

Aileen's reaction. It was not every day someone dared to challenge Aileen.

"Yer come crawling in here in the dead of night, yer care about something daughter of mine," Aileen scowled. "Eight goddamn years I hear nothing from yer and now yer come in here dressed up like, I don't know who." Aileen pressed her face closer to Tessie's and jabbed her finger at her chest. 'But I see yer, Tessie Fisher. I see who yer really are. I know who yer are and I got no inclination to lift a fine finger for yer until yer bring me something worth my fucking time. So either get in there on yer back girl, and earn me something, or get the fuck out of here."

The rage in Tessie riled up like vomit, but it was no use. "I'll be back," she said. "We ain't finished yet."

"We'll see, daughter. We'll see."

Tessie pushed past the onlookers and burst back out into the storming night. The cold outside ravaged her damp clothes, but hot with rage, she felt nothing.

CHAPTER 21

*P*acing by the fire in the hotel parlour, Tessie's damp dress and loose hair clung to her body as her heart raced. In one meeting it had all spilled out fresh before her. The remnants of Aileen she had taken so much care to bury were laid bare again. She ached with it. A familiar bile rose up from her belly and she couldn't tell if it was anger or grief, but it was an old feeling that rumbled to her core.

To Aileen, everything had a price. A cost. Whether it be money or affection. Tessie should have known if she had allowed her thoughts to go there. In all her years away, she had found something else to be true. Her love for Finn had no price. And his love for her cost her nothing. It was not an exchange. Not a negotiation. Not everything was a trade.

Daylight crept in through the windows as guests passed through on their way to breakfast. Though they kept their distance from her, it wasn't long before Ruby and Kyran appeared, brows creased in question and accusation.

"Here you are," Ruby pressed.

"Have you been down here all night?" Kyran looked tired and weary. "Are you alright?"

"I'm fine."

"You're all wet. You've been out in this storm."

"Yes." Tessie pulled on her coat as if preparing to leave.

"You're not leaving again?" Ruby put her hands on her hips.

"No." Tessie didn't know what or where she was going. She just wanted to be away. Away from the questions. She set her coat down again. "No, I'm not."

"Where have you been? We are supposed to see your mother, has something happened?" Ruby perched on the edge of the sofa, seeming hurt and confused.

Tessie clenched her eyes shut and took a deep breath. "I've already been. I've already seen her."

Kyran frowned. "You went last night? On your own?"

"Yes."

"Why?"

Tessie held her hands out in front of her, trying to reign in her anger. It was not for Kyran and Ruby, yet it bubbled up just the same.

"Well, what did you find out?" Kyran asked, managing to be the only one between them to keep a civil tone.

"She wants money." Tessie sighed, rubbing her face wearily. "If we want to get anything out of her we'll have to pay her. And even then I don't know what we'll get. Perhaps a slap in the face and a punch in the guts."

"How much money?" Ruby shifted her posture.

"However much it's worth to yer. I have nothing to give her so it hardly matters, does it?"

"She's your mother. Will she really not help you?"

"No. That's not how she thinks. I tried to tell yer," Tessie countered, her voice croaky and tired.

"Then we pay her," Kyran agreed, shrugging. "If that's what it takes."

Ruby didn't seem so keen to rush in. "Hold on. How much?"

Kyran looked ever optimistic. "Enough to make her talk."

"You expect us to just hand over the money to you?" Ruby asked of Tessie.

"I don't expect yer to do anything."

"Well, how do we know you won't run with it yourself?" Ruby dipped her eyes, as if guilty to even be posing the question.

Tessie turned back to the fire, fighting off the cold seeping through her damp dress. "I didn't come for yer money or anything else yer have. I came for Finn. And I came for answers. Just like yer did."

"If you run off on your own again we won't be getting any answers. We have no idea whether you already have them and are choosing not to tell us."

"I had to." Tessie bit her tongue, unsure how to finish her sentence. "I had to go alone."

"Why?"

"So yer don't see who she is!" she snapped. "Where she is. I didn't want yer to see."

Ruby stepped forward. "We don't care who she is."

"Yer say that now. But she is my cross to bear and I'll be the one to deal with her."

"Then we can't give you any money, Tess." Ruby crossed her arms, and though Kyran looked on with less conviction, Tessie picked up her coat and strode away.

IN THE ROOM, Tessie stood watch over the dresses laid out to dry. None of them were hers; all of them lavished on her by Ruby. Was she wrong to push back at them now? Pressing her fists to her eyes, the pressure built up. Could she afford to walk away from them? They'd brought her this far, been generous and trusting, even if she didn't understand why. Were they expecting something in return? Were they just like her mother and wanting something in exchange? What was the cost going to be, she wondered? Did she still need them after all?

Behind her, the door opened and Ruby closed it softly, resting back against it. "I should not have been so rash," she said, meekly.

"It's yer money. People are rash about their money and have a right to be." Tessie stared down at her hands, tugging at the ribbons on the front of her skirt.

"Kyran is milder than I, but trust is a difficult thing. You are wary of us and we of you."

"That is fair."

"It's the price we pay for dealings with the Angel. Suspicion everywhere. Never resting. Never letting one's guard down. It is exhausting." She stepped closer. "But Kyran has scolded me...so." She smiled, in an effort to lighten the mood. "And I suspect we still need each other. At least for now. Can that not be enough?"

"Enough for what?"

"We both want answers, Tessie. When we have them we'll be free to go our own way."

Tessie wanted to relent, but it still meant letting them into Aileen's world. Letting them see the dark mess and squalor from where she came. Could they ever look at her the same? Why did she even care?

As if reading her mind, Ruby took Tessie's hand. "Kyran said he met you in the room on Bethnal Green."

"Aye." Tessie remembered it well. "That's where I delivered the note."

Ruby sat on the bed and took her time as if conjuring the picture in her mind. "I lived there with my sister not so long ago. I didn't know he was still paying the rent on it."

Tessie searched Ruby's face. She had lived in that bare room not a stone's throw from the slums? She could not picture Ruby, her skin shining bright and her elegant charm, in such a dark and grimy place.

"I didn't know yer had a sister."

Ruby looked down at her fingers. "She died of smallpox before all this. She was 14."

"I'm sorry."

Ruby cocked her head to the side in thoughtful repose. "She was more a beauty than I. But she was not meant for this world. We came with our father from Vienna when we were very young. He was a cobbler. That's where I got my love of shoes I suppose." She played with the lace on her sleeve, drawing on something genuine. "He passed in his sleep one night. No sickness. No fuss. He just didn't wake up. I think he'd had enough is all. And my sister was all I had in the world until Kyran came."

"Must our lives be so full of loss?"

"Only mostly full." Ruby smiled wryly and reached out to squeeze Tessie's hand again. "We will find our way free. We have to believe it. And you must believe Kyran and I do not begrudge your past any more than we begrudge our own."

Tessie looked at Ruby and felt it a genuine moment.

"We must trust each other, at least this far. For this moment," Ruby urged. "Now come, change your dress and let's go on to breakfast. Travelling makes me hungry as well as tired."

～

As evening fell, Tessie guided Ruby and Kyran back to The Cleary where they watched for a time from their carriage.

Kyran seemed strangely on edge and lit a cigarette. "You're sure this is the place?"

"Of course." Tessie nodded. "I was here last night."

"Maybe we should wait here," he said slowly, pulling back from the window.

"What are you talking about?" Ruby frowned. "We're not letting her go in alone. We're going in with her."

Kyran sunk back in his seat and before Ruby could press him more, Tessie opened the carriage door and they made their way to the Cleary's red door.

Inside, the barman's eye twitched when he saw her, and without a word, he stepped back out of view. A ripple of drunken laughter demanded their attention before they could properly look about the room. Seeing Aileen through the crowd, Tessie braced herself. She was laughing, telling jokes — likely with a lewd punchline. When she saw Tessie across the room she dramatically shushed the crowd around her.

"Well look who it is," she said, relishing Tessie's approach. She nudged her sidekick, a stout man with a grubby face. "Yer must have a better offer to come waltzing back in here." Inspecting Tessie's companions, Aileen lingered curiously on Kyran. He shifted his feet and held her gaze. "I was half expecting a visit at home. The girls would love to see yer, though I suppose yer didn't want your new friends seeing from whence yer came. I'll save yer the mystery, new friends, she sprung from the whorehouse on Summer Lane. The Black Bonnet if yer looking for it." She paused on Kyran again and winked. "I suspect yer will find yer way. Though if anyone asks it's a boarding house, yer mind?"

Tessie set her jaw, the back of her neck burning. She had

to give over to this now, to let it all out loose to fall where it may. She had nothing else to lose.

"Sit," Aileen demanded.

Tessie did so, though Kyran and Ruby remained standing behind her.

"Well, out with it. What have yer got for me?" she quipped, switching to seriousness.

"We'll pay yer," Tessie said. "Since that's what yer want. We'll pay yer if yer tell us about the Angel."

"How much?"

"10 pounds," Ruby said.

Aileen let out a croaky chortle. "I won't scratch my tits for 10 pounds, love." She nudged at her sidekick again. "Ain't that right, Donald?" She grabbed his head and rubbed it in her sizeable cleavage, laughing outrageously.

Tessie and the others shifted uncomfortably, Donald surfacing with a goofy smile and his thin hair in disarray.

Aileen's sober gaze returned. "I told yer not to waste my time."

"Name your price then," Kyran said, losing patience. Tessie noticed the eye contact between them. Why was she looking at him like that?

"100 pound," she said.

Kyran nodded. "Very well."

Aileen slumped back in her chair. "So what is it yer want, prodigal daughter of mine?"

"I told yer what I want."

"Tell me again." She rustled her fingers in her tobacco pouch and rolled a cigarette.

"Why was I attacked?"

"How the hell should I know? Am I to be blamed for every calamity to befall yer in the last eight years?"

"They said yer owe him a debt."

"I don't owe him a goddamn thing!" Aileen jabbed her finger in the air. "Owe him." She looked set to launch into a rant, though she swallowed it down. "What else yer got?"

"He tried to have me killed."

"And yet here yer are!" She feigned disbelief. "The absurdity of it."

"Yer aren't telling me anything. What did we pay a hundred pounds for?"

"What do yer expect me to tell yer? We are at war, that much is true, but what the Angel does back in London has got nought to do with me, no relevance to me, no care, no mind, no fucking interest to me. Yer get it?"

"He were to send me home to yer in a box!" Tessie's fist pounded the table. "So don't tell me it had nought to do with yer."

Aileen's eyes flickered and, slowly inhaling her cigarette, she blew the smoke at Tessie, letting the statement linger.

"Who told yer that then?"

"Someone who knew what their plan was."

Muttering under her breath, she swigged back her drink and slammed it down again. "Send me daughter back to me in a box, will yer?" She beat her fist against her chest. "I'm Aileen fucking Fisher, damn yer."

"What is it about?" Tessie pressed. "Money? Territory? Smuggling? I know what yer get up to over here. What is it?"

"A dispute about the smuggling?" Aileen mocked. "This is a bloody joke. What have yer even come to me for? This man waltzes in here and pays a hundred pound for stuff he can tell yer himself. There ain't nothing I know, that he don't." She flung her dark eyes at Kyran again.

"What are yer talking about?" Tessie frowned. "What do yer mean?"

"I ought to crack my hatchet over his skull right now."

Tessie turned to Kyran. "What is she talking about?"

"I don't know what he told yer, love," Aileen stood up. "But that there is the Angel's man behind the scenes. Anything yer need to know, he can tell yer."

"Stop it! Stop it now!" Kyran cut in. Tessie's mind reeled. What on earth was going on?

As Kyran opened his mouth to speak, the back door flew open and a flood of men burst in. Throwing fists and knives at anyone within reach, the room burst into a mass of fighting bodies.

"Yer have got to be kidding me." Aileen cursed under her breath. She screamed out a gruff call to arms and upended her table as men about her were drawn into the fray. Gripping the hatchet at her waist, Aileen leapt onto her chair, ready to swing.

"I told yer, love, it's war. Best get out the way."

Tessie whirled around at the men wrestling on the table tops and breaking chairs. Glasses smashed on faces and heads. Their exit was blocked. Ruby screamed as Kyran pulled her close and Aileen cracked her hatchet down on a man's head as he ran towards her. Blood slashed across her skirt and she wiped the blade on her sleeve.

"Fight em' lads! This is our house! Don't let them have it!"

A man falling past Tessie grabbed her skirts and twisted it around her legs. She struggled to pull away and kicked her boots wildly at his head. Finally striking his face, his hold loosened and she jumped over him in time to dodge another man flying past in chase. Kyran and Ruby had made it to the other side of the room and Kyran called to her, but Tessie hesitated. Maybe he was the Angel's man, or maybe her Mother was lying. Whatever the truth, this next part she had to do on her own.

Turning toward the back exit, she left the room behind her writhing in violence and Aileen cleaving her way through the crowd.

Outside, her boots beat against the cobblestones. She ran until her lungs hurt. Faster and faster she went, deeper into the city, weaving and winding her way through the alleys. It was dark and the streets near deserted as the midnight gale blew through, but she did not stop.

CHAPTER 22

The cold stones beneath her seeped a frozen ache into her bones and as she woke, she unfolded herself in a painful stretch. Hiding beneath a stairwell, a cart and donkey fumbled by, dumping a crate of bruised turnips at the door she'd been watching. Around her, the alleys unwound with their usual morning clatter, discarded glass bottles kicked to the gutters as both animal and human trudged the murky borough. A faded sign flapped above the back door. It simply read "A.F." with a picture of a black bonnet.

She had memories of this alley. Oh yes, she did. Boring everyday ones of ricocheting pebbles against the staircase, skipping mud puddles and feeding scraps to stray kittens. But there were other memories too, of brash men and women, drinks and foul mouths, violence and clawing hands, and another, being dragged kicking and screaming, her mother marching coldly and staunch.

Tessie stood to straighten her back as the door wrenched open and a girl peeked out. She was older than Tessie, with a cherub face and rosy cheeks. Her doughy eyes squinted at the turnips. "God save us," she muttered. "Turnips again." The girl bent to pick up the crate revealing her open cleavage to the alley. Her skin was perfectly white and pudgy with warmth as if just rising from a warm bed. She had only a blanket thrown over her shoulders, though seemed to glow untouched by the cold.

"Faye," Tessie hissed. "Faye!"

"What's that then?" The girl called louder than Tessie would have wished. "If that's yer Willy Cradle yer can come round the front like everybody else!" Tessie stepped out from her stairwell and waited for the girl to see her. Faye nearly dropped the turnip crate as she caught a glimpse of her, a few tumbling to the ground with a muted curse. She put the box down before leaping across the alley, barefoot. "Tessie Fisher, if that ain't your ghost?" Faye swore, and Tessie's smile burst forth with the recognition. She couldn't remember the last time a smile had stretched her cheeks.

"Jaysus," Faye whispered, crouching down to meet her. "Where have yer sprung up from?"

They squeezed each other tight. "I'm so glad to see yer," Tessie cried.

"But what are yer doing out here, girl?"

Before she could answer, the door opened again. It was Aileen.

"Why in God's name is this door swinging around like the balls of St. Nick?" Last night's clothes were bloodstained, her hair knotted and wild with a stripe of blood down the side of her face.

"Faye! What are yer doing, girl?" Aileen stepped out of the doorway. "I don't want yer girls outside right now. Yer know that. It's not safe."

Faye gasped at the sight of her. "Is that your blood?"

"Only some of it. Now get yer arse back inside, come on." She nodded towards the back door, but paused, seeing Tessie beneath the stairs. "Well, well, well." Aileen lifted her arms to block her path. "How quickly they fall."

"We aren't finished are we," Tessie said.

Aileen clicked her tongue, tired and weary. "On with yer then." She urged her toward the door impatiently.

Standing in the kitchen, Tessie found it both changed and the same. She took in the familiar grease spattered stove and scratched table top. Eight years had not seen significant change. The chairs were different, with lumpy fabric seats stained with grey and greasy blotches. Two girls slept in the hallway sprawled over each other on a pink couch. They had seen Tessie come in, though registered no comment and Tessie didn't recognise them. Faye stood at the sink on her tippy toes cutting turnips and plunging them into the already boiling water. In the store cupboard, Aileen clattered with the pots. "Christ Almighty, where is Siobhan?"

"She's upstairs."

"If she's used the last of my ginger I'll smack the piss out of her."

"Does that mean they're coming?"

"What?"

"The blood on yer clothes?" Faye pressed, anxiousness creeping over her quaint features. "Are they coming for us or not?"

"Oh." Aileen looked down at herself. "Look at my damn shirt. No," Aileen brushed it off. "It don't mean nothing."

"That were the Angel's men last night?" Tessie asked. "They are here in Dublin? They are bleedin' everywhere."

"I told yer already," Aileen said, pointing at Tessie in warning and then turning her attention back to the pantry shelves. "I need my ginger."

Aileen tossed another pot into the hall and Faye put it on the stove as if she had needed it anyway. Aileen charged through, nudging Tessie toward the table. "Take a seat, girl, yer in the way." She raced up the stairs and they waited below, listening as Aileen opened and slammed doors.

"I'm sleeping!" Siobhan yelled.

"Where is it?" Aileen demanded, followed by further ransacking of Siobhan's room and what sounded to be the knocking over of tables. The shrieking raised higher before Aileen's voice was the only one left. "I knew yer had it. Prime slut, I'll have yer out, I tell yer! I need it for my guts, so I do."

Faye gave Tessie a reassuring wink. "Leens gets her ginger tea from Mr Chin at the docks. She's pretty precious about it. And Siobhan, gets a bit big for her boots, so she does."

"It's the Angel coming for yer?" Tessie whispered.

Faye bit at her nail. "Aye. It's been a bloody winter. One of the girls got stuck with a knife on her way home only yesterday as a message for Leens. She's been playing it down but she's not letting us leave the house and I know she has men on the lookout in the alleys to keep watch. I'm right shakin' they're gonna run through the place like they did when...yer know—"

Aileen emerged, ginger triumphantly in hand and Faye and Tessie pulled back as if they'd been sitting in silence. The two girls on the sofa dragged the covers over their heads avoiding her as she trampled past.

"Anyone would think laying about with yer legs in the air was the queen's work. Queen fecking Victoria." Aileen slammed a smaller kettle on the stovetop and rolled herself a cigarette. "When's that soup ready?"

"I only just put them turnips in."

"Christ, girl."

"Yer want crunchy turnips or not?" Faye said and they exchanged a familiar glare at each other.

Tessie's eyes fell to the table, something prickling up inside her. She knew this place, knew it like home. A strange suture formed down her middle, half foreigner, half-kin, the line burning as it surfaced.

There was safety here with Aileen. It was why the girls stayed. It was why Faye had stayed. It may even be why her legs had carried her here in the middle of the night when she had nowhere else to turn. Aileen had a vicious bite, that much was true, but within her walls, you could see her, you could dance to her tune just enough to stay out of the way. And all the while she blocked the entrance, stopping the black leeches of Dublin, whose talons would pluck those girls raw from the nest. Aileen was the gatekeeper. Ferocious. Indomitable. If you were hers, she kept you.

Though Tessie's memories of being dragged to the workhouse clambered for space. Aileen hadn't kept Tessie. Hadn't minded her. Hadn't been her gatekeeper. The pain of it rose up like mangled twine in her throat and she erupted in a choking cough, trying to expel it. Hunching over, she had drowned out all other conversation and when she looked up, Aileen was watching, her eyes suspicious.

"Right then, Faye. Bring me up some soup when you're done, and don't let these girls sleep past noon." She pointed at the two on the hallway couch. "They'll need to beat those sheets out for tonight."

"We still need to talk," Tessie interjected. Aileen stretched tall and croaky, swilling the hot water in her ginger tea.

"Not now we don't. Right now I'll be sleeping."

"What am I supposed to do?"

"Wash yer face. There's a rag over there. Sorry, we don't got any of that fancy stuff yer used to." Aileen disappeared up the stairs. "Faye'll take care of yer."

Faye nodded in agreement, scooting up next to Tessie. "Don't worry about her. She'll sleep it off and be down later. I couldn't be gladder to see yer."

Tessie squeezed her hand. "Aye. Yer wouldn't believe what it means to see a familiar face."

"Yer eyes tell the story. But yer ribs..." She jabbed at Tessie's waist. "Yer have been eating more than turnips."

Tessie laughed. "Yes, that much is true."

After finishing a bowl of soup, Faye set her up on a pallet in the front room, buried beneath a layer of musty blankets. Tessie covered her face, listening to the sounds around her. She might have been her younger self, listening to dirty jokes and the jostling politics of young women vying for themselves. It simmered in the background, wrapping her in a foggy cocoon of memories and the disjointed reality she had succumbed to.

Her mind wandered to Kyran and Ruby. Were they looking for her? Though if Kyran really was the Angel's man, he would know where to find her. Taking a deep breath, she let her chest sink into the pallet. None of it made sense. Why bring her here? She had been used by the Angel to get back at her mother in a war about imports and territory. Was Kyran really a part of that? And Ruby? She couldn't get the story to gel, though perhaps it explained how he could interrupt the attack in her tenement and whisk her away. Was he more powerful than she thought? Had they simply let him walk in and take her without fighting him?

As Tessie lay there, the questions grew thicker still. If the Angel wanted her dead in order to send a message to her mother, why involve Kyran at all? They could have easily plucked her off the street and packed her home to her mother without any of that charade. And the note, was there more to that than Kyran had let on? She believed Kyran's reaction that night had been genuine upset. Perhaps above everything, the note was the key.

~

IN THE EVENING the girls lit their lanterns, moving around Tessie's pallet to shake out their cushions and pillows, preparing a sultry welcome. She woke in the haziness and hidden in a veil of shadow she sat up. Looking at the girls, now preened and plumped with shiny faces, she had the instinct to slip out the back door without a word, but she still had unfinished business.

Shaking off the cobwebs of sleep and wrapping her cloak around her, Tessie weaved her way through the girls in the front room and headed upstairs to Aileen's room. Hearing a rasping burst of coughing and spluttering, Tessie pushed open the door to see Aileen folded over, beating on her chest.

"Close the door," Aileen barked, and flung herself back again, catching her breath.

"Are yer sick?"

"No. It's like this when I wake up."

"Yer need to rest and stay out of the cold with a chest like that."

Aileen stood out of the bed in a drab and shapeless nightdress and drank from a cup on the nightstand. "Thanks for yer concern and keen medical advice. It's called getting old, love."

Tessie looked down at her mother's bedside knick-knacks. A small figure of St. Brigid had toppled on the bed stand, lost amongst the stray pennies and rubbed out cigarettes. It was like the one she had left at the docks for Finn.

Aileen had never taken Tessie to church, even when some of the girls went every Sunday, though St. Brigid was as familiar to her as the rest of their house. She had been born a slave, so Aileen had told her, and it had been St. Brigid's prayer that Aileen repeated over Tessie's bed at night. Memories of a watchful mother clashed with those of being dragged across the cobblestones by her hair. Of Aileen marching forward without mercy and without explanation, flinging her at the workhouse gate. Watching Aileen now gasping for breath in a stained nightgown, a sour taste flooded her mouth.

Aileen's small room was one of many in the crumbling box of damp wood and floorboards. For whatever money Aileen made, none of it showed in this establishment. She had a newish bed, a plush quilt for herself and a few odd pieces of furniture about the place, but there was little to distinguish the building as anything more than a dilapidated and ignored whorehouse.

"What?" Aileen accused, seeing Tessie's inquisitive eye. "Not fancy enough for yer?"

"My home in London was much the same if it makes yer feel any better."

"Aye. The poor never have money, even when they do. Remember that." Aileen picked at the cut on her hairline, dabbing at it with a rag as she looked at her reflection in a fogged up broken mirror. "What do yer want then?"

"Yer have to call it off. In London I mean. Yer have to stop it."

"Stop it?"

"Stop the Angel coming after us. Finn and I. He's out there and I can't find him. Call it off before it's too late."

"I told yer. What the Angel does in London has nought to with me."

"But he's doing it because of yer. Call it off!"

"Use your head, girl." Aileen tapped her finger at her temple. "That ain't going to happen. It don't work like that. Nobody calls the Angel off."

Tessie stared at her in amazement. Had she been naive to think it would be that simple?

"Then settle it! Settle this war. Whatever it takes."

"You've lost yer marbles, girl. I ain't giving that man a

damn thing and whatever plans he's got are his, and his alone. I don't know what yer want from me. I really don't."

"I paid for the answers. I paid for...something..." She trailed away, her conviction weakening. Was it so hopeless?

"I suspect your friend did that."

Tessie slumped, thinking of Kyran. "Does he really work for the Angel?"

"I ain't seen him for years. But that were him sure enough."

Tessie fidgeted with her hands and perched on the edge of the bed. "Why did he know who I am?"

'What?"

"How did the Angel know I existed? I haven't been home in eight years. No one in London knows our connection. Why would he even think of me?"

Aileen got back under the covers as the walls erupted in a dramatic burst of moans and gasps. Picking up a broom handle and hitting against the wall, she called out. "It's too early for that lot, Trudy, tone it down." The noise dulled and Aileen fluffed up the pillows behind her. "Pass me tobacco."

"I want to know—"

"Alright!" Aileen snapped. "Give me a bleeding minute."

Tessie folded her arms, watching her slowly fashion her rolling paper into a perfect cylinder. She snatched the candle on the bedside table and urged her to light it. Aileen inhaled slowly and deeply, before turning her cranky eyes on Tessie. She looked hesitant, her mind whirring backwards through time.

"He's always known," Aileen said, inhaling. "He's yer da."

"What?"

"Yep." Aileen nodded and a slow chuckle rumbled from her rasping chest. "That's the truth of it."

"What?"

"That's the answer. Yer asked and I told yer."

"What do yer mean he's my da?"

Aileen shook her head in disgust. "I mean what I fucking said. Arthur is his name. I can tell yer that much. And it's his seed what stuck yer in my belly."

Tessie stood up, stamping her boots hard on the floor. How could that be the bloody truth?

"I didn't always look like an old leather boot. Let me tell yer," Aileen said. "And I knew as soon as I fell ill, it was his. I rooted out every bub that got stuck in here." She pointed at her belly. "But not yer. Know why? Coz I knew yer were his! And I thought to myself, that might be fucking useful to me. Having the Angel's baby might just be worth the bleedin' hassle. I had plans, I did. I always did. And when push came to shove I threw your name out there like the weapon I always intended. That's me. That's yer old Mum. That's who I am." Aileen bristled up, defending herself before Tessie could even respond. "Didn't work in my favour but that's life ain't it?"

Tessie's mouth opened to speak but no words formed. Anger glared from her eyes, clashing with her shock and outrage. "The Angel of Bishopsgate is my father?"

"Yes. My Lord, yes!"

"All of this is because I'm your daughter. He was gonna kill me. And I'm his daughter?"

Aileen drew back hard on her cigarette, stubbing it out roughly. "There yer have it."

"I've lost everything. I've lost Finn. I have no idea where he is or what happened to him."

"Whose Finn? Don't tell me all this is about a fucking boy."

Tessie snapped back into reality. "It's about my life. He were going to kill me."

"But he didn't."

"He still might! And Finn. Where the hell is he?"

"Christ, love. You've gone lost yer rocker. I don't give a fig about Finn."

"Yer don't care about nothing but yourself!" Tessie screamed. Aileen leapt forward, pointing her finger in Tessie's face.

"Yer keep your bloody voice down."

"Of course yer don't understand. Yer have never cared for anyone but yourself. Yer are dead on the inside. Dead and rotten. Always have been!"

Aileen's face contorted, her wild hair shaking with the sharp movements as she stood before Tessie. "I know who I am. And I know what I've had to do. Yer might not like it, but this is how I am, daughter of mine. I'm not soft and I'll not coddle yer, and I'll not apologise for it neither. Any one of these girls can walk out of here free as a bird, any day of the goddam week, and they don't! Yer know why? Because in here is better than what's out there. I won't be judged. Not by anyone and certainly not by yer!" Aileen's chest heaved as she spoke and Tessie's cheeks flushed with the scolding.

"Why the fuck did I get stuck with yer? The best thing yer ever did was drag me to that workhouse!"

"And even then yer didn't go easy. Don't knows what's good for yer. Never have listened even when yer should."

Tessie paced back and forth, the anger in her looking for an exit. Bearing it no longer, she stormed from the room, slamming the door behind her.

"Don't walk away from me, girl!" Aileen hollered. "This is what yer came here for ain't it? Let's have out with it." But Tessie didn't stop, tumbling down the stairs and bursting through the Black Bonnet's front room.

"Stop, Tessie, wait!" Faye trailed behind her.

Tessie's boots slowed as she pushed through the crowds on Great Britain Street.

"Yer can't let her get to yer," Faye urged. "You've been away too long you've forgotten what's she's like. You've gotta ignore her carry on."

"How can anyone ignore that?"

"It's how she is and it ain't worth upsetting yourself."

Tessie took a deep breath. Hot tears of anger stung her eyes but she swiped them away with the back of her hands. "It is so unfair. All of it."

"Aye. You'll hear no argument from me."

Tessie stilled herself. Faye was right, there was nothing to gain by letting it all get the better of her now. It was just the frustration. The overwhelming frustration, and the ever-changing mixture of rage and vulnerability she felt for her mother.

As they walked toward the river, a market stall hummed with barrels of mulled wine and hot apples. Carollers grouped near the lanterns and passersby dropped pennies in their buckets. She had forgotten about Christmas. She looked at the work-weary people, relaxing into the quaint scene. These were her people. The poor and the workers, the tired and downtrodden. They weren't fancy or pretentious, but they laughed and cherished the small victories; an extra lump of coal or a stocking without holes. How she had longed for them. She imagined Finn amongst them. It felt like home.

"We should be getting back," Faye urged, looking about. "We ain't supposed to be out, yer know."

"Aye," Tessie nodded. "Just a moment longer? Let's have a cup of mulled wine before we go."

Faye looked hesitant though nodded and they sauntered towards the beckoning lights.

Their warm cups in hand, they moved to the sidelines to watch the carollers. "Have yer never wanted to get out of here, Faye?" Tessie asked.

Faye cocked her head in consideration and shrugged. "Sometimes. Charlie Simms proposed last winter and I thought to go with him out on the farm."

"Did yer? Faye the farmer's wife," Tessie teased.

"Aye. But with the famine and all the potatoes shrivelling up, he were but starving out there. He turned ill not long after."

"That's a shame, Faye. I'm sorry."

"Argh," she dismissed. "He were a good lad. We might have been alright, but I'd never been outta the city so I were nervous about that, I won't lie. But here I am. Still whoring. Probably will be for as long as I can get my legs up."

Tessie tugged at her lip and nodded. It was tough times in Dublin, and everywhere it seemed.

Faye sighed. "Could be worse, couldn't it? These girls ain't so bad. And Leens, well she is and always will be Leens."

Tessie nodded. Yes, things could always be worse.

"She went mad when yer left, yer know," Faye broached the subject. "She tore this city up looking for yer."

"Yer remember?"

"I'm older than yer, Tess, for god's sake, but I ain't lost my marbles yet. Yes, I damn well remember."

"What do yer mean?"

"She tried to find yer. Had us out there night and day, checking alleys and rooftops. We all wondered why you'd left."

Tessie shook her head, indignant. "Why'd she put me in there then? In the workhouse?"

Faye frowned. "Yer don't know?"

"No. I don't."

Faye pushed herself off the wall in shock. "She never told yer?"

"Told me what?"

"Oh my Tess..." Faye faded at the realisation she had no idea. "She were trying to protect yer."

"Protect me?"

"Listen," Faye insisted. "The Angel's men were set to run through the place. Back then, it was like it is just now. Attacks back and forth. One of his men had come into the Bonnet as a customer and tried to murder Aileen in her sleep. Lucky she woke first, but after that, she knew they were coming. She wanted yer out the way, girl. She knew the Angel would take yer. Or do worse. She didn't know where else to put yer, so she put yer in the workhouse thinking to come get yer when it had all blown over. But yer had already gone."

Tessie's mouth hung open, a frown frozen on her brow. "I don't remember her being at war with the Angel then...I don't remember her..."

"Yer were 12, Tess, and yer know how she plays things down. She didn't want to scare yer, but I can't believe she didn't tell yer she were coming back. I guess she thought the less yer knew the better."

"She dragged me by my hair. She didn't say anything at all."

Faye bit her lip. "She never could say a soft word. She don't know how, Tess. She's a fighter and that's what she does. But it hurt her to do it. I know it did. I seen it in her. She didn't cry, or talk about soft things like others might. But she was ready for war. And when she found out yer had gone she flew into such a state."

"And the Angel? Did his men come?"

"Aye, not a day after yer left. The girls put up a fight, so they did. But it were bad. I'm no fighter, yer know that, and I were one of the lucky ones. They came with knives and axes and they didn't care we was just girls. Lucy and Maura died right there in the front room. Sometimes I still hear the screaming. There was so much of it. It was Aileen who singlehandedly fought them off, one by one with her hatchet. She were legendary after that. The Black Bonnet of Dublin. I tell yer, that night spread the name of Aileen Fisher further than the edges of this city."

Tessie closed her eyes, imagining the bloody scene.

"And yer ma was right, Tess," Faye continued. "They were looking for yer too. Turned the house upside down looking for any space a 12 year old could hide. They would have taken yer. And God knows what would have happened. They're animals, Tess."

Tessie stared down at her mulled wine, blowing into the steam, her heart pounding. Her mum had fought for her, and while she'd been fighting, Tessie had run away. Her emotions swung like a pendulum, surging her belly with seasickness. "I don't know what to make of anything anymore, Faye. Maybe this has all been my fault. Right back at the beginning."

"No, girl. It's the Angel. And it's those animals. And don't think Aileen don't care about yer. Not all love looks the same. If yer think it does yer will go yer whole life blind to it."

Tessie thought on it. Trying to merge the story with her memories and the feelings biting at her chest.

"But let's get back now." Faye took Tessie's empty cup and handed it to the stall owner as they set on the pathway home.

As they walked, Faye's words settled over her, and the images of her past rose up around her on the streets in every echo on the cobblestones, against the backdrop of stained tenements, mud and muck.

"Yer gonna bake us a cake while yer here?"

"Oh, I don't know." Tessie smiled, memories of hovering over the old stove, with not just ginger cakes, but apple tarts and shortbreads too. Cake made for simpler times.

"I could do with some warm cake from the oven, so I could."

As they turned off Capel Street towards the Black Bonnet, Tessie noticed a figure lingering a few yards behind them.

"Let's walk faster, Faye," Tessie urged, gripping her hand.

"What is it?"

"Someone's behind us."

"Oh sweet Jaysus." Faye clenched her eyes shut as they picked up the pace. "I knew it, I knew it, I knew it."

Tessie cursed herself. Why had they stayed out so long? As they turned the alley corner another figure appeared in front of them, but they could see Aileen's door up ahead. They just needed to make it a little further. Tessie squeezed Faye's hand, her chest hot with fear. The figure behind them was gaining ground and Tessie broke into a run though the figure in front left them nowhere to turn.

He was upon them. His arm looped around Faye's neck and he yanked her down. His knife blade caught in the light, his hand smothering Faye's mouth as he slashed deep and hard across her throat. Strong arms held Tessie back as she struggled to break free and get to Faye. Releasing a scream so loud it echoed off the alley walls, the figure punched her in the stomach and ripped at her hair as she gashed her nails along his face. "Somebody help us!"

Breaking free and flinging herself towards Faye, the door of the Black Bonnet opened and Aileen emerged in her nightgown, hatched in hand. She gave out a long whistle, summoning her guard points who emerged from the shadows. But they were all too late. Blood gushed from Faye's throat, flooding onto her dress and cobblestones beneath her.

"No! Faye!" Tessie cried as the colour drained from Faye's face, her eyes bulging with raw panic. Tessie gripped the wound trying to stem the flow of blood but there was too much. The wound was too big.

Aileen rushed upon them, her nightgown flaring and her hatchet raised but seeing Faye, she dropped to her knees and cradled Faye in her lap.

"He cut her throat! He cut her throat!"

Faye gurgled and choked for breath, tears squeezing from the corners of her eyes. Her mouth gaped open as she stared up at Aileen, unable to speak.

"I'm here child, hush now." Aileen rocked her back and forth, stroking her hair as the light faded in her eyes. Faye's hands fell away exposing the violent gash across her throat and Aileen clenched her eyes shut and looked away. "I'm here, child," she repeated.

Tessie collapsed beside them, throwing her herself over Faye's body and howling.

CHAPTER 24

"We have to get her inside," Aileen commanded. "Grab her feet."

Tessie roused herself, smearing the tears away with her fists and taking hold of Faye's ankles as Aileen heaved her limp body up by the shoulders. "Lift child. Lift, dammit."

Tessie stumbled backwards to the open door of the Black Bonnet, the girls crowded at the doorway in a mass of wails and whimpers.

"Move!" Aileen directed. "Clear off the sofa. Do it." The distraught onlookers leapt into action knocking cushions and papers to the floor as Tessie stumbled to keep pace with Aileen's strong stride.

"Bolt the door." Aileen pointed and one of the girls slid the thick metal bolt across and placed the wooden post in its bracket. "Now who's here?"

"Just Walter and Mr Wickens," another girl sniffled, staring wide-eyed at Faye's bloodstained corpse.

"Get'em out. Get 'em out now!" The girl ran from the room and there was a flurry of action as the girls ran in circles trying to follow directions but so distraught not knowing what to do. The two men were ushered through the back door and the girls finally stood quietly with muted cries awaiting their next instruction.

"Now yer all to get to your rooms. There's to be no more hysteria. Our Faye has gone. There's nought can be done about that. On with yer now and comfort yourselves while I take care of our Faye best I can." The girls herded out of the room leaving it quiet.

Tessie paced by the window rubbing the blood in her fingernails as Aileen returned from the kitchen with a pale of water and cloth. She moved mechanically as someone used to the practicality of death, though her face was sombre and her eyes dark.

Without a word, Aileen crouched beside Faye's body and swept her blood-soaked hair to the side, gently smoothing her round cheeks with the cloth. "I suggest yer help me, or fetch her blue dress from her room. I'll not leave her here soaking in her own blood."

Tessie stood still a moment, processing the request before striding from the room.

"And bring her quilt."

Tessie's limbs felt heavy and her face swollen as she rummaged through Faye's room, returning with her blue church dress and the quilt from her bed.

Aileen's eyes didn't move from Faye as Tessie lay them beside her. "There yer are girl, we'll make yer as comfortable as we can."

"She was out there for me," Tessie said, rocking back and forth from foot to foot. "This is my fault."

Aileen's eyes darted briefly from Faye. "What's done is done."

"It was the Angel weren't it? He's everywhere."

"Hush now." Aileen rose up quickly. "I'll not hear yer voice now. And I'll not hear of him."

Tessie bit down on her lip, turning back to the blood in her fingernails, pressing so hard it tore the skin.

"Take off her shoes," Aileen said, and Tessie dropped her head in obedience. How could this have happened? Why had they stayed out so long? Why hadn't she returned when Faye had asked?

Working methodically, Aileen moved in quiet tenderness as she bathed Faye's pale white skin until she was fresh and clean. She helped Aileen carefully change her in the blue dress and then wrap her tightly in her pink quilt. Pulled up to her chin, she looked simply to be resting on the couch, her pretty face perfectly calm.

"That's all we can do tonight." Aileen stood in the corner, her eyes drained and weary and fixed on the figure in the pink quilt. "Yer should sleep. We have things to do in the morning." With that, Aileen ascended the stairs to her room leaving Tessie alone with the cocooned body beside her.

AT FIRST LIGHT, Tessie woke to Aileen's strong hands nudging her awake. She had slept sitting upright in the front room, her eyes closed but never resting. All she could see was Faye. In the hours of silence, her heart quick and her breathing shallow, she couldn't shake the fog away, nor the lump in her throat. None of it could be undone, and the shame rumbled and slithered inside her. Why had it not been her throat that caught the blade across it? Why had she drawn Faye away from the Bonnet?

"Come with me," Aileen said.

"Where?"

Aileen opened the door, spilling light into the gloomy room as Tessie peeled herself from the sofa. Taking a last look at Faye's still and lonely frame, her limbs stepped one after the other, numb and heavy. Aileen kept a strident pace along Capel Street so that Tessie struggled to keep up as they cut along the dark tenements. The wind off the Anna Liffey beat against her as she followed behind and finally, taking a canal bridge to the south side and tucking into an alley just shy of Crampton Quay, they stopped to catch their breath.

"Here," Aileen said, holding the coin purse Kyran had given her only days earlier. "It's all there." She pressed it into Tessie's hands, still heavy with coins,

"What's this?"

"There's a boat leaving for Liverpool in an hour." She nodded toward the Quay. "Best be on it."

Tessie looked out at the boats lining the harbour. "Yer sending me away?"

"Yer need to get out of the city."

"Yer want me to go?"

"This's got nought to do with what I want," Aileen said. "These are my streets. And this is my fight. Mine. I'm Aileen Fisher. I run my house. I run my docks. But yer don't belong in that house. Probably never have."

Tessie stung all over. "What about Faye?"

"She don't need yer now, does she? Yer want to be next?"

"Any of yer could be next? It should be me back there on the sofa. Not Faye."

"Dammit girl." Aileen cursed under her breath. "Yer came here for answers and yer got'em. Ain't nothing here changed and ain't nothing here for yer. We both know it."

Tessie looked at the city surrounding her, struggling to remember the reason for all of this. A rush of nausea hit her belly and tears stung her eyes. "Faye told me about the workhouse. She told me why you took me there."

Aileen held her gaze, swallowing hard. "Well now yer know."

"All these years..." Tessie shook her head.

"Don't yer cry," Aileen cut through. "Don't yer dare. Yer know what I am. And yer know all I have to give yer is more of this shite. More throats cut. More blood. More thrashin' about, fighting for every measly bite. Yer'll be cursing me if yer stay. Yer know it."

Tessie's shoulders slumped with the weight of it, the wind off the river blustering against her. "I don't even know where to go now. I don't know how to find Finn and the Angel..."

Aileen pushed herself off the wall. "Yes yer do. Yer the daughter of Aileen Fisher and the Angel of Bishopsgate. Yer know what that means? That means yer take shite from no one. Not a fucking soul."

Gritting her teeth, Tessie choked a sob in her throat and Aileen gripped her chin in her hands. Aileen's own voice cracking and her eyes shiny, she forced Tessie to look at her. "Yer bow down to no one. Yer hear me? Yer get your revenge. Yer find your Finn or whatever his name is. Yer take this money and go where ever yer need to go, do whatever yer need to do, but yer keep fighting. And yer keep fighting and yer never stop. This world will eat yer alive if you let it." Aileen released her grip on Tessie's chin and slumped against the wall, her energy expended.

Tessie held herself, trying to replicate the steely fortitude in her mother's jaw, her heart surging and her legs shaking. Whatever her mother's sentiments, she was being sent away again. This city didn't want her.

"On yer way, girl. On yer way." Aileen nodded towards the Quay.

Taking a last glance at her mother, their eyes locked, Aileen's dark and resigned, her wild hair whipping at her back and hatchet tucked in her waistband. Tessie turned away, and though something inside her screamed, twisting and wringing her insides, her eyes turned forward. She was going after Finn.

CHAPTER 25

rthur stood in the dark, a damp-ended cigar resting between his thumb and forefinger. The fire had long gone out though he hadn't called to have it re-lit. His eyes sagged with weariness though he would not retire to bed for more hours yet. Sleep was something that eluded him more than most things in this world.

From his vantage point at the window, he couldn't see the dark alleys stretching through the East End, nor the river writhing through the centre of London — but he knew they were there, carrying the ever moving pieces of his empire. This was usually the part he loved. The planning and the poetry of strategy, though his sight across the Irish Sea was more obscured than ever. Was he losing his grip? Had he lost his hold over the city? Kyran was certainly holding out, and it put a crick in Arthur's neck so that he stretched his shoulders and tried to shake it off. "It's that damn girl he is with," Arthur spoke into the empty room, tucking one hand into his waistcoat. "Flirty harlot. Golden-haired twit." She had gotten under Kyran's skin and he should have seen it coming. He should have taken care of it long before. But it would catch up with him soon. If there was one thing Arthur prided himself on, it was seeing things through.

Without a knock, the study door pushed open and his father entered. "Have you seen Artie? I need me nickels."

"No, Pa." Arthur's gaze didn't shift from the window.

"Where is Artie?" Otis persisted. "Nickels. I need me nickels." Otis moved to the desk and rifled through the drawers, knocking things over in a boisterous and clumsy assault on the quiet that had been. Arthur's shoulders sank and he narrowed his watery blue eyes, suffering the old man's shaky hands on his belongings.

"Pa!" Arthur reprimanded. "Don't be touching my things."

"Artie has my nickels and I need a drink. I want my marbles."

Arthur closed the desk drawer shut with his knee as the old man looked into Arthur's face without recognition, tears springing in his eyes. "I need my nickels." Flashing with anger, Otis whipped his arm up to strike and Arthur caught the blow on his forearm. Guiding him back towards the door, Arthur wrapped his arm around his father's shoulders in a gesture of warmth, holding him close. "Come on, Pa. Where's Betty? You've gotten away from her again."

Out in the hall, Arthur called for her, holding Otis's hand as he stared into space. "You are having a time of it, aren't you, Pa?" Arthur sighed. "Imbecile or monster. Flick from one to the other."

"Hey?" Otis barked, none the wiser.

Betty came running in her nightdress and dressing gown. "Oh, I'm sorry, sir." Seeing Otis in one of his states, she quickly took his arm. "Come on, Mr Crabbe, come with me."

"Get him some warm milk, Betty. That seems to settle him down for the night."

"I will do, sir. I will do. Thank you."

Arthur ushered Otis towards her and watched as he

trailed away with her. By all appearances, he was the same sturdy man who chastised him over breakfast, though in these moments his shoulders sagged and he lent his head to the left.

Betty turned back to repeat again, "I'm sorry." Arthur lightheartedly waved his hand in reassurance.

"Will you not be coming to bed?" Cynthia spoke from behind him, her voice probing and shrill so that his eyes winced at the sound.

Turning to see her wrapped in a gold-spun dressing gown, his face fell in a greeting of disappointment. "Not just yet, no."

"This staying up all night business is not good, Artie. Not good at all."

"What point is there of coming to bed if I'm laying there awake."

"The point is rest, husband. Something that fails you."

Arthur shrugged her off, moving swiftly toward his office. Cynthia followed, not yet prepared to give up chase. "The cracks will start to show if indeed they are not already."

"What are you talking about now?"

"You've let it get to you. This Kyran business."

Arthur's eyes flared up at her now. "You know nothing of my business, woman."

"He must come back of his own volition. You cannot control everyone and everything, Arthur."

"If I do not, then who will? Tell me that then! Who will step in where I do not? Who will make sure things happen as they should?"

"That's not how things are supposed to work, grinding the world beneath your thumb. No one will survive that. You work against yourself!"

"Go back to bed."

"You drive him away. You are unbearable."

"You overstep your place, woman," Arthur warned.

"My place? My father is the cousin to the Earl—"

"Distant cousin."

"This is my place. You are the one borrowing, stepping on my head to buy your way—"

"No one else would have you!"

Cynthia paled. "I am not an ugly woman, Arthur Crabbe. I may not be the fair lady of your dreams but I have fortitude enough to withstand your constant dismissal and degradation. You drown out everyone and everything around you. Suffocate it to the bone. You will die alone and unloved."

"Loved? You waste your breath."

"You know nothing of it. Nothing at all."

"What is better, to be loved or obeyed? I'll tell you which one I want in this very moment. One is real and one is fantasy…and whim."

"You have no capacity for it. That is why you don't understand it."

"Get out!" Arthur bellowed, and lunging, he grabbed Cynthia by the shoulders and marched her backwards from the room. She screeched, gripping his hands where they held her. He thrust her from the room and slammed the door.

CHAPTER 26

"You can't just keep sneaking up like that." Billy cursed as Finn popped his head over the stable door.

"Yer know I can, Billy." He hoisted himself up and over, landing with a thud beside the hay Billy was hacking with a pitchfork. It had been a nearly a week since he'd sent Billy home on the hunt for information and even though the morning light would soon be in full flare, he'd risked a venture into the East End.

"Well, I ain't got anything for you."

"I'll keep coming back until yer do, rest assured of that."

Billy swallowed and gestured towards the chestnut mare eating from the food trough beside him. "I'm supposed to saddle her up. Mr Smith's coming to fetch her in about 30 minutes."

"Saddle her up then. I'm not stopping yer." Finn slouched against the wall. "Yer said yer was going to the Seven Bells last night."

Billy continued brushing down the chestnut horse in front of them. "I went."

"Well don't hold out on me, Billy Brittle. The sooner yer give me something I can use, the sooner I leave yer alone."

"You sound just like them now, you know that? Throwing your weight around."

Finn set his foot down and braced his shoulders, though the words settled on him. "I'm not like them. Tessie ain't like them neither. Yer know that. We need yer help and yer should be offering it willingly if there was any use in yer."

Billy paused, keeping his eyes on the mare in front of him, brushing her slowly. "I said I'd help and I went, alright."

"So what did yer see?"

"Nothing really."

"What, anything? Were any of the Angel's men there?"

"Yes. Plenty of them. Of course. Drinking and carrying on. I was keeping my head down, wasn't I? Anything can happen in there."

'Well? What did you see?"

"Who knows? How would I even know if I was looking at something? I don't know what I'm looking for."

"A person."

"A person?" Billy tossed the saddle mat over the horse. "What do you mean a person? I saw plenty of persons."

"Yer know." Finn splayed his hands in exasperation. "Someone who stands out. Someone important."

"Someone who stands out..." Billy trailed away as if Finn was talking nonsense.

"Was Moses there?"

"Yeah, he was there."

"What was he doing?"

"Drinking. Talking."

"Talking to who?"

"A few people."

"Think, Billy. Anyone who stood out and caught yer eye?"

Billy grimaced as he tightened the saddle girth and moved

around to the front of the horse to adjust the bridle. "There was one bloke." Billy shrugged. "I thought he looked a bit odd."

"Odd how?"

"I dunno really. They spoke out the front by the window before Moses came in. Over to the side, like."

"So the other man didn't come in?"

"No." Billy stepped back, admiring the horse. Taking a rag, he started polishing the saddle's leather. "Wait. No, he did come in at first, but I guess he was looking for Moses because he only poked his head in and walked out again and that's when he bumped into him out by the window."

"Was he wearing an Angel's cuff?"

"No. He wasn't. I looked and didn't see one."

Finn slumped and rubbed his forehead. "No cuff. I guess that means he's out."

"Well..." Billy paused and rubbed his patchy adolescent beard as if his thoughts had finally been stirred. "It's only...they all seemed to know him, like."

"How do yer mean know him?"

Billy thought on it. "It's more like a feeling I got. Like they... I don't know...moved out of his way." Billy bowed his head acting it out. "They acknowledged him. Gave him a nod, like. It was small, but...could be nothing."

"What did he look like?"

"That's it too. He were dressed nice. Not like the others in there."

"So he was dressed nice."

"Yeah. A nicely dressed, African-looking bloke."

"African?"

"Yeah. Black skin. Dark, like."

Finn pushed himself off the wall, staring hard at his boots. "This might be something, Billy. It just might be something."

"You reckon?"

"Only one way to find out. That's yer next job then."

"Hold on, what?" Billy stood back from the horse, dropping his hands to his side. "What now?"

"Follow him." Finn scooped up an apple balancing on the stable wall. "Find him, and follow him, and tell me where he goes."

"That's my bleeding apple!"

Finn took a bite and hoisted himself back over the wall. "A delicious one it is too. Mind yer follow him."

"I was keeping that for Anne."

"Whose Anne?"

"A girl." Billy turned away, hiding a blush in his cheeks.

"Sweet on her are yer?"

"It's you who should be giving me apples."

"Mark my word, Billy. If yer actually pull this off, I'll give yer anything yer want and more."

HE'D TAKEN a risk crossing the bridge and wandering into the East End as morning broke, though pulling his cap down hard and falling in sync with a hay wagon, the buzz in his chest told him it was worth it. They had a lead to follow and that was exactly what they needed. Maybe Billy would come through for him after all. Until this morning it had felt like nothing but a sad hope in the grass.

Around him, the city was deep in the throes of Christmas preparations with butchers parading their prize cuts of meats, destined to take centre stage on any extravagant Christmas table. Turkeys, geese and even swans were out on display. The smell of roasted chestnuts hung in the air.

Finn had a craving for Tessie's humble ginger cake as the hay wagon dragged him back over London Bridge and halfway to Bermondsey. He thought of her and all those early mornings with the smell of fresh-baked cake over the stove. Maybe he was one step closer to finding her.

Back in town, Mickey was pulling on his boots at Cora's bar as she set down a bowl of lumpy porridge. As Finn walked in, he was inspecting it.

"I could make a better batch myself if yer let me in that kitchen," he quipped, staring at his lumpy oat stew.

"Mr Finch'll knock you silly if you so much as stick your head in there," she came back at him.

"I ain't never heard a word outta Mr Finch." Mickey stood on his stool and leaned over the bar to peer in.

"He don't talk much but you'll feel him when he slaps you. Don't say I didn't warn you." She whipped him with a teacloth, but she was teasing. "Mr Finch, this lot out here is complaining about your porridge again." She set off back to the kitchen.

As Finn sat beside him, Mickey slid the bowl in his direction. "It's all yours, brother."

Finn took a deep breath at the sight of it but dug in none the less. "Where are yer off to?"

"If I don't get a day's work soon I'll be outta cash, and I need to be saving for Boston while we carry on here. Was gonna head to the railway or tannery, I guess. See what I can find."

"Not the tannery. Please. The stink'll get on yer and yer won't be allowed back in here."

"There are some smelly blighters in here already, my friend, let me tell yer."

"I might as well come with yer. Sitting around here waiting for a break ain't helping anything and I'll be scraping the bottom of my pockets very soon myself." Finn looked over at his new friend. "I'll put everything I can towards yer fare. I hope yer know that."

"Argh." Mickey shrugged though acknowledged the gesture and lowered his eyes.

"Why Boston though?"

"Hey?"

"Could be New York or anywhere else yer fancy to make a pound. Why set yer heart on Boston?"

Mickey looked to the ceiling and pursed his lips. "That's me son's name."

"That's his name?"

"We called him Boston. My Ciara and I. That was the new hope for us yer know. To get him away from the dying farm. A new life. Something different. She believed in it, even if her parents don't."

"Yer son's name is Boston Bell?" Finn tried to keep with the serious tone though his mouth tinged with amusement.

Mickey chuckled. "Boston Connor Bell. We call him Connor."

Finn wrapped him on the back playfully. "Well my friend, we'll get yer there one way or another." Finn's attention diverted to the window where Madochée's face pressed to the glass looking at him. "There she is." He gestured for her to come inside but she shook her head and he moved to the doorway to intercept her path outside.

"Do you need to find somewhere? I show you?" she offered.

"No. I don't."

Madochée tucked her hand away where she had held it out expectantly. "Alright." And she started away.

"That doesn't mean yer can't stay. Have yer eaten today?" He stepped back around the corner and grabbed his lumpy bowl of porridge. "Here, eat the rest of this."

Madochée took it and scoffed it down quickly, scraping it clean with the wooden spoon. He watched with his arms folded and she handed back the bowl and started back into the crowd.

"Where can I find yer?" he called. "If I do need to find somewhere?"

"I find you. You see me." And she turned again into the crowd. Finn watched after her, wondering if she'd stumbled across him by accident or if she'd been watching him all along.

"Hey," Cora called to Finn, interrupting his thoughts. "You ain't going anywhere. You've been summoned."

"Summoned?" Finn frowned.

"That's right. You need to head over and see Ryder first thing."

Mickey held his arms out. "I've been sitting here all morning and you haven't said a word?"

"It was him that was summoned, so it's him I'm telling. Go with him if you like, it don't mind me. But Ryder called for Finn."

Finn shoved his hands in his pockets and slumped his shoulders. As much as he needed Ryder on his side, he didn't much want his company.

CHAPTER 27

Finn and Mickey moved back out into the Bermondsey streets, busy now with wagons on their way to central London with farm wares and produce.

"What yer think he wants?" Finn asked as they crossed the street, sloshing over icy puddles.

"No telling."

"What did yer make of him when yer were there?"

Mickey shrugged. "Seems like he wants to be more important than he is. That'll make a man dangerous, yer know."

"Yeah. Or useful. We'll likely find out one way or another."

They pushed on towards the old tenement Madochée had led them to and Finn knocked ominously on the door. It was Charley who opened it, his face dark with bruises and one eye swollen shut. "Sheesh," Finn let slip.

"Get in here," Charley said, clearly not wanting to acknowledge or discuss fight night.

"Come in," Ryder called from the back. Finn and Mickey found him stooped over his desk, fluffing papers as if looking for something. "Come in." He was without his long overcoat and Finn could see just how tall and gangly Ryder was, bending low to meet his desk.

"Yer summoned me?" Finn floated out there, a whip of irony in his tone. Ryder darted him a look, pausing from his desk to stroke his long beard.

"That I did, my boy."

"Why?"

"Bold aren't we?" he asked, slowly moving to pull on his coat after all. "There is a draft in here, Charley. Find it will you, or stoke the fire."

"Yes, sir." Charley shot Finn another look as he pushed past and checked the low windows behind Ryder's desk.

Ryder moved around the other side of his desk leaning back on it like a chair. "I wanted to look into your eyes again," he said plainly, his own eyes shiny with something sinister and cunning so that Finn felt his throat dry up.

"To look into my eyes?"

'That's right," Ryder said, smoothly and slowly, again seeming to enjoy the way he spoke the words. "It's all happened very quickly, wouldn't you say? I snatched up your friend here and low and behold we are suddenly in the midst of something together."

Was this all about to backfire? Where was Ryder going with this?

"I was sitting there watching Charley do his job, you know. He took his beating, made it look convincing, didn't you Charley?"

Charley didn't answer but took his place at the back of the room with his arms folded.

"I need reminding why I should trust you." Ryder shot a steely glare at Finn.

"Maybe yer shouldn't trust me, nor I yer."

Ryder pursed his lips, bringing his hand to his chin. "Every man likes the idea of moving up in the world. No one likes the idea of moving down. I work hard. You work hard. Charley works hard, don't you, Charley?"

"I do, sir."

"He does. I'd like nothing more than to gain a little ground from the great Angel of Bishopsgate. I run my own little world down here. Have done forever. For as long as forever. But times change. Things move. Small things so that you don't even notice. But they are changing." He pointed a long finger at Finn who nodded, though he found it hard to piece together the thread in all this talk. What was he on about?

Ryder ran his hand down the length of his beard. "I think the Angel wants a piece of what I've got down here. I mean a larger piece. I pay my dues like every good scoundrel will, but that's what happens when you do a good job, isn't it? Everybody sees and then everyone wants a bigger piece. And then a bigger piece until everything you've worked for looks nothing like it did. Do you follow me, Finn O'Shea?"

"I think so," he lied.

"I might have been the Angel's scrapper and a scrapper may I stay, but this is my territory. My place. My world south of the river. This is my message I want to send. Will we send it together?"

"Sits well enough with me, Mr Ryder."

"It had better my friend." Ryder's eyes darkened, giving Finn a glimpse of what could follow. "If you double-cross me, there will be no coming back. You understand."

"I understand." Finn squared his shoulders.

Ryder hesitated, holding a thoughtful glare before releasing the tension in his expression, exchanging it for an amiable sigh. "Good man. Alright. Then a plan is what I want. What of your boy, Billy?"

"He's found a lead. A man to follow. Someone who could

right get us closer to the Angel's whereabouts. His real identity. I want to strike him where he feels safe."

Ryder nodded. "Alright, alright. Let's see how that pans out. But if what you say is true. You'll do something for me."

"What will I do?"

"You'll make my collections today."

"That's my job." Charley unfolded his arms and stepped forward, cutting eyes at Finn. "I'll do it. I always do it."

Ryder held his hand up to stop him, and Charley shut his mouth.

"Collections? What collections?"

"After a fight people have bills to pay. Even at Christmas. They've had five days. Time to round up the stragglers."

"I'm not a debt collector."

"Today you are." Ryder rolled his angular jaw in dismissal. "I like you two. You've presented me an opportunity. But Charley did your job, and now you'll do his."

"The people know I'm your collector," Charley argued. "They'll think I've been demoted. They'll think he's your new man."

"I'm interested in coin, Charley. Not favourites. And take a look at your face, man. You'll scare the children."

"Let Charley do them if he's your guy. Why am I to do his collections?"

"Because men like to move up in the world, Mr O'Shea. Making my collections is no small honour. I'm bestowing it on you. I'd be suspicious of a man who doesn't want to make his way up so do not take it lightly. See here on Charley's face. I've taken something from him and given it to you."

With that, Ryder strode out of the room, leaving Charley huffing and Finn looking at Mickey in trepidation.

Out on the street, Charley pushed Finn up against the wall. "I tell you straight, you'll not get between me and Ryder. I've worked too hard and put up with too much."

Finn shoved his arm away. "I don't want to be between yer. I said what I want and it has nought to do with yer and whatever yer got with Ryder."

"Well, he's taken a shine to you and that puts me out in the cold."

"What am I to do about it?" Finn shrugged. "I don't want your place and I don't want to do yer damn collections either."

"You'll do them, alright," Charley threatened. "And you'll do them properly."

Mickey laughed. "You don't make no sense, brother."

Charley threw him a look. "Laugh all you want, scrapper. But I survived the Angel and I've earned my stripes here. You come swanning in and if I end up on the street, there'll be hell to pay."

"Relax, would yer?" Finn urged. "We'll be outta here as soon as this is done."

Charley pulled a list of scribbled names from his pocket. "Can either of you read?"

"I get by," Finn offered.

"Didn't think so."

"Guess yer got me there, Charley boy. Feel better now?"

"Slightly."

"Give it here." Mickey snatched the list from Charley's thick fingers, his eyes scanning it over.

"They got their amounts next to their names."

"How are we supposed to know how to find them?" Finn asked. "We barely know where we are."

"That ain't my problem. Go ask Cora seeing as she's taken a shine to you as well." With that, Charley turned his back on them. "Ryder will be expecting it all in full by six this evening. Don't come crying to me if you're short."

~

HAVING RUN the list past Cora, Mickey and Finn were directed first to the canal worker's post behind the railway.

"We didn't even ask how much we was to get paid for this?" Mickey sighed, rolling himself a cigarette.

"I think we're being paid with his good graces."

"His good graces won't keep us fed."

"No. But here's hoping it gets us closer to the Angel and Tessie. But go ahead to the Tannery if yer want. I can take care of this."

"Ah, there'd be no fun in that, would there?" Mickey kept walking, though faded away and stopped dead in his tracks.

"What is it?" Finn turned back to see him.

"I heard something yesterday that I haven't told yer about."

"What's that?"

Mickey hesitated, scratching the back of his neck. "I was debating whether to tell yer."

"Tell me."

"I don't know if yer want to know. Or if it's even relevant."

"Then why bring it up?"

"Because yer might want to know, and it might be relevant."

"Well why didn't yer find that out first?"

"Because I can't."

"Well spit it out then, man." Finn threw his arms up, though his belly stirred with possibilities. He could see in Mickey's face it was something serious.

"I heard a rumour. The lads on the canal were bringing a load in from across the river."

"Alright."

"They were all a chatter about something found at the docks on the other side that morning."

"What?"

"A body. A woman." Mickey dipped his head as if there was more he didn't want to say.

"And?" Finn coaxed.

"She had red hair. They don't know who it is. Said her face..."

"Her face what?"

"They said her face were so badly eaten by rats there's no telling who she was."

"It wasn't Tessie if that's what yer getting at."

"Alright." Mickey nodded his head in agreement. "I just wanted to tell yer before we get all tangled up with this lot here in Ryder town."

"It's not her."

"I don't know if it is."

"She bloody hated rats. If it were her she woulda died somewhere the rats couldn't get her."

'If yer say so, brother."

"And if it was her then I have more reason than ever to beat that man to a pulp."

"Alright." Mickey nodded.

Heading toward a group of workers on the canal, Finn pulled the list out of his pocket. "Mr Gordie? Where's Mr Gordie?"

"Who wants to know?" A brawny fellow lifted his head.

"I'm collecting for Ryder this morning."

"Where is Charley?"

"Who knows, but I have his list and it says yer owe a full pound here, so hand it over, come on."

"I'm not giving anything to anyone but Charley." He shoved his hands in his pockets and turned back to what he was doing.

Finn huffed and looked over at Mickey. "What's the bet we have to repeat this conversation all bleeding day?"

Mickey stepped forward. "Yer seen Charley take his

punches the other night, didn't yer? He's in no state to be out here collecting off no one."

"Yer seen him didn't yer?" Finn pushed when the man still hesitated.

"Yeah, I did."

"Well then. Come on. Ryder has us on a schedule, don't have time to appease yer sensibilities. Pay up like yer supposed to and we'll be on our way."

The man grumbled under his breath but reached into his pocket.

"Thanks," Finn said, slapping the money into his coat and turning away. "One down. 15 to go."

CHAPTER 28

Tessie had travelled across the Irish Sea with the weight of a hundred pounds in her skirts. Her mother's words carried in her ears and images of Faye fluttered always close by. Picking incessantly at her hands where the blood had stained her nails, a quiet rage smouldered in her chest.

For five days she'd let the stench of London settle over her, and exchanging Ruby's extravagant dresses for some more practical, she'd walked the harbour each evening hoping and praying to run into Finn. Christmas was over. The city forged on, and with her cloak hanging low and the smell of hot pies and river water swirling around her, she knew the Angel's men were still out there looking for her. She wondered if they would even recognise her should they look into her eyes. She did not feel the same girl who had left the Old Nichol.

Watching now from a quiet spot across the bridge, the city before her held all the answers. All its working pieces moved before her; hackney cabs and horse-drawn carriages, patrolling bobbies, pedestrians in city clothes and the occasional couple strolling in the winter sun. Wharves and warehouses loomed in the background while on the river, workers unloaded barges of esparto grass.

Out there somewhere was a man called Arthur. A faceless man, with a voice that stretched across the city and all the way to Dublin. He rode in those cabs and carriages below her, reading newspapers and sipping English tea. And somewhere was Moses, his long maroon coat whipping as he strode the streets with his alcohol stench and dark eyes. They were men who gave orders, and men who followed them.

Out there somewhere was Kyran and Ruby, returned to their quiet parlour and their crackling fire, their fine parties and silky garments. She longed to see their faces and find out the truth about Kyran and the Angel, but that would not be today.

And maybe, just maybe, down there somewhere was Finn. She recalled his arms wrapped around her. His warmth and smell. His rough hands. His closeness. How she cherished him! Had they pushed him far from the East End, or was he out there searching for her? She imagined his brown eyes looking back at her from somewhere across the bridge, though as quickly as her hope surged, it sunk away again. If he believed her dead, would he even have stayed in London? He could be weeks away by now, having jumped on the first ship that sailed and be lost to her forever. Whatever the case, he had been alive after the attack, that much was true, and she had to find out what happened to him. She had to stop the Angel squeezing them further apart if she was to ever find her way back to him.

Thinking always of him and the wailing in her heart for Faye, the heat flared in her, rising sour and sharp in a sizzling mist. Turning her eyes to the docks, it was something more sinister that bubbled up inside her now. Something that demanded action.

Sipping warm sassafras bark tea she'd bought from a vendor, she pulled a knife from her boot and held its weight in her hand. If her mother couldn't call off this mission of his, she would have to find her way to the Angel herself. But how on earth could she do such a thing?

She had not lived a life of violence like her mother, but there had to be a way to hold her own. She had the blood of Aileen Fisher and the Angel of Bishopsgate running through her veins after all.

Eyeing a wooden post a few yards away and again bouncing the weight of the knife in her hand, she launched it. Ricocheting off the side, it hit the ground. Without flinching, she marched forward and picked it up, launching it again. It was a meditative exertion, as she formulated her plan, and she threw it over and over.

She needed a closer vantage point, somewhere she could watch the Angel's men without being seen. Close enough to make sense of what she saw, but far enough to be safe. She couldn't do it from outside the East End. She needed to be in there amongst it.

She threw the knife stronger and harder until her shoulder hurt. Again she pulled back her arm and let the blade fly, lodging it in the post with a satisfying chop. Tessie's eyes widened and her heart thudded.

Her mother had said it was a smuggling dispute, a trading war between thieves. She wanted to strike her own blow. Even a small one. All on her own. Something to signify the tides were turning in her favour. Something to let him know she was here. And she was coming for him.

SINCE RETURNING, she had taken a small room in Clerkenwell above the Willnock family shopfront, a small ironmonger on the corner of Woodbridge Street. It was just far enough from the East End that she could relax her paranoia to properly sleep and to not look over her shoulder should she cross the street to the market. It gave her comfort to bide with an ordinary family, people untouched and oblivious to all that had transpired. Life was going on around them, and it would stop for no one.

Mrs Willnock was a sour-faced woman who swept the floors with a constant scowl. She'd lost the two youngest boys to pneumonia the previous winter, and the family had moved on like a well-oiled machine thanks only to her sheer determination. She was curt and no-nonsense, and Tessie appreciated the security of knowing exactly where she stood. They gave her a safe home base to work from. And tonight, she was going to work.

The more Tessie thought on it, the more she narrowed her focus. Moses. It was he she wanted. She wanted those beady eyes of his in front of her. Wherever he went, she needed to be. And that was her plan. After dinner she would excuse herself and under the cover of evening darkness move back to the East End to find that man. He had gained himself a shadow, only he didn't know it yet. How different it felt to be the hunter, instead of the hunted. It brimmed up inside her, the anticipation and chase.

As Tessie entered through the shopfront, Mr Willnock was just closing up, dragging his display trolleys inside.

"Evening." She nodded, passing through.

"Evening love," he called.

In the back, Mrs Willnock was busy at the stove, her children cleaning up at an iron wash tub by the fire. Tessie quieted in Mrs Willnock's presence, as she always did, but still beamed with a gift of meat she placed on the table. "I've brought you some salted pork and a chicken," Tessie said, taking off her shawl and tidying up her hair which had become loose in the wind.

Mrs Willnock seemed alerted to Tessie's change in demeanour. "What's brought this on?" she enquired shrewdly.

"I've had a good day is all." Tessie smiled, sweeping her hand over the hair of her eldest daughter sat at the table in waiting.

Mrs Willnock inspected the packages. "It's not necessary, your board covers your meals, but I thank you."

"You're welcome."

"Lucy, put these both in the ice chest please."

"Yes, ma'am." The eldest daughter rose and followed her instructions.

"Supper is almost ready if you want to wash up," Mrs Willnock continued.

"Of course, thank you, ma'am," Tessie said, reminded she hadn't eaten all day. She was in need a good meal before stepping out on her secret undertaking this evening.

Throughout the family meal, Tessie could barely keep the gleam from her face. She bit at her top lip, covering the small gap in her teeth, in an effort quell any misplaced or ill-timed smiles. Her foot tapped furiously below the table. It was the thrill of it. She had no idea what she would possibly do or what might happen later that night, but for the first time she felt empowered. She had something in her corner, instead of waiting on someone or something to show itself and help her. She was making it happen on her own.

She did her best to respond to polite conversation throughout supper, but she could barely keep track of what was going on around her. Her mind was whirring and eager for the house to retire for the night. The Willnock children were usually in bed by 8 o'clock, with Mr and Mrs Willnock retiring by 9:30pm but Tessie was desperate to leave as early as possible if she was to reach the East End in time to properly survey the scene.

With her room upstairs, it would be difficult to walk through the main room where the Willnocks were likely to be sitting before the fire. It would be suspicious for her to leave the home at that time of night, unescorted and for no specific reason, and so Tessie made up her mind to leave straight after supper. She knew she didn't owe the Willnocks an explanation, but she did not want to arouse suspicion and thought to give the excuse of visiting an ill friend where she would likely stay for the evening.

Tessie assisted Lucy to clear the dishes. She scraped food into the slop bucket, passing them to Mrs Willnock who wiped them over in a tub of water. Upstairs, Tessie exchanged her woollen shawl for her dark cloak that covered her from head to toe. She quickly scanned the room for anything she might need. Spotting the satchel Kyran had given her, she checked over the contents; tallow candles, matches, a small bottle of paraffin oil, a pocket knife, handkerchiefs, a coin purse, and a needle and thread. She slung it over her shoulder and re-laced her boots.

"I thought to visit a friend a little down the way," she said, returning downstairs. "She was poorly this afternoon and has little ones to care for. I wanted to check on her and help for the evening."

Mrs Willnock frowned her pinchy frown but nodded curtly. "Very well, dear."

Tessie felt her skeptical gaze but was in too much of a hurry to let it slow her down.

"Walk quick, mind yourself," Mr Willnock added. "The riff-raff come out this time of night."

"Do you want to take some food with you?" Mrs Willnock asked, just as she was about to close the door.

"Oh." Tessie hadn't expected that.

"We have some spare." Mrs Willnock set a pot from below the counter and scooped in the leftover stew, layering the top with cheese and onion scones still warm from the oven. Wrapping the pot in a tea-towel she handed it to Tessie.

"It'll sure be appreciated, thank yer." Tessie quickly made her exit.

Now what was she to do? Carrying it all the way through Shoreditch and beyond was surely going to slow her down. She needed her hands free. She thought to hide it in an alley, or throw the contents into the river, but she could not in good conscience waste food when there were so many going hungry.

Stopping at a crossroad and ducking into the alleyway, Tessie knew there was a dosshouse on the corner and anyone who had been thrown out, or who could nought afford a night often squatted in an abandoned factory house close by. Approaching, Tessie saw a fire lit in the side alley, and it set her heart beating fast. Was this really a good idea? Her feet kept moving forward. An old woman's face, dark in the shadow, peeked out from a red shawl. She was the closest to the road and Tessie stood beside her and called out to the others. "I have food here."

A small crowd stirred.

"Come, come. I have food," she called again. A small group of about eight moved towards her. Placing the pot on the ground she backed away and let them inspect it. In moments there was competitive moaning as they dug their hands into the stew and whooped at the flaky scones.

"I'll be back for the pot in a few hours," she said to the woman closest to her. 'You'll only fetch a few pennies for the pot should you pawn it. I'll give you a shilling if it's still here when I return."

"Yes, ma'am," the old woman said, baring her nubbed teeth. "God bless yer."

Back out on Church Street she was back in Nichol territory and kept her head down and her pace quick. It was a cold night, and the last of the eating houses and storefronts had closed.

She was veering towards Wapping, knowing the Angel's men often drank at the Seven Bells on the border of White Chapel and the industrial warehouses. Looking up at the storefront roofs, she needed a way up to watch them from above. Seeing a staircase up the side of one of the warehouses, she quickly ran to the corner, assessing if she would be able to jump from roof to roof across the length of Leman Street. The warehouses were connected, and she took the staircase to the top of the stone warehouse roof.

It was quiet up there, and dark across the space as below lanterns strung the length of the street outside the Seven Bells Public House. They were rowdy in there already at barely 8 o'clock. Tessie leapt to the next roof, and then the next, landing with a thud that hurt her ankle. Dismissing it, she would not be injured and hobbling, she told herself. She curled herself into the corner and peered over the stone ledge to the Seven Bells below. She had a perfect view of the entrance and could see in one of the windows. Some patrons lazed at a table playing cards while a fiddler was playing somewhere inside and she could hear some of them stomping their boots on the floor. They were a rowdy lot. She saw no Moses. But nonetheless, all she had to do was wait. "Come on, Moses, dear, dear, Moses. Do not let me down."

CHAPTER 29

As evening light faded over Bermondsey, and workers filled the public houses on their way home, Finn and Mickey returned to Ryder's, their pockets weighed down with coin. Satisfied they completed their round, but exhausted and ready to be done with it, Finn pounded on the old tenement door expecting Charley to open it. Instead, it spilled open to a room filled with other men who, just like them, appeared to be reporting back with their day's collections.

Finn and Mickey fell into line behind another chap. However, they only lingered a moment before Ryder saw them.

"Finn, my boy, come forth. Come forth," he beckoned. The men before him cleared a path, turning to see who had drawn Ryder's interest.

Ryder threw his arm around Finn's shoulder and led him back to his desk. "How did you go?"

"We got it done," he said, as he and Mickey emptied their coat pockets, loading their collections onto the wooden desktop.

Ryder clapped his hands together in a childlike moment, embracing Finn again. "Everyone, this is Finn O'Shea and Mickey. They are with us now. They are with me." Ryder pressed his hand to his chest in playful theatrics. It was an unusual announcement and Finn felt awkward with all the eyes upon him, particularly Charley's, who watched on from the back of the room. Ryder seemed oblivious and gripped the back of Finn's neck with his hand, roughing him up affectionately.

"Charley, get them a drink," he called out the to room without making eye contact with his bruised and loyal worker. Finn tried to throw him a blameless and apologetic shrug.

Charley sullenly followed his orders and shoved drinks into both their hands as the crowd folded back around them, returning to their orderly reporting.

Ryder seemed to be checking off a meticulous list in front of him, taking great joy in keeping a tally of what was collected and what remained. He barely made eye contact with anyone; in fact, his eyes firmly held the numbers and tallies in front of him, updating the markings next to each name with what Finn assumed to be a blunted quill, but soon recognised as a twig of sorts, scratching the ink into a thick notebook.

Finn and Mickey looked for somewhere to sit, hoping to blend into the background, when Ryder, without looking away from his precious list, indicated a bench behind him. "Sit here." Without arguing they obliged, letting their weary feet kick out in front of them. They sat quietly as man after man reported their quota. Ryder received them each with a click of his tongue and a strike of his inked-up twig.

As Finn watched the crowd, he spotted Lance Tanner at the back of the room, the boxer filled with bravado from

Jacob's Island. He was talking to Charley in the back. What a strange gathering of misfits this was. Were they safe here in Ryder's presence? Finn felt a rumbling deep in his spine.

Handed drink after drink, the hours passed, and Finn's plans to quietly slip out the back into obscurity were going nowhere. Ryder was keeping them close and it was getting late when a commotion burst through the door just out of view.

"Where is he? Where's Finn? Finn O'Shea?" It was Billy, his face burning red and his chest heaving as he struggled to suck in a breath. Pushing through the crowd, he paid no attention to the orderly ceremony he'd interrupted, or to Ryder sitting at the head of his writing desk, eyes ablaze at the intrusion.

"Here!" Finn leapt up from his spot behind him. "Here, Billy. Sweet chips, what are yer doing? What's wrong with yer?"

Billy doubled over, struggling to talk. "I did what you said. I followed him. I've been...I followed him." Billy was pointing behind him, gesturing wildly outside.

"Take a minute to breathe would yer. What is it?"

"I followed him like you said." Billy gripped his chest. "That's where I've been. The African man. The one with dark skin."

"Yes, yes..." Finn waved his hand to hurry him. "Yer found him."

"Yes. I followed him and...and..."

"Come on, man!"

"I followed him since the whole day and now the night. And he went to a house in Mayfair..." Billy shook his head in shock, expecting Finn to understand his confession.

"What! What are yer saying?"

"And it's him. I swear it's him. It's his house!"

"Whose?"

Billy swallowed, and looking around him at the strange faces, he took a step closer to Finn, his eyes growing wide with fear. "I hid in the bushes to see. He were in there for ages. And...right there in the bushes, they came out. He looked right at me. I think he seen me." Billy's face broke into a panicked sob, but he quickly composed himself.

Finn's eyes locked on his, urging the answer. "Who did yer see, Billy?"

The colour drained from Billy's face leaving only his cheeks seething red and flushed. He swallowed again. "The Angel." The words stuck in his mouth. "I seen the Angel. Dead in his eyes."

"Holy Christ!" Adrenaline jolted through Finn's chest. He'd done it! He'd bloody done it!

"He seen me. I think he seen me." Billy's panic was flowing now. "The Angel of Bishopsgate seen me hiding in his bushes. I'm a dead man, now. I'm a dead man."

"Pull it together." Finn gripped him by the shoulders. "Yer did good. Yer did good, Billy." He slapped him on the back and Mickey too stepped forward with a drink, thrusting it into his hand and wrapping him on the shoulders.

Billy guzzled it down as Ryder rose from his desk. "The dark skinned man?"

"That's what he said," Finn agreed.

"I've heard of such a man. Castor Adams."

"Yer have not seen him?"

"No, but it's known a dark-skinned man is as close to the Angel as any might get."

"It's not him yer pay up to?"

"My lads meet an errand boy at the bridge and he carries it back." Ryder seemed to resent the words as he spoke them, as if it confirmed his place further down the pecking order than he wanted known.

"Do yer think he's right? That he's followed Castor to the Angel himself?"

Ryder slapped him on the back. "Only one way to find out, my boy!"

At those words, Finn was ready to move.

CHAPTER 30

*H*ours passed, her back turning cold against the stone roof wall. Changing position to stay comfortable and keep watch was a difficult task. Her legs were stiffening and the cold was wearing her out. But as the church bells struck 11 o'clock, she felt a tingling sensation, the anticipation building. He was close. She watched the corners of the building with eagerness. He would make his appearance, she was sure of it.

There, his maroon coat swooped around the corner, and in his loping gate he strode towards the door and disappeared inside. "Yes!" Tessie gasped, though quickly followed it with a sigh to herself. A three-hour wait for a glimpse of but a few seconds. But it was a triumph, she encouraged herself. Now she knew where he was. She had him. She just had to wait for him to leave. Realising it could be hours, her adrenaline subsided again and doubt tickled at her toes. Was she to wait all night only to see him stumble home drunk in the early hours near dawn, with nothing achieved except to establish him a drunk? It was possible, she realised with a sigh. She may have to spend many nights in this cold stony corner to discover anything of use at all.

The weariness dragged in her eyelids, as she thought of her warm bed and the food she had given away. Why hadn't she saved a few cheese scones for herself? She should like a snack to nibble on to pass the hours. Or some water. As the rain started to patter on her head, she cursed to herself. "Bloody hell, woman. What are yer playing at out here?" She was not a master of this, but she had to hold steady.

The midnight bells rolled over the rooftops and Tessie imagined Moses to be drunk and sprawled out half asleep at one of the tables. Could she pass by the window? Could she creep upon him? She wondered at the urges that might arise in her should she stand so close to him. Could she restrain herself? What if his beady eyes darted in her direction and he recognised her? She couldn't risk it, however strong her frustration. Patience. It was all about patience now.

The twelfth bell sounded and the door opened. His maroon coat gleamed in the light of a gas lantern as he strode away from the building, two men in tow. He did not go back the way he came but turned towards the river.

Tessie leapt from where she sat with her legs splayed out in front of her. This was it! Gathering her satchel and her wits, she ran to the edge of the building and around a row of smokestacks dividing each of the warehouses. Pausing to look over the side and keeping Moses in her sights, she continued along the roof and reaching the last rooftop she saw them turn towards the West India Docks. They were following the river. Straining to see a way down, she rushed to a set of stairs at the back of the building and dashed to the ground clinging to the shadowed walls.

The river water swelled and lapped at the muddy embankment to her right as she walked, daring not to look around or even pause to catch her breath.

As the docks came into view, their dark figures wandered ahead of her. Barges rested along the horizon like sleeping beasts on the water, and tugboats knocked up against the wharf, the ropes stretching and pulling as the water ebbed and rose. All around her it was quiet and she knew if she lost sight of them she might not find them again.

She hung back in the shadow. She could see no one, but the large gates of the West India company loomed large with a hanging padlock. The men moved past it and followed the long fence line around the back of the structure where they disappeared into the darkness. She cursed herself for lagging too far behind, but then a small light flickered to the far end of the docks as a door opened, exposing a light within, and quickly closed again. That was where they were going. Seeing their three figures walking across the yard, she breathed a sigh of relief. But how did they get in?

Moving further around the yard, she couldn't tell if she had passed a gate or not. The backside of the building was hidden by the shadow, sheltered from the moonlight and the few gas lanterns along the entrance. And then, the door swung open again.

Tessie ducked to the ground, her knees hitting the dirt with a painful thud. A man came out, and holding her breath, she kept her chin to the cold ground, and watched him. He was talking to someone back in the room as Moses and his two companions joined him. She could hear the distant murmur of low voices. The figures moved back towards the water and Tessie couldn't see them anymore.

Caring not for her dress as she lay on her belly, she snaked further forward to the fence, reaching out to one of the metal posts to pull herself forward. The fence wobbled under the exertion and Tessie notice the next post wobble more than the others. Touching it, she found it loose. "Dear God, this is it!" Taking one more look to make sure the door was still closed, she pushed the metal post to the side and slipped inside the enclosure.

Crouching, she scuttled away from the makeshift entrance, and catching a wave of adrenaline, her feet moved on their own. They carried her quickly, the dark cloak wrapping around her as she ran to the corner of the building. Running without even looking, she hit the outer wall as voices echoed off the water. Breathing hard, she gulped and tried to steady. They were close, their voices urgent now.

"Easy, man," Moses barked. "Bring 'em up slow. Slow!"

"I'm trying!"

"They'll gulp the water if you bring 'em up too fast."

They were tugging on ropes hauling barrels from the water. They were surely stocked with brandy bottles or tea and had been floated underwater to avoid the tariffs. The men were rolling them back towards the building.

Tessie allowed herself a moment of satisfaction. Without knowing it, he'd led her right to the action. She edged to the corner and readied herself to peek around at them. Before she did, there was movement behind her, and what she thought was the door opening again.

A flood of panic rushed through her and looking ahead an unhitched wagon loaded with crates and barrels waited off to the side. She ran for it, every muscle in her back flinching as if it would feel the blow if they caught sight of her. Diving behind the crates, her breath caught as indeed another man walked around the corner. He was annoyed, jabbing his finger about. One of them had dropped the barrel back in the water.

"What the bloody hell was that?"

Tessie's chest heaved though she was in a better position here, free to watch through the crates and barrels and away from their thoroughfare. There were four or five men. She recognised only Moses, but there were three others with an older one getting frustrated and bossy.

Her brain whirred with adrenaline. She was watching the Angel's operation unfold before her eyes. This was something precious to him. Something secret and valuable. She wanted to hurt him. But how? What could she do here with this?

Deep in thought, she heard one of the men approaching. He was rolling one of the barrels again, this time towards the wagon. "Oh god," Tessie thought. "They're loading them on here." She sunk down low behind the wheel. Whatever she was going to do, she had to do it fast.

Desperate for inspiration, she opened the satchel and rummaged through, spilling the contents into her skirt. The knife, the matches, the paraffin oil. The man thudded dry crates from the barrel onto the opposite side of the wagon and it shifted with each new crate.

When he left, she inspected them. She had nothing with her to crack them open, even using her knife to wedge along the top would take too long. Holding the paraffin oil and matches, she hoped whatever was in it, was also packed with straw. Tea would be the best. Having no time to think, she bit down and pulled the cork from the paraffin oil, dousing the closest crate and soaking its edges in hopes the oil would seep into the straw or tea inside. Then fumbling with the matches, she struck one. Snapping it quickly and flicking its end into the darkness. "Blasted thing!"

There were only 3 matches left! Her fingers were clumsy with impatience, and she tried again. As soon as it struck she would have to run for it. Taking a deep breath, she dragged it across the lighting strip and the spark took hold. Without a thought she flung it at the oil-soaked crate, and gripped the front of her skirts together to catch all her belongings, she ran with all her might for the fence. Hearing nothing but her heart and the sound of her feet thudding against the ground, she slid back through the metal posting and lay flat on her belly. She expected to hear men hollering or see them hurrying behind her. But no. She saw nothing. Beside the panting in her lungs and the thud in her chest, it was silent. She lay in wait and watched the corner where she expected the men to enter into sight. But there was nothing.

"What!" she cursed. "How is that possible. Bleedin' useless paraffin oil!"

And then, there it was. A small glow. The flame flared up from the back corner of the wagon. It was small, but as it cut through the layer of oil and caught at the wood in the crates and the straw inside, it grew quickly.

Tessie waited, her eyes bright with triumph. Moses' voice boomed over the yard, and he waved his arms about as the others came running. They cursed as the flames bore higher, running back and forth with pales of river water. But it wasn't helping, the whole wagon erupted, upward of 30 crates would soon be alight. "I wonder how much that is worth to him?"

The men were hollering now, bewildered and panicked. Surely the Wapping Police would have to respond to a fire on the dock, even if they were aligned with the Angel.

Tessie wondered whether she should wait, but moved quickly and quietly back towards the front gates of the West India Docks. Keeping to the shadow, she moved back along the river, turning back for the most spectacular view. The fire had taken over the wagon, its embers spilling to the floor. Tessie had no desire to damage any other merchant's goods but found herself willing the fire to jump to the main building where the men had been. The men were nowhere to be seen and she imagined, having no way to put out the fire they had no choice but to run. How would they explain their presence should the police arrive?

Tessie found a place to crouch down and relax, taking in the view of the Angel's hoard going up in glorious smoke and disappearing into London's night sky. As she watched, she heard a boat coming. Surely, it was the marine police, Tessie thought. Hurray! She waited as the small boat chugged into view, and she heard yelling, and a horn blow. It was them! The small figures hit the dock and sprung up onto the wharf. Behind them, another boat came. The alarm had been raised.

Turning for Clerkenwell, Tessie's eyes were wide with adrenaline. Her pupils beamed large as if she had looked upon the face of God. She knew if anyone looked at her they would think she possessed. But no, she thought to herself. It was just the magnificent taste of power.

CHAPTER 31

*R*yder clapped his hands together in glee. "The Angel's not gonna know what hit him." He turned to Charley who in the midst of the announcement, had left his hiding spot in the corner and now stood beside him as Ryder whispered something into his ear.

"Wait," Finn said, trying to slow the swell in the crowd. "We need to be sure. We need a plan to do this right. It'll be the only chance we get."

"We've got a plan, lad." Ryder rummaged in his desk and pulled two pistols from the drawer, jamming one into Finn's hand and keeping the other for himself. "Now is the time to seize what we want. Now, lad."

Something hummed in Finn's lower back. This could quickly spiral out of control. He needed this to go right. "We don't know what we're walking into. Let me and Mickey check it out first. We want to know who's there, what the set up is-"

"We'll know when we get there. Now you can stay, lad, if that's what you want. But me and my lads aren't letting the night grow cold on this information. You said it yourself, no longer the Angel's scrapper. So come and get yours, that's what you wanted. Come and get it!" He gripped Finn's shoulder, urging him on, the intensity in his eyes beckoning him. What choice did Finn have? He couldn't let them go alone and mess things up! If this opportunity went begging, he may have no hope at all of demanding answers from the Angel and finding Tess.

Finn gave a discerning nod and Ryder's moustached mouth curved into a smile. "That's my lad. Let's go," and Ryder turned his attention to Billy who sat slumped against the back wall, nursing his empty whiskey cup.

"I ain't going back there. No, I ain't."

"Up lad. Show us the way." Irritation rang in Ryder's voice. He was on a mission now and he wouldn't be slowed down.

"No." Billy's voice wavered as he looked back and forth between him and Finn.

"He'll be right," Finn cut in. "Tell me where it is, Billy."

"No. He's coming. We have to be sure. They'll be no guessing. No guessing."

Billy scrambled to his feet, forlornly looking to Finn for direction. "It'll be alright, man. I'll make sure of it."

Turning to Mickey, Finn searched his face for inspiration, but they both knew their choices. The only way to control this now was to lead from the front. They followed Ryder outside to a waiting horse-drawn wagon where they pushed Billy up and into the corner, before sitting either side of Ryder.

The man seemed on edge with glee and Finn wondered what Ryder imagined awaited them if indeed it was the Angel's home. He barely knew this lanky bearded man and had only an inkling of his temperament. Was he a violent man? Rash and prone to unpredictability? A man likely to dash all hope of getting information about Tessie? Finn tried to reassure himself and focus on his own plan. They needed to wait, and to watch, and choose their moment carefully. Perhaps with the home in their sights, Ryder's enthusiasm would be quelled enough for thoughtful consideration.

There was five of them in this small wagon, Ryder, Finn, Mickey, Billy, and Charley driving, though a select bunch of Ryder's men had been swept up in the mission and followed in another wagon behind. Charley drove them north through Bermondsey toward the London Bridge and as they turned to cross it, Finn saw Madochée's head bobbing up and down as she sprinted after them.

"Go back!" he called, waving his hands at her. "Go back!" But she didn't appear to slow down and as they turned onto the bridge Finn lost her in the shadow. He felt a bolt of panic that she would find her way into the middle of the mess about to unfold and urged the wagon to pick up its pace so there was no way she could follow.

To his dismay, it slowed down just shy of the bridge, leaving them to walk through Cheapside as the bells of St. Paul's rang out 12 o'clock. Looking behind them, he saw no sign of Madochée. He felt responsible for that girl now. He'd tried to fight it but it was too late. She'd gotten under his skin.

It was dark and quiet on those Cheapside streets as they made the rest of the journey on foot. Onwards towards Pall Mall they marched, the angst stirring in Finn's underbelly as they all walked quietly, their footsteps scuffing the cobblestones.

"Where?" Ryder demanded at each major crossroads.

Billy simply pointed in whichever direction was needed, lifting his long arm.

They were moving into Mayfair now, the homes growing larger in shadow and stature as they stuck strategically to the hedges, their frozen breath fogging out in front of them.

Finally, Billy stopped, and pointing at a home across the street, lights in the rooms either side of the door softly beckoned. "It's that one," he said, already retreating.

"Are you sure?" Ryder barked, pushing through the men and gripping Billy's arm tightly.

"I'm sure. I crouched in them there bushes," and he pointed to some just inside the gate. "That's where he seen me. The Angel looked dead in me eyes." And then he turned and ran, his boots belting heavy and loud against the icy pavement.

Ryder turned his gaze back to the windows, biting his lip in thought.

"We should move to those bushes too," Finn hushed. "We'll have a good view from there."

"Then what?" Ryder mused, tugging on his beard.

"Then, when the time is right...*if* the time is right," he stressed. "We make our move."

Ryder squinted at him as if he was about to disagree, though gave a quick nod.

As they moved into place, Finn felt the lump in his throat. Was this really about to go down? Was he about to look upon the man who had destroyed his life and taken Tessie from him? It built up in him, roaring in his ears so that he wasn't sure if it was silent around him or if he had blocked everything out.

Sandwiched between Mickey and Ryder, they crouched in the shadow of the shrubbery watching the glow in the windows. From time to time they saw a movement, though nothing distinguishable. "What are we going to do?" Mickey whispered to Finn, and all Finn could do was widen his eyes in growing uncertainty.

"We need to get closer," Charley said a little too loudly for Finn's liking.

"Not yet," Finn hissed.

"What are we bloody waiting for? There can't be more than 2 or 3 people in that room. We storm in and it's a done deal."

"We don't know who's in there," Mickey quipped, not hiding his dislike of Charley.

"Well go and have a look then if you're the big bloody man."

"Alright—"

"We'll both go," Finn cut in, and elbowing Mickey off to the side they moved around the far edge, first keeping to the fence and then the outer wall of the house.

"How yer want to play this?" Mickey asked when they were far enough from Ryder and Charley.

"I'm making it up as I go. Any ideas?"

"Not a damn clue." Mickey crouched as they approached the window. "But it doesn't feel right, does it?"

"What yer mean feel right?"

"I don't know," Mickey kept low and turned his head to the window. "It's the parlour or whatever rooms the rich people have. A bloody sitting room," he whispered.

"Are people sitting in it?"

"I see two pairs of legs. Men."

Finn couldn't contain himself and inching further he too peered in through the bottom of the window. "Do yer think that's him?"

"I don't know. Billy seemed damn sure, I know that much."

"Well Billy might have an imagination on him."

"Aye. It's a gamble."

"The mighty Angel in his sitting room..." Finn shook his head. "He's about to get a damn surprise. Or some other poor toff." Turning around he used his fingers to signal to Ryder that there were two people in the room.

"Alright, we should do a lap though, check the other

rooms. For all we know he has twenty men in the back room. Servants. Who the bloody hell knows. There are probably women in there too. Then what?"

"Tessie could be there." The realisation just hit him. Could they really be this close? No, if the Angel had caught up with her she would be dead, but the sting of it lingered in his chest.

"Aye. And we should wait till the house goes to sleep. It's already after midnight. It can't be long now," Mickey continued, oblivious to Finn's internal wrestle.

Nerves danced along Finn's back and down his legs. He'd never done anything so brazen, even in his years living on the streets. Pickpocketing, sure, opportunistic thievery, sometimes, but never had he been a voyeur, looking through the glass with the plan to burst in with sudden violence. It stirred a fear in his belly, even if the man was the Angel. But he thought of Tessie. What had he done to her? Where was she now? This man had the answers and he didn't want to wait a moment longer. The adrenaline surged in him with such force he wanted to reach out and smash the window right then and then.

"Finn!" Mickey grabbed his arm, drawing him back.

"Yea."

"We have to do this right."

"Aye," Finn agreed, though his heart thudded louder than ever.

They turned back to the shrubs, though as they took their first steps away, Ryder and Charley charged towards them, their men in tow. What were they doing!

"No, go back, go back," Mickey mouthed, but it was a stampede. Flying past them, Ryder grabbed Finn by the arm, urging him onwards. They too could not wait a moment longer.

The rush of movement ignited in Finn, pulling him in a

rush towards the front door. This was happening! They were doing it!

Ryder held his pistol at the ready as Charley burst through the front door in a loud clatter, his face wild and rabid, hollering obscenities. Finn felt Ryder at his back pushing him inside, while Mickey too rushed along with the group, trying to find his own footing as they dragged him along.

Charley moved quickly to the parlour door and in a flash the room spun around them. Finn gripped the pistol in his pocket, struggling to pull it out. They were going to get him! They were going to get the Angel! As he raised the pistol, not even knowing yet what or who to aim it at, a blow struck him hard on the back of the head. He went down with a thud.

The fuzziness cleared in Finn's head as the figures in the room loomed over him. Before he could get up, his arms were wrenched behind his back, his hands quickly bound. They had him pinned and surrounded as the room still spun around him.

"You right down there, Mr O'Shea? You comfortable down there?" Charley's face was the first to float out of the crowd and come into focus. With a wide grin, he kicked Finn in the ribs hard and fast. They were still in the parlour, though as Ryder stepped forward and snatched the pistol from the floor beside him, he wondered if any of this had been real at all? Was this the Angel's house? Was he even here?

"Sorry lad," Ryder said. "I told you. I'm interested in coin and not much else. And this here paid a pretty penny."

The sick feeling tumbled over Finn in heavy waves. How had he been so stupid? He couldn't bear to look at them, rolling his eyes to the floor in disgust as Mickey too was dragged over to lay beside him.

At the back of the room, Finn saw the dark-skinned man

Billy had spoken of - Castor Adams. He was leaning back in his chair, a cigar still in his mouth, seemingly unperturbed by the commotion. Then another man stepped forward who didn't say a word. Finn felt his eyes on him, and despite his effort to resist, something of a gravitational pull demanded he look up.

The man's piercing eyes set on him, unwavering and cold. "I hear you want to see me, boy?" he said, crouching low and blowing cigar smoke into his face so that Finn coughed and spluttered. "Pick him up," he barked and returned to his chair by the fire.

Charley gripped Finn by the back of the neck and dragged him. "Here, Mr Crabbe, sir." The man pointed to the ground in front of him and Charley pushed Finn onto his knees. Finn's chest thudded and he stared back with all the hatred he could muster. It was him, after all. Mr Crabbe? It had to be. The Angel was right in front of him!

The Angel's gaze was penetrating and full of purpose as he glared down at them. "Who is who?" he asked of Ryder.

"The one on the right is Finn O'Shea. He's the one. The other is Mickey Bell. He's a nobody."

"A nobody?" Mickey shot back. "I'll have yer—"

The Angel backhanded Mickey across his face and leaned forward on one elbow, all of his attention on Finn. "Found yourself in the hornet's nest, haven't you boy? It's you I want to hear from."

"I was coming for yer. I would have got yer too if he weren't a backstabber."

"He is loyal to me as he should be and he will be rewarded."

Ryder watched on from the background, his eyes still ripe with glee. Why hadn't he seen this man for what he is? An opportunist. A thief. Finn's stomach sunk with it. He had orchestrated his own capture. What a bleeding fool!

"I'm sorry, lads." Ryder held his arms out wide as if taking a bow, his expression absent of any apology at all. Beside him Charley watched on, his arms folded tightly and a smirk on his lips.

"You're the one who killed Moses' boy. Stuck your nose in well and deep where it didn't belong, didn't you?"

"I don't care about Moses. And that Johnny shouldn't have been there. I care about Tessie and what yer did to her."

"Well he cares about you, boy. He cares about you. Johnny was an up and comer. A get in there and get it done. Someone who might have been useful for years to come and here you come bowling in. A man's son is his pride. His legacy. His bloodline. It's just like stealing, isn't it? Just like stealing."

"Yer stole from me! From us. Tell me what happened to her!"

The Angel pressed his lips together and slit his eyes. "I think you know what happened to her, boy. Else you wouldn't be here."

Finn's insides churned. What did he mean? Is she alive? Is she dead? Did he think he already knew? Finn's brain whirred so fast he felt dizzy. Was he going to come all this way and find out nothing more?

An unexpected knock wrapped on the door and all heads turned to see it open. A blonde woman popped her head in and seemed surprised by the gathering, though showed no reaction to the bloodied man on his knees before the Angel.

"Dammit, Cyn, I'm in the middle of something, can't you see that?" The Angel threw up his arm in the air. "These vagrants stormed the house to do us harm. What have you to say about that then?" He spoke in full cockney embellishment.

She cut her eyes at him. "Well when you're not indisposed, there's another of your men here beating on the door like a savage to wake up the neighbours. Says there's been a fire at the docks—"

Castor leapt up. "Fire where? What fire?"

The woman stepped aside and Moses burst into the room, out of breath and his eyes wide like a maniac.

"A fire, sir. A fire..." He looked set to launch into detail, but stopped, his eyes scanning the gathering. Finn's heart thudded with the recognition as Moses jabbed his finger at him. "What's going on? That's him." He rushed at Finn and Castor leapt up to block his way, as the woman let out a shriek of feminine dismay.

"Hold him!" The Angel barked at Castor, holding his arm up as if to pause the room in motion. "Close the door, Cynthia. You've seen enough. Close the door. Now."

Cynthia flashed her curious eyes about the room as she withdrew, peeking through the crack as she left the door ajar.

"Go!" he boomed.

She slammed it shut with a loud thud.

"What's this?" Moses demanded, shaking free of Castor's hold and bowing out his chest. "What's going on with him that I don't know about?" Moses posed his question to the Angel, but quickly re-directed it to Castor. "You dare leave me out of this? You dare bring him in without me?"

The Angel scratched his sideburns as if frustrated he had to explain himself. "You're a loose bloody canon ain't you? Fire off at any damn thing, so yes! How about you stick to your job and tell me what's it at the docks? What fire?"

Moses threw a hard sideways glance at Finn but continued as directed. "We was pulling up the goods, you know. And there must have been someone there coz the wagon caught on fire and there weren't no way it was an accident, there weren't no lanterns, no nothing close by. It spontaneously burst into flames-"

"Spontaneously burst into flames, my arse." The Angel rose up from his seat. "How much was lost?"

"It jumped to the roof and when the Wapping lads showed up we had to leave it, sir, so...I don't know. I don't know how much. Enough to matter."

Finn waited silently as the Angel flared his nostrils and looked like he might devour Moses whole. "That's her, isn't it?" He flashed his eyes at Castor whose brow too was furrowed deep in thought.

"Aileen? It could be."

"Ain't no could. We sent men her way. So she's sent them back this way to burn us to the bleedin' ground!" He clenched his fist, his face flushing red. "Aileen Fisher ain't gonna have her way on this. You understand me?"

Finn kept his eyes low, his mind racing with the conversation around him. This had been about Tessie's mother after all. He tried desperately to put the pieces together.

The Angel turned away from them, tossing his cigar into the fire and pacing back and forth. Finn felt the room around him waiting with bated breath. The man was on the trail of something. He could see it growing in his expression.

"Castor?" The Angel turned to the window. "When was the last time we had a public hanging?"

Castor squinted his dark eyes. "Not since that Hewson bloke back in July."

"Yes. That was his name."

"It stirred up quite a storm."

"It's a storm we want ain't it?" The Angel swung around and smiled at Finn, clenching his fist as if grasping the opportunity in front of him. "You're the bait now, boy. You're the bait."

Finn's chest seized as he and Mickey exchanged a worried glance. What was he talking about? A public hanging? "She's still alive, isn't she? She's out there!" Finn riled up in panic. If she was alive, he could not bear to be the cause of her downfall.

"We'll soon find out thanks to you, son." He was grinning now, a smirk of cunning and victory. "And then her bloody mother will get what's coming."

Finn's stomach twisted. They were going to hang him in the hope of drawing her out. "She won't fall for it. She won't."

"You fell for this easy enough, didn't you? Right down to Castor here catching the attention of your half-wit, Billy Brittle. You think that boy has half the smarts needed to find us if we didn't want him to. That was the play, boy! And you missed it."

"She's smarter than I am. And she's survived this long with all of yer men out there looking for her."

The Angel gritted his teeth, glaring hard at Finn. "You talk now, son, but you haven't got yours yet either. Castor, send for the sergeant. Tell him we've got two in custody to be charged with burglary with violence."

Castor ran his eyes over Finn and Mickey. "With pleasure." Placing his hat on his head, he strode from the room.

The Angel crossed his arms. "Moses."

"Sir?" He stepped up his posture.

"I need him alive. But you have from now until the sergeant arrives. Beat him to a pulp if you will."

Moses's beady eyes lit up. "Yes, sir. Alive."

With that, the Angel strode from the room. Finn gritted his jaw as Moses locked his eyes on him. He knew what was coming. Taking a run up, Moses drew back his leg and kicked Finn hard across the jaw.

Snow flurries dissolved on the cobblestones of Albemarle Street as Tessie's eyes fixed on Number 22. An hour passed before a carriage pulled to the front of the grand terrace home and the navy blue door opened. Kyran stepped into the cold, securing a top-hat on his neatly groomed hair. His breath fogged as he strolled quickly to the carriage.

Striding across the street Tessie pulled herself up and slipped inside the cab. Kyran's eyes widened as he realised who it was. The driver clicked at the horses and they pulled away from the house. It was a while before either of them spoke.

"I wasn't sure I'd see you again," he said, finally. "You could have just knocked on the door."

"I didn't want to come inside." Tessie's eyes flashed as the carriage rumbled along Pall Mall and the quaint terrace houses moved by the window. "I need to know if it is true what she said," she added, cutting right to the point. "Do yer work for him?"

"No." His eyes fixed on hers.

"She said yer are his right hand man?"

"I'm not. Not anymore."

"But yer were?"

"Not anymore," he said more firmly.

"What then? Yer have to tell me everything now."

Kyran took a deep breath. She thought his face had changed or was incredibly sad. He reached into his pocket and pulled out a silver locket. It was a simple design. Smooth and undecorated. He clicked it open and shut again, before passing it to Tessie.

"This is the necklace he asked for. A locket. Though he cares nothing for it."

Tessie held it in her hands. This small little object had started it all. This is what she had demanded from him just weeks ago.

"What does it mean?" Tessie asked as she opened it to look inside. There was a portrait of a woman, her hair blonde like Kyran, a faint smile on her lips.

"My mother," Kyran said.

"The Angel wants a portrait of your mother?" Tessie raised a quizzical eyebrow.

"No, he doesn't want it. I told you. It was never about the locket."

"Why did he ask yer for it then?"

Kyran shifted in his seat, pulling at his collar as if it was suddenly choking him. "As answer to the question he posed in the note."

"The note," Tessie repeated. "Yer never said it asked a question. What question?"

He took a deep slow breath. "I wasn't truthful about what it said. It pointed to you, yes. But not in the words I told you before."

"What did it say, Kyran? Yer must finally tell me!"

He turned his eyes on her, again searching her face for something. "The note said that you are my sister. And that if I did not return to him, you would be killed. I was to hand over the locket as assurance of my return. Without the locket, my answer was no."

"The note said I am your sister? And yer knew he would kill me and still did not hand it over?"

"It was a trick, Tessie."

"My mother said the Angel was my father. So how then are yer my brother? How!"

"I'm his son," he said quietly.

"What?"

"Yes," he said. "If you are indeed his daughter. Then I am your brother."

"Yer are my brother?" Tessie's eyes scanned the cab as if looking for something to confirm the revelation. Kyran's eyes were dark with intensity as if it was the first time he himself had heard the words out loud. "I have a brother." It fell on her with an unfamiliar sensation, and a wave of calm sat heavy in her chest. Never had she imagined a sibling, someone of her very own blood. Someone she could call family. Her brother. She had a brother.

"Yer are my brother," she repeated.

"Yes, it seems I am." Kyran cut a light smile and they both sat stunned with the reality of it. Could it be that all this time she had not been alone in this world? To not be alone? To have more than Finn in this world to be her family. How strange the thought!

"Why did yer not tell me? All this time, Kyran. We could have worked it out together."

"Yes," he looked down again. "I did not imagine it was true. I thought it only a lie to lure me back in. A fabricated guilt to corner me into a decision. How could you be my sister? I thought if anything we must share a mother, and yet you look nothing like her. I wanted only to disprove it to ease my conscience or to uncover whatever connection my father might have conjured up to wound me."

"And it was true..." Tessie held his eyes, the wonder of it filling them to the brim. "The Angel is your father too."

Kyran called through to the driver to go around the block so they could keep driving. He grew quiet wringing at his gloves and shrugged. "I never had the same nature as my father. Even though I tried. He raised me up, always pushing me. I wanted to please him, of course. I wanted to be everything he wanted of me." Tessie sat back as all the missing pieces of Kyran clicked into place.

"He was never married to my mother and he took me from her at a very young age. I went everywhere with him. I saw the most gruesome things as he made his way up in the world. Excruciating violence and he would not let me look away. It was the family business and he wanted me to be there with him. As he made more money and asserted himself into respectable society, he distanced himself more and more from the front line. That was my job. I was another buffer between his work and the persona he created for himself. But try as I might, I couldn't do what he was asking, the way he was asking. I was a disappointment. Always. I'm not violent enough. I'm not cruel enough. I'm soft. Weak." It clearly pained Kyran to speak of it. His brow contorted as he pulled the memories up for her to see.

"What happened?" Tessie asked, a lump in her throat.

"He gave me a job to do. He wanted me to get rid of...well...someone who had worked for us for some time. Someone I knew well and cared about. Someone who knew all our secrets."

"And...?" Tessie prompted, desperate to know what happened.

"I couldn't do it," he said simply. "Of all the things he had asked me before I had found a way around them. A way to solve the problem a different way or delegate it away from me because I was too weak. But this, I couldn't do. I wouldn't do. I think he knew that from the beginning. It was a test he knew I would fail."

Kyran leaned back in the cab, letting out a deep sigh. Outside the window the snow was falling heavier now. "It was Ruby," he said quietly as if releasing a terrible secret.

"Ruby?" Tessie asked, the shock tumbled through her in waves. "She worked for him too?"

"Yes, and no, she was a chess piece he moved around. She gambled with rich men's wives, drawing out information, people and their plans and business, and he used it to his own end."

Kyran squinted his brow as if it was all too hard. "In order to save her, we had to move fast. Father had already presented me to society as Kyran Luther, an associate, and the only way I could think to save Ruby was to bring her out and make her visible as well. If she died in the slums no one would have cared, you know that as well as I do. The poor are invisible. The river will swallow multitudes without the city paying heed. So I presented her as my cousin and I her chaperone. It took work and Ruby is resourceful and incredibly astute. A pupil of culture and repose. She took to it very easily."

Tessie's anger in him quietened. The sorrow in his brown eyes, the pain in his jaw as he clenched it showed his path had not been an easy one.

"Yer love her," Tessie spoke the truth she had seen out loud. "Yer love each other."

Kyran looked at her and didn't speak, but his eyes confirmed it.

She sat back in the carriage and fidgeted with her sleeve, folding her leather wristband out of sight. "We have to stop him, Kyran. We have to expose him for everything he is."

"I tried to help you, Tessie, because I felt responsible, but I think now I haven't helped you at all. I think you need to let it go. We all do, and get on with our lives. Fighting him does nothing but suck the life out of us. I should not have let it carry on so long for myself."

Tessie shook her head, the idea of letting go lighting a panic in her guts.

"No, Kyran, listen." She moved to sit beside him, clasping his hands in hers. "He thought to destroy us. He brought us together thinking it would bring us down. But look, we are stronger together. We can stand against him."

Kyran took a deep breath. "There is a change in you," he said. "I see it. A bitterness in your eyes. The first time I met you there was benevolence there. And now I have seen where you've come from. I've seen the harshness of it, and yet you didn't let it swallow you up. Don't let this now be the thing that defines you, Tessie."

Tessie wrestled with his words, and even if they were true she refused them time to settle. "Finn saw the good in me," she insisted. "Without him to see it, what use is it to me? I must find him. And to do that we must be free of the Angel and his power."

"Vengeance is a disease," he urged. "It will get us even if the Angel doesn't."

"Who cares about vengeance? It is justice, I want. This is our chance to end it. For yer and Ruby, and Finn and I. To end him and the power he has over us!" She paused, the ache in her heart filling the small space. "I cannot bear this pain in my body knowing that out there he is untouched by it. He is free of it. A pain like this cannot leave him untouched!" She clenched her fist, her eyes piercing his. "Do not underestimate me, Kyran, I will find justice with or without yer." Kyran looked out into the snow, the white frosting gathering deeply in the guttered edges of the street.

"Are you sure?" he asked a final time.

"It's the only way for us to live."

CHAPTER 34

There were no soft edges in their cell, only a cold hard floor that clawed at their bruised bodies no matter how they tried to be comfortable. Finn had taken his beating from Moses, Mickey too copped it from Charley, though it left him heaving in each breath with broken ribs and horrible welts on his face.

In the corner was another man, half-naked and curled into himself, who had not moved since they arrived. The stink was putrid, thick with human waste and stagnant water. It was hard to breathe it in.

They had been charged with burglary with violence, and as ironic as it was, Finn had little to defend himself. He had every intention of busting into the man's house and had no legitimate or lawful reason to be there. The only justice to be found existed beneath the law, but here he was chained at his feet and a prisoner, with any semblance of it far from reach now. He just wanted Tessie to be safe. That was the most he could hope for now, that in spite of this all she might find a way to live on. To survive. The Angel had not found her yet, and he hoped beyond hope that his failure would not bring her down with him.

They had not seen another soul except the hefty-framed albino who fed them a bowl of gruel each morning. The cells were full though. They heard the calls and conversations of many men lilting up and down the dark corridor, crazy voices, some loud, some quiet chatter, but all of it foreign and haunting.

"So this is how it ends, brother?" Mickey squeezed a wry grin. "In a stinking English cell."

"I'd rather they shot us where we stood instead of this misery."

"They want us well degraded before that happens. And it'll be a rope around our neck, not quite long enough to make it quick." Mickey made the noose action and hung his head to the side as a rat trundled too close to Finn's foot and he kicked it away.

"Nothing like rats and shit to break a man's spirit. The perfect bleedin' marriage."

"Told you I find you." Madochée's small face appeared at the window grill by the ceiling. "Even here I find you."

Finn's heart sunk at hearing her small voice. "Aye, yer did. But yer shouldn't have. Not around the prison. Yer need to find somewhere to go, Madochée."

"I'm checking on you." She moved into a cross-legged position and pulled a wrapped bundle from her pocket. Unrolling it, she had 4 scones though they were starting to crumble and break from being squashed in her coat pocket. "Here." She squeezed them through the grate and Finn leapt to his feet at seeing her offering.

"Oh sweet cailín, what have yer done?"

"I got them at the market," she whispered, and Finn's chest ached.

"If yer be doing that yer will end up in here with us. Yer mustn't."

"You're hungry."

"Aye. We are." Finn reached his hand through the grill and brushed her hair. "Thank yer. Please don't risk yourself for us. Not for us."

She nodded, though Finn knew she was lying. She probably did it every day. She had before he met her and would long after he were gone. How else was she to eat? Finn passed the bundle to Mickey who took a scone in each hand, ripping a bite from one of them. Finn moved to the corner and savoured the light sweetness of the biscuit. "Look at where I've got myself, now. Relying on a girl to feed me stolen scones through a prison grate." Finn shook his head at himself. "I think it was always destined to end this way. Tessie should have rid herself of me long before this happened."

"What are yer talking about?" Mickey said. "I've never met that girl, but I have no doubt yer the world to her."

Finn reflected on his life, whirring through years past. Had it all come to this? Had he been fighting off this very moment since it all began? "I had a brother," he announced. It was a confession and Mickey waited for what followed. "I lost him too when we were younger."

"What do yer mean yer lost him?"

"We were in the square like every other morning. Looking for something, or someone to get us by another day. There was a shoe-shiner there and I made off with a handful of pennies from his takings. He threw something at me as I ran and I still don't know what it was but it just about split my head open." He touched the faint scar above his eyebrow where it cut a small dent into his forehead. "Hurt like buggery, and we ran. I thought we both ran. I was holding my head and laughing. I thought he was with me, but when we got back to our place, our spot behind the square, I was running alone. I went back for him. I looked for him for days, but there was no sign of him."

"Yer think someone took him?" Mickey frowned.

"I wish I knew. I've prayed for the answer. But truth be, anything might have happened in those moments with my eyes turned." Finn shrugged. "But it were my job to look after him and I didn't. It were my job to look after Tessie and I couldn't." And he turned his eyes to Madochée. "And Madochée as yer can see. I can't look after yer either. I'm sorry. Yer should find someone else to follow around these streets. Someone yer can rely on to be there for yer. I can't protect anybody."

Madochée crouched low into a ball, pressing her face to the grill and giving a dismissive shrug. "I don't follow you to protect me. I followed you because you can see me. You can see me still, can't you."

She delivered her words as a simple statement of fact, but they hung with a poignant air of wisdom.

"Aye. I can see yer." He lifted his hands to squeeze her fingers wrapped around the cold grill.

"She has a point, brother." Mickey swallowed the last of his scone. "And yer didn't lose Tessie or your brother any more than I lost my Ciara. We didn't lose them. Life took them. Life throws shit at everyone. All we can do is throw something other than shit back at it. It's got nought to do with what yer deserve or what yer don't."

"I just want her to be safe. That is all. I'll go to my death happy if I know that to be true."

Mickey's head slunk to the side, at the macabre tone that swept over them. "Aye. At least I know my boy is well. I know he is safe with his grandparents. And he'll never know his da died with a rope around his neck."

Finn let his head tilt back against the damp wall as the half-naked man in the corner suddenly stretched out his leg and moved his head. Mickey jumped.

"He's alive." Finn held out the last of his scone. The decrepit old man reached out and took it without a word.

CHAPTER 35

The moment Tessie set foot in the terrace home on Albemarle Street, Ruby threw her arms around her.

"You've come back to us!" Her ever pretty eyes blinked back a bright sheen as she squeezed her hands. It took Tessie by surprise and she struggled to mirror her warmth even though she was happy to see her. She hadn't expected them to miss her so, or to even really worry about her. Were they friends now after all this? Is this what friendship was?

After the initial rush of greetings, Kyran filled Ruby in on their discussion in the carriage, and the three of them moved to the parlour. Tessie was itching with plans and schemes and could barely stop the thud in her chest. She needed to win Ruby and Kyran over to the idea.

"I have a confession to make." Tessie perched on the edge of her seat. "Some nights ago I went into the East End after dark and followed Moses to the docks. I watched him and three others haul barrels from the river filled with brandy and tea."

"That sounds about right." Kyran did not see the importance.

"They loaded the wagon and taking my chance, I set the whole thing on fire."

Ruby choked on her tea. "Goodness!" She covered her mouth. "What a risk you took."

"On fire?" Kyran's mild disposition startled.

"All of it. Burned to a crisp."

"What on earth were you thinking?" He wasn't catching the excitement as Tessie would have liked though she pushed on, the urgency rising in her voice. "I want to do more. To burn it all. Every time he plans to bring in a haul, I want to burn it down."

Kyran rubbed the back of his neck, staring hard into his drink.

"He has taken from us. It's time for us to take from him."

"You want to start a war?" His brown eyes searched hers as Ruby looked on at her in confusion.

"But why, Tessie?"

"Why?" She frowned. What did they mean, why? How could they ask why? "To show him we won't be pushed around no more, that's why. To make him call off this mission against me and Finn. So yer and Kyran can be free as yer wish to be."

"This isn't the way." Kyran shook his head.

"Why ever not! Are we to be sitting ducks forever? I'll not sit back any longer and neither should yer."

Kyran took a deep breath and shoved his hands in his waistcoat pocket.

Ruby looked back and forth between them. "We don't want a war with him, Tessie. A war we could never win. You are plotting against a man and you do not know who he is."

"I hardly care who he is. I care about stopping him so I can find Finn. Don't yer understand?"

"Finn?" Ruby leant her head down and pinched her brow.

"What am I to do? Wander the London streets in hopes of bumping into him? I cannot show my face in this city. He may think me dead, he may be far away, or he may be hiding right beneath our noses and unable to get free of these animals, but he is alive! The only way to find out is...."

"Is to what? Start a war with the Angel?"

"Do something that will make him sit up and take notice. Make him talk to us, make him or Moses or whoever tell me what happened to him. Or call this whole thing off. I need to know where he is!"

The expressions on Kyran and Ruby's face were sullen and heavy. Not at all the show of grit that Tessie had imagined. "How can yer not want to fight him?"

Ruby pursed her lips, though it was not an expression of surrender, but one of experience. "We have been fighting. For longer than you, Tessie. Much longer. It is a burden that only grows heavier and now we want to be free. That is it. We want to be free of him."

"Then be free? What is keeping yer here? Yes, he is your father, but yer have the means to go and yer do not."

"It may look like that from the outside, Tessie. But everything we have is tied up in companies he owns. Connections he can squeeze shut at any moment."

Kyran hung his head low and put his hand on Ruby's shoulder. "That is why the deal in Paris was so important. It would have given us some independence and let us branch out on our own. We'd have had something that didn't have his stamp on it. Something he couldn't touch."

Ruby's expression pained at the mention of it. "The Angel has only allowed things to continue as they are because he hopes for Kyran to come home. That is it. We could be out on the street at a moment's notice. Everything would be gone."

"Then be out on the street!" Tessie cried, though she knew it was cruel and it was not that easy. Even if they chose destitution over this life, the Angel would not so easily let them go. It would not end there. She moved away to Kyran's desk by the window, hunching over as her chest thudded madly.

"You can't know for sure that Finn is alive." Ruby turned the attention back to Tessie, her tone was gentle but it was a cutting remark nonetheless.

"Yer saw him. He was alive not a few weeks ago. Why should he not be alive now? I know he is."

"Let's assume he is then," Kyran said. "For argument's sake. What does starting this war with the Angel achieve?"

"It gets his attention." Tessie bowed her head over the desk; the frustration draining and heavy. This was not so easy as she had planned. Her eyes darted over the stacked papers on the desk, her eyes catching on a folded copy of the *London Times*.

A tattered edge peeked out from beneath a stack of books, and there on the top right corner of the page was an etched portrait. The lower half of the man's face was obscured by books so she could only see upward from the bridge of his nose. Tessie's mouth gaped open, but not a word escaped as she reached her hand to the unknown face. Seeing a distinct scar above his left eye, she knocked the stack of books to the ground.

"Tessie?" Ruby rose to her feet, though Tessie stood frozen to the spot. The man's face stared back at her. She gripped the paper with her fist and braced the other to her chest.

"It's him," she said, quietly. "It's him."

Holding out the etched drawing towards Kyran and Ruby, the head and shoulder portrait of a man with a scar above his left eye stared back at them, his face weary, and his mouth downturned.

"What does it say?" She thrust the paper at him. "That's Finn! What does it say?" The excitement rippled out of her, giddy and urgent.

Kyran took the newspaper with a confused expression and studied the portrait picture, reading the article himself before speaking it out loud.

"What is it, Kyran?" Ruby rose to see for herself.

"Is that the man you saw?" he asked of Ruby and held it to her face.

"It's him!" Tessie urged.

Ruby faded away as she tried to read the article. "It could well be..."

"For goodness sake, read it to me!" Tessie cried and Kyran took it back, shaking the newspaper out and clearing his throat.

"On the evening of January 3rd, there was an attempted burglary at the home of Mr Arthur Crabbe, a most prominent public figure in Mayfair. The assailant, named here as Mr Finn O'Shea, in the company of Mr Michael Bell, was restrained at the scene by the house staff and Mr Crabbe himself. Mr O'Shea is currently being held at Newgate Prison awaiting trial, though the case is drawing particular attention as Mr Crabbe has petitioned the court for a public hanging, despite the trial and sentencing having yet taken place. Mr Arthur Crabbe has made a statement to the writer of this article that members of the populous so inclined to thievery and thuggery, must be given, often and publicly, a stronger deterrent than the colonies. Mr Crabbe described the assailants as armed and rabid, and insisted the good fairing classes refuse to live in fear of those delinquents who dare come from the East End in the early hours of the morning to wreak havoc and destruction. They need to see the consequences swinging in front of them..."

Kyran trailed off at the end and looked to Tessie, whose eyes were alight with urgency.

"He's at Newgate Prison, and they wish to hang him. Now will yer help me?"

~

RUBY AND KYRAN struggled to pull on their gloves and jackets, having followed Tessie into a cab without time to properly dress. Without a thought Tessie had rushed out the door, urging the cab onward to Newgate Prison. To think, just that morning as she had woken in Clerkenwell, he had been not a 15 minutes walk away, in a cell!

"He needs someone to help him. Who can get him out?" Tessie quizzed them, leaning forward in the cab as if to make it go faster.

"If there's to be a trial he'll need representation. A defence lawyer."

"Do yer know one?"

"None that will represent him against Arthur," Ruby asserted. "That's for sure. Not in this town." Ruby's eyes slid past her, serious and concerned as the streets outside whizzed by.

"There must be."

"Tessie, not even Ruby or I can be publicly seen to go against Arthur without it causing a fracas. I am a known associate of Arthur's. Our long-standing business connections know me, know us. It would be social suicide. Business suicide, to publicly show support for an armed robber who has attempted to burgle and do God knows what else. It would only serve to weaken our position in London and that will not help you."

"He is not an armed robber!" Tessie cried. "Damn this city. Damn the whole lot of yer!"

"Let me make some enquiries of the less public kind, but we cannot rush in there and make a scene, it will only hurt your cause!"

'He's done this on purpose," Tessie lamented, crossly shaking her head. "This whole charade. It was me he wanted, not Finn, and now look where he is. And who knows what they've done to him. I told yer he was out there. I told yer."

"Yes." Ruby squeezed her hand. "You did. But you still must wait."

She had to see him, and as her eyes raced the landscape for any trace, the horses dragged her in the slowest motion. "Urgh. I could run faster!" She wrung her hands, moving from side to side of the carriage scanning in each direction.

Finally the driver stopped and without another word, she leapt from the carriage.

"We'll be right here, Tessie. We'll be here waiting," Ruby called after her, though Tessie hardly heard her.

CHAPTER 36

Composing herself, Tessie straightened her gloves and tidied her hair as she approached the entrance of Newgate prison. In the foyer, she saw the check-in desk and a man in uniform shuffling papers and serving an older couple. What was she to say to him? What was she to ask? They were hardly going to allow her, a woman, to waltz inside and visit him. Kyran was right - if this was a trap, they would be expecting her to announce her name. Her mind going blank, she scanned the room before leaving and quickly moved to the long side of the outer prison.

Slipping down the alley, she saw low window grates towards the back. The holding cells were her only hope. Perhaps he was still held there. She ducked beneath the office windows and made toward the back of the alley.

Crouching by one of the grates, she peered in to see they were windows to the basement cells. She could barely make out shape or form in the dark space below as the smell human waste wafted over her. "Finn," she hissed. "Finn, are yer here?" A small chorus of voices mocked her and she moved onto the next cell. "Finn, it's me. Are yer here?"

Hearing the clang of a heavy door opening, she flung herself against the wall and waiting till it closed, she called out again.

"Who are you?" said a small voice with a Haitian-creole accent. Tessie swung around and saw a young dark-skinned girl crouching at the end of the alley. Tessie wasn't sure what to say and turned back to the ominous grate in front of her. "Finn!"

"They are over here," the girl pointed to the grate closest to her.

Tessie's brow creased with confusion. Did this girl know who she was looking for? Did she know Finn? Keeping herself low, she moved along the wall closer to the girl who calmly watched her approach. As she did, she pointed with a stick at the grill. "In there. He is in there."

Hesitant, Tessie crouched. "Finn? Are yer here?"

"Tessie?" His voice, croaky and strained, echoed up from the dark chamber and she threw herself on her belly to get closer. Finn's tall frame emerged from the shadow as he pulled himself to the grate. "Tess!"

"Oh my God." Tears sparked in her eyes and she strained to get her arms through the gaps in the bars. "I've found yer." His hands reached for her and the realness of his touch washed over her.

"My love. Are yer alright?"

"Yes, yes, oh I can't believe it to be true!" She kissed his hands, relief flooding her in waves. "They put yer picture in the paper. I saw yer picture. Oh, I can't believe I've found yer." Pressing her forehead and cheeks to the cold bars, she breathed in the warmth of him, letting the moment settle.

"Let me see yer. Look at me," he beckoned and she sat back, peering at him, bruised and battered though his familiar smile beamed back at her.

"You're hurt," she said, reaching back toward him.

"I'll be fine now I know yer made it. Yer will be alright. But yer shouldn't have come. They're looking for yer, Tess. This isn't over."

"I know. I know. I was careful."

"I was trying to get back to yer. All this time. But it all went wrong and I just want yer to be safe."

"It's alright, my love. Listen." She hushed her voice and bowed her head as footsteps encroached from outside his cell. "I'll find a way to get yer out. I will."

"No. They are going to hang us, Tess. That's the truth of it. Mickey Bell is to be hung with me and we don't have long." He moved back so she could see the equally battered man behind him. Mickey only looked up in her direction and waved.

"They'll both die," the girl said over Tessie's shoulder.

"No. No, yer won't. I'm going to get yer out." Her heart burst and she yanked angrily at the grate, though it did not budge. This could not be their end. This would not be their goodbye. "I will find a way. Yer have to believe it."

"It's a trap, Tess. I found the Angel and he's done this to draw yer out. Don't fall for it. Don't go and make a fuss. Stay away from the Old Bailey. Stay away from here. It's enough for me to know yer are free. I love yer. And yer must go on, now. Go on."

"Don't speak such things to me. Not now," she scolded. "I will not say goodbye to yer."

'You must. It will kill me to see yer here in such a place. Look at yer now. Cleaned and cared for, wherever yer have been. Yer shouldn't have come here for me."

"I will always come for yer! Always."

"That's Madochée." Finn nodded to the girl watching on. "She needs a home. Someone to care for her. Take her with yer."

"Uh," Tessie nodded, overwhelmed. "Alright, but wait.

They can't just hang yer without a trial. There must be time first."

"The trial will be a joke, Tess. Listen to what I say, yer mustn't return here. They'll be watching. Please. Promise me."

Finn lost his footing and dropped out of reach, struggling to pull himself back up. Behind him, the door clattered and Tessie ducked to the side out of sight.

"You must go," he hissed. "Go, my love. "

"I'll get yer out," she urged. "I will."

"Mo chroí, mo teas."

"Always. Always!" She squeezed his hand one last time as he pulled away.

"Go. I love yer. Go."

"I love yer."

Tessie hurried to her feet, fighting back the wail in her chest. "Come," she said to the girl. "Come now." It took everything she had to keep walking, though she stumbled towards the road, the Haitian girl in tow. He was alive! After all this, he was alive! And she had to leave him there in that damned place.

Bringing her hand to her mouth to disguise herself as she approached the road, she eyed the waiting carriage and paused to crouch beside the girl. "Yer are a friend of his and so yer are a friend of mine." Madochée looked back towards the cell, her mass of frizzy hair flopping over her eyes. "Yer must come with me as he said, somewhere safe, but we'll get him out. You'll see." Tessie took her hand and led her across the street.

CHAPTER 37

*B*ack at the house, Ruby and Tessie stood back with their arms folded as Madochée pushed a small toy horse on wheels across the rug of her bedroom. Behind the screen, Martha was pouring warm water into a tub, as a younger maid laid out an undershirt. "This is the smallest one, miss," she said as its length hung off the bed.

"Oh. Here." Ruby shook her head. "Send Lucas to the Moseleys for two sets of day clothes. Tell them she is up to here." She put her hand just above her hip measuring Madochée's height. "And of slight frame. Go."

The young woman nodded, and in a bit of a tizzy, rushed from the room.

Tessie watched on, but her thoughts were elsewhere. It had been so hard to see Finn, to have him so close within reach, only to return to the house without him. It pounded in her chest and flushed her cheeks. She had to get him out.

"Let's get yer in the bath," she said, rousing herself. "Have yer had one like this before?"

Madochée flashed her dark eyes and stood up though she still didn't speak.

"I know yer can talk. I heard yer, remember." She kept her voice teasing and calm.

"I talk," Madochée confirmed.

"Well, yer probably hungry. We can eat when you're through."

"Lots of lajan." Madochée averted her eyes, pushing her hand into the warm water of the tub.

"Lajan?"

"You are a rich lady."

"No." Tessie almost laughed. "I am not. Miss Ruby and Mr Kyran, though. Yes."

"Do I live here now?"

"We are guests here. Yer and I are guests. Now, do yer need help, or can yer do it on yer own?"

"I can," she said, and kicked off her loose and well-worn boots, both without laces.

Tessie gave her some space and took her place by the window, where Ruby too watched over the street below. Rich? Tessie mused at the notion she might be confused for being wealthy. Little did this young girl know that Tessie herself had been just as grimy and threadbare only weeks earlier. She looked down at her coffee-coloured skirt and crisp white blouse, the faded stove burns on her fingers and palms. Had she changed so much?

Tessie turned her thoughts again to forging a plan. "I know yer think I'm rash." She glanced at Ruby. "With setting his goods on fire, and now rushing into the prison. But I can't bear to sit still..."

"I understand, Tessie. I do." Ruby's brow creased with thought. "If it were Kyran in there I would feel as you do. I'm sorry I doubted you. Finn was out there and you believed it."

"Lady, you are going to save him?" Madochée asked from behind the screen.

"We will do everything we can."

"He thinks you should forgot him."

"What do yer mean?"

"He said he failed to protect. Echwe. Failed. So you should. That's why. But I told him I didn't want him to protect me. Did you want him to protect you?"

It dug deep in Tessie's chest as she thought of Finn feeling he had failed. "I wanted to protect him too."

"We protect each other," Madochée said.

"Aye. We protect each other." Tessie pressed her palms her to her eyes. Taking a deep breath, she perched on the end of the bed, listening to the sound of mild splashing as Madochée settled into bathing. That man she loved more than anything, feeling any blame or failure, churned her insides. It was not him, but this world that had failed them. It had failed them both.

A lot had happened in such a short period of time, it was a lot to hold out before them, too much to have any perspective. They were deep in, muddy and tangled. How could they find a way through?

"You heard in the article his name is Arthur Crabbe," Ruby broached, quietly stepping into the silence. She was crossing a threshold. "But you do not yet know who he is. He's the Owner/operator of Criterion Merchants and Shipping. He chairs the Council of Spice Merchants, advises the Board of Trade and holds a number of other fancy titles in the shipping industry I can barely recall. He is a popular figure, Tessie, with many connections across the shipping world and in London society."

"But he's a...villain? A murderer. How is he all of these things?"

Ruby stood to turn about the room, her skirts rustling as she moved. "He didn't start out all these things. He was poor as poor can be. A dockworker. Labourer. He worked his way up the ranks to supervisor, eventually starting his own small business. It grew as he grew. The more power he had he used to orchestrate partnerships, positioning rival businesses right where he wanted them, ultimately swallowing up their businesses. He made it look like they didn't deliver their merchandise, when all along his little minions were siphoning them off." She was a buoyant storyteller, her voice relishing the drama of it all. "He is a businessman first. Always. And he accepts no competition. No loose ends. No uncertainties."

"So yer saying we can't fight him. It's impossible."

"No. I have to believe it's possible too. But we have to be careful. And for Kyran..." Ruby trailed away, but Tessie understood now it was more complicated for him. "He is your brother. You will see the toll of it for yourself."

"Perhaps. I might be the daughter of Arthur Crabbe, but I have never known him. I have never looked into his eyes."

"They're eyes that pierce you to the bone, I will tell you that. It takes energy just to stand him looking at you."

Tessie let out a sigh, pressing her thumb to the small gap in her teeth. "But we know what he wants, and we know who he is. That at least should earn us an audience."

Ruby shook her head, and Tessie could see the worry in her eyes. "That would be for Kyran to orchestrate. Let's wait to see what he brings us."

With that, Madochée splashed water across the room as she leapt from the tub. "Oh wait, wait." Ruby rushed forward and wrapped her in a sheet.

Hours passed as they waited for Kyran's return, and sitting down to tea in the parlour, he finally opened the door.

"What did yer find?" Tessie stood from her chair.

"The trial is set for Tuesday."

Ruby set down her tea. "So early?"

"What day is it?" Tessie looked back and forth between them realising she had no idea.

"It's Wednesday."

"We have only a week." She fell back in her chair as Madochée looked on from the table in a new play dress that fell just below the knee. She looked different, awkward, the colour in her fresh cheeks bright against her collar. Her fizzy hair pulled back in a neat bun, though she dug her fingers into it so that it was pulling loose and fraying about her face.

"A week until what?" she asked with big eyes.

Tessie looked to her boots quickly before touching her hand to Madochée's. "A week before Finn's trial."

"So a week and they let him out. Or he dies?"

"Yes." Tessie nodded. The truth of the statement felt cruel in its simplicity. A tight ball held in her stomach.

"Can I have my old clothes back? My mama gave them to me. Where are they?"

"Oh," Ruby interjected. "They are being washed. Yes. You can have them."

Kyran unbuttoned his coat and loosened his tie. "He'll be expecting and hoping you show up at court, wailing at the top of your lungs. We cannot walk into that trap."

"I'll beg him, anything, to get Finn out." Tessie thought hard. "Yer need to get me in front of him."

"A minute ago you wanted to wage war."

"I still want that. I want the earth beneath his feet to shake. I want to look in his eyes and know that he has felt the pain of what he has done to us. I want him to feel unsafe as we have felt. But I have to get Finn back first. I will beg and crawl, fight and kill to get him back. Yer just need to tell me how."

Kyran rubbed his brow in thought. "I can't think on an empty stomach. I need to eat."

Tessie slid a plate of tea biscuits towards him. "I've been eating all day and it hasn't helped me an ounce."

They fell silent in their thoughts as Madochée munched loudly on her own stack of tea biscuits. Tessie picked up her plate and moved toward the door. "Here, take this down the hall to Martha and tell her you're still hungry. She'll find yer something even better."

Madochée seemed skeptical at being asked to move and looked at each of her newly acquired adults. "Are you going to talk about killing him?"

Ruby's mouth opened but she didn't answer. None of them did.

"Finn wanted to kill him too. Finn and Mickey."

"Aye." Tessie looked into the young girl's eyes and recognised something in her. She was adrift, unanchored to anything but perhaps Finn. If she didn't keep her close she was just as likely to run and disappear back out into the streets. Instead, she closed the door and Madochée returned to her seat as Tessie ushered Ruby and Kyran to the other side of the room and lowered her voice. "Between the three of us, is there nothing we have against him? We know who he is. We know what he wants. Can we not threaten him?"

"He is not a man who crumbles at a challenge, Tessie. He thrives on it. He even invites it."

"If he thrives on it, he'll at least meet with me. What else can we do, Kyran? Yer know him better than anyone. What can we do to engage him?"

Kyran gave a lopsided smile of exasperation. "Engage him? He will engage. That is what I'm afraid of."

"The ball!" Ruby suddenly piped up. "The Arlington Ball is on Saturday. He will be there." She looked to Kyran who mulled it over.

"Do you really want to be in a room with him?" he pushed

back at her. "This involves you too, being in the same room as him, after everything that has happened."

"I had planned to go. The Belfords have written to us. The Swansons. All of them expect us there. I shall not miss it. I know he will be there, but it will be in public. That's safer than giving him warning or time to arrange something privately, surely?"

Tessie added, "Will he talk to me?"

"Talking to you is the least of our worries." Kyran seemed to be slowly changing colour, fading to a sickening yellow. "We need to be clear on our objective. That's what we need to be clear on." He was getting frustrated, and Tessie didn't press him on it. She had gained a brother in this, though there was still much she did not understand about him.

"Our objective is to free Finn and then ourselves. It cannot be clearer than that."

"And what is our threat? To expose him? Tell everyone who he is?" Ruby was growing in confidence. "We could write letters to people of influence."

"It would all be dismissed." Kyran dusted biscuit crumbs from his chin. "Conjecture, accusation. It is near impossible to prove he has anything to do with the Angel and then we have played our trump card. It is over and snuffed out and we've done nothing but aggravate him."

"Alright," Ruby shot back. "We're just thinking out loud here."

"So how can we prove it?" Tessie ignored them. "For the threat to have any bearing we have to be able to tie him to the smuggling racket and everything else he does?"

"It would require a serious betrayal of someone close to him."

Tessie's large eyes pleaded with Kyran. "Yer the one close to him, Kyran. Yer are the one."

He set down a half-eaten biscuit and looked into the fire, his brow strained.

"Yer could testify against him, Kyran. Yer could do that."

Tessie watched him struggling and slumped back in her seat to stare at her fingernails.

"Find another way," he said, though she'd already known his answer.

"Ugh. This is twisting my head in knots." Tessie gripped her head in her hands.

Ruby's eyes widened. "Kyran won't testify, but the Angel doesn't need to know that," she said quietly. "He just needs to believe he is at risk, that it is possible."

Kyran raised his head as Tessie too wrangled with the concept. "Yes."

"Alright. So we threaten him. What then? What if it doesn't go to plan? It is in public, yes, but it is no guarantee of safety. He is unpredictable."

Ruby moved to a desk in the corner of the library and took out a box, placing in front of Tessie. Opening it, inside was a small pepperbox revolver. All three of them looked at it silently, understanding what it meant.

"You can hide it in your skirts as a last resort," Ruby said, matter of factly. "We can do this."

It was becoming real and the weight of it swirled in Tessie's belly. She was talking with confidence, but could she really see this through? The hefty anticipation pressed on her chest so that she flopped down on the chair behind her. This very moment Finn was sitting on a cold floor in Newgate Prison. "Alright," she said, and looked up at her companions.

Kyran's eyes were sullen. "Are you a killer, Tessie?"

"It's what he deserves," she said. "He's a thief and murderer a hundred times over."

Kyran pressed his palms together in solemn contemplation.

"If he will not free Finn, or let us walk away from him, what choice do we have?"

"We can't take back what we start."

"Neither can he."

Kyran pressed his lips together, as if he were about to speak, but instead he walked swiftly from the room.

"Is this too much?" Tessie asked with concern. She had sat across from him in the carriage that very morning and learned he was kin. It was new and fragile, but still she felt it, a connection. Despite the rage she felt toward the Angel and the need to get Finn back, she did not want to lose Kyran.

Ruby looked at the doorway after his exit, considering it. "It is one thing to hate your father, it's quite another to plot his destruction."

IN THE QUIET of the house, Tessie stood before the mirror and wondered if she had, in fact, lost her mind. The pistol box rested on the mantle and her heart quickened at the thought of its weight in her hand. Her eyes wide, she caught a mad glimmer lurking in the half-light — a spark of lunacy born of sorrow and rage. Who had she become? she wondered of her reflection. A murderer? A pretender? A vengeful soul who could not rest? The titles did not sit well with her, and yet, the ache in her heart thudded louder, much louder, than her doubts.

The days past in a busy flurry of preparation. Tessie had never been to a ball and Ruby took great pride in educating her in the etiquette and expectations. She wanted to prepare her for every step and bow, and one or two dances should she feel compelled or be drawn out in duress.

They selected her outfit, she rehearsed her lines and backstory, always in a perfect English accent, and all the while her heart pounded with such force that it kept her awake.

As Saturday approached, Ruby received more and more mail, sometimes several a day from a steady stream of dedicated followers all hoping to see her there. Tessie had no idea she held such notoriety — so much so that she had Anna, the younger maid, send thank you replies on her behalf with assurances she would make sure to spend time with them at the ball.

While Ruby seemed invigorated by the plan and the many preparations, Kyran had made himself scarce. He was solemn at dinner and stressed throughout the day, busying himself with business and menial tasks.

On the day before the ball, Tessie watched him from the parlour as he lingered by the hedges in the rear courtyard. He had on his coat and hat as if he were going somewhere, but instead was pacing back and forth. Tessie, taking her own coat, went to join him.

"Are yer alright?" she asked as she approached, the foggy breath floating out in front of her. "It's freezing out here, Kyran."

"I'm fine," he said, though she could tell he had been out there longer than she'd thought as his lips were pale and cheeks flushed red.

"Why are yer out here? You'll catch your death."

"It gets so stuffy in that room with the fire, I just wanted some air."

"I'll walk with yer. Shall we go around the block?"

"We still shouldn't let you be seen around here. It's too risky. Even now."

"Alright. We'll just walk in here then." She indicated the small area of the courtyard.

Rubbing his hands together, he acquiesced. "Alright. Let's do that. Are you warm enough?"

"I'll be fine." Tessie smiled and they moved around the small group of hedges. It was a glum and miserable day, every facet of the landscape doused in frost with London's ever grey clouds hanging low and ominous.

"Are yer concerned about the ball?" She broached the topic subtly, though they locked into a fairly hasty walking pace in an effort to keep warm.

"We should all be concerned about it, Tessie. There is a lot to be considered."

"I don't want to push yer into anything. I really don't. I know I can be forceful and I don't mean to be."

Kyran dropped his head with a wry smile and tucked his hands behind his back. "I need to find the courage, Tessie. That is all."

Surprised by his response, she reached out to touch his arm. "Yer have already shown so much."

"Not to his face. Not to his face. There is something there..." He struggled for the right words. "And I buckle. Perhaps when you look into his eyes you will feel it too, or perhaps it is my burden alone. Something in a father's eyes that only a son can see. But to have his eyes, piercing through me...it's something that strangles me. I cannot explain it."

They came to the corner and Tessie spun around to speak directly to him. "You're right, I have not looked at him, nor have I had his eyes upon me. But we must think ourselves worthy, Kyran. We must think ourselves worthy of the freedom we demand. We have a right to ask for it. We do."

"Yes. Of course, you are right in principle. But principles fail us in the moment. I have seen him do things you could not imagine. I can barely imagine them myself, and yet I still want to believe there is good in him. How can a person be entirely void of any good? I cannot grasp it."

"If there is good in him then he will have a choice to make too."

Kyran's eyes looked to the sky. "Maybe there nothing there, but I attach it to him because that is what I want to see. I want to see good in him so I hope. Ever disappointed. I spin myself around thinking there is no point to any of this. Fight as we might, hope or pray. It is destined for nothing but more of the same."

"Think of how far we have come." Tessie looked around herself for inspiration. "Yer did not judge me for my past as I thought yer would. I am wearing finer dresses than I ever felt worthy of wearing. And I thought Finn was all I had in this world. And here I have yer, and Ruby, and back there young

Madochée asleep in my room. We are not alone, Kyran. And we were never alone, even when we thought we were."

"Sweet words, dear Tessie." Kyran drew in a breath and she could see the burden heavy on his chest. "As I said, I just need to find the courage. No one can give it to me, I must find it for myself."

They walked a little further, each holding their thoughts as the cold air singed their cheeks. Tomorrow would be the ball and all would be known. Kyran at least had a landscape to envision, whereas Tessie had never attended a ball at all. She would know no one and had no expectations to navigate. She was going in fresh, with one goal only. Kyran, on the other hand, would know many people there and perhaps many more would know him. And his father would be there — a meeting fraught with history and weighed down with meaning. Their experiences in the same moment would be very different and it was never more evident to Tessie than it was now.

They rounded the corner again, Tessie feeling the turn of breeze rushing at her back. "My dear friend, may God rest her soul." She crossed herself. "She told me all love does not look the same, and if we think it so we may go our whole lives believing we've never seen it. The same can be said for courage. Not all courage looks the same."

"Then maybe I do not have the kind of courage I want. The kind that will get us what we want."

"Do not judge yourself so harshly. I do not know what will happen tomorrow. I don't know if we will fail. If I will fail. Or if we will be dead in a gutter and Finn hung the next day. But we will have tried, dear brother. And for whatever happens. For whatever courage yer find or don't find. I will not judge yer for it."

CHAPTER 39

Snow fell gently past Tessie's reflection in the window. She stood in a turquoise ball gown with rich taffeta cascading over a hoop skirt with lavish splashes of gold and billowing silk. It was a stunning dress. Her auburn curls glistened, pinned at her neck with a delicate net of pearls and a small jewel rested on her chest. She looked every bit a portrait of opulence, but for the gnarled leather band at her wrist, and the heavy concern at her brow.

Beneath her petticoats the pepperbox revolver pressed against her thigh, her knife tucked safely into her stockings — a reminder that tonight was far more than a winter celebration. With only a few days of practicing and rehearsing her movements, her voice, her posture and manners, the pressure of it rose in her chest. Everything depended on this evening. Everything.

She gulped back a glass of whiskey. It burned down her throat, sizzling with the wave of anger in her belly. It was still there, and gritting her teeth and rolling her shoulders, it wanted to be released. She wanted the Angel to feel it thunder out of her for all he had done, but Finn needed her composed. He needed her focussed, and she needed the Angel alive. Justice would have to wait a little longer yet.

Ruby entered in a flowing gown of pearly hues, her golden hair a mass of beautiful curls as she glided towards Tessie, catching her as she put the whiskey glass down. "Darling," she smiled. "You'll be ahead of us all at that rate. I'm surprised Martha let you have this up here."

Tessie paid no heed and poured another. "I took it from the parlour, and here, you probably need one too." She thrust the glass at Ruby, who nodded approvingly.

"Your accent is passable. You needn't worry about it." And she too downed the glass of whiskey and held her chest as it burned.

"We will know in a few hours if we have failed or succeeded. What if I can't do it?" Tessie's voice was ominous and she pressed her hand to her stomach to quell the sick feeling.

"None of us can guarantee how we'll handle ourselves tonight. Kyran has been pacing the library for over an hour."

"What if I can't get him to free Finn?"

Spinning her back around, Ruby tapped her on the chin. "Relax. Stay focussed on the plan. That's what I'm telling myself anyway."

"Is it working?"

Ruby widened her eyes and shrugged. "I guess we'll find out later."

"It is wrong to speak my fear now, but I feel it. Have I pushed yer all too far? Have I–"

Ruby placed her hands on Tessie's shoulders and held her eyes. "He tried to kill me, Tessie. He tried to kill you. Kyran carries scars that perhaps we will never understand and he will have Finn hung from the walls of Newgate Prison. This is not a burden you carry alone. It is for all of us, and we must go through this. It is the only way forward. I see that now."

Tessie breathed deeply, though the weight of it was heavy, she turned her gaze to the window. "Perhaps the weather won't clear in time?"

"I wouldn't worry about that." Ruby moved to Tessie's dressing table and rifled at the contents. "The Rochesters are a force of nature. Come rain or shine they will not be outdone. Not even by the weather." She paused to inspect her reflection and pinch at her cheeks. "Before the night is out I'm sure you'll hear the story of Prince Juniper. They say he died in a blizzard near a century ago, desperate to make it to the Arlington ball. They are *that* important!"

Ruby put her hands on her hips and looked Tessie over. "Well. You look magnificent. I shall never be able to wear that dress now. Will you not take this off?" she asked of the leather band.

Tessie shook her head, needing Finn close tonight of all nights. Ruby retrieved a long length of lace and gently bound Tessie's wrist as a makeshift accessory.

"Are you sure he's going to be there?" Tessie asked, swallowing another surge of anxiety and pulling on her gloves.

"He will be there." And Ruby swigged back the last of the whiskey glass.

THE SNOWFIELDS either side of Arlington Manor were the perfect backdrop. A string of gas lanterns led guests from the driveway in a whimsical trail, the large home beckoning with festive music and lights. In the carriage, they sat quietly, resting their feet on the foot-warmer, nerves cramping in Tessie's belly as they moved slowly up the progression of carriages. Kyran sat stiffly in a black dress coat and barely uttered a word throughout their journey, though wiped his brow often with his handkerchief and spent the rest of the time repositioning it in his pocket. Ruby, her face strained and eyes serious, held her smile at the ready, prepared to step into her role at just the right time.

Pulling up the ranks, a footman opened the door and Ruby graciously stepped out first, holding her arm with elegant expectation. Tessie followed suit, though with doubtless less grace and Kyran escorted them to the greeting hall. Giving their names to the steward they were presented to their hosts, a portly and eccentric Mr Rochester, his four grown children, and his wife, who was snapping at her daughter between greetings.

"If it isn't the effervescent Miss St. Clair," Mrs Rochester crooned. "Delighted you could join us again this year, dear."

"The Arlington Ball is always my top priority, Mrs Rochester. I wouldn't miss it for the world."

"If you please, Ladies and Gentleman," the steward continued. "The ballroom has been opened. Beverages and refreshments are being served at the far entrance."

Following the flow of guests in extravagant gowns and elegant tailcoats, a sizeable orchestra beckoned guests to the ballroom as the ceiling above loomed in an intricate painting of angels and men in golds and silvers and royal purples. A large rose chandelier hung low in the centre and it was the grandest scene Tessie had ever seen.

"Are you strung too tight? What is it?" Ruby asked.

"No, no." Tessie shooed her away. "I'm just..." She breathed again, the enormity of it all pooling in her chest. Ruby squeezed her hand as they moved through the luxury and grandeur, through the gaudy displays of jewels and preened faces, plucked and drawn with makeup, cutlery polished to flicker in the lights, pristine glasses and shining centrepieces of crystal in silvers and golds. It was blinding, and as she breathed it all in, other scenes flashed before her.

Finn reaching from his dark cell.

Faye gasping in her dying breath.

The twisting agony of Moses plunging his knife into her side.

And her mother's grip on her chin. *You bow down to no one.*

It had all come to this. The Angel was amongst them, and she was here, exactly where she needed to be.

IN THE BALLROOM, guests turned to greet Kyran and Ruby as they entered. They were popular and well-known, though it seemed often people knew Ruby even when she was entirely unsure of them.

Inviting circles of chairs had been arranged for guests to take refreshment and they were called to join a Mr and Mrs Walters who had travelled from York. Mr Walters spoke with most familiarity of Ruby, though flashing a smile at Tessie it was clear she had no idea who he was or if they'd met before.

"Miss St. Claire, tell me, I was in Vienna recently, where is your estate?"

"Oh sir, it's been so long since I've been home I pray I could barely tell you," Ruby effortlessly teased and an appreciative laughter rippled through the onlookers.

"Must be near the river, is it? So many beautiful properties along there, my dear."

"Indeed, Mr Walters. Now stop or you'll have me homesick and I'm having such a good time. You don't want to see my moods when I get like that," she teased.

"No, sir," Kyran chimed in. "I believe last time it ended with Mr Wickman's wig on fire!"

The crowd chuckled and Tessie's nerves relaxed as guests

made their introduction and did not immediately take her for an imposter. Ruby brimmed with charm and grace, captivating in every way as she worked the ebbs and flows of the crowd. Her words floated back to Tessie. *I make them feel good and they make me feel empty.* This was how the Angel used her - to grease his unsuspecting targets with her graces, plying them into submission with compliments and flirtation. She was good at it and it was the making of her prison.

Kyran stood beside her, men in all manner of colourful tailed coats approaching to shake his hand and wrap him on the shoulders. They spoke on serious matters of business and she could see he too was held in high standing and well liked. It was peculiar to see them in their element, working their graces and plying their skills. This was their world.

Around her, polite conversation was littered with frivolities. What passed for upper-class gossip swirled around her as the guests settled in their circles. Tessie did her best to stay an invisible ghost, though she was caught in the crossfire a number of times. A Miss Brimsley and her brother took a distinct fancy to her and engaged in polite and proper conversation.

"So, my dear, where have you been hiding?"

Nodding politely, Tessie swallowed. "I have not been hiding madam, I assure you. Though my Uncle did keep us quite away from London revelry I'm afraid."

"I see." Mrs Brimsley persisted. "How is it we are finally graced with your presence this evening?"

"I am just now a guest of Miss St. Claire. We met while on a brief stay in France and spent a good deal of the voyage home making great acquaintance." Tessie felt her mouth roll the last few words in a slight lilt and bit down on her lip.

"And what does your father do?" Mr Brimsley asked without noticing.

"My uncle, sir. My parents passed when I was very young. But my uncle has an estate, madam, north of Cumberland." Tessie answered and was most grateful when Kyran cut in and steered the conversation elsewhere.

As Tessie recovered, Ruby subtly caught her attention and turned to the side. Nodding her head to the right and looking discretely forward. "The one facing us," she whispered, widening her eyes with a sideways turn. Tessie's eyes darted to a small cluster of guests not twenty feet away. There he was, the man whose name had burned in her guts.

Arthur Crabbe, in a short-tailed coat and white cravat, leaned casually against the window frame enjoying the revelry. His trimmed goatee moved as he spoke, and other guests buzzed around him, craving his blue eyes, ripe with confidence, to catch theirs for just a moment. The thought his eyes might lock on hers gripped Tessie with fright as if he might see through her in an instant. But still, she could not look away. He was a man, after all, enjoying the Arlington Ball with two hundred others and a glass of champagne.

"That's his wife," Ruby whispered of the woman slightly behind him in striking and over the top make-up and an excessively broad skirt so that no one could stand within three feet of her.

"Wife? I hadn't even thought about that."

"Cynthia Crabbe. She is older than he. A strategic marriage on his part I believe as she was a tad worse for wear when they joined, but she is from a very well to do family, if not the black sheep. And there is Castor. On his right." She nodded to the dark-skinned man just outside Arthur's circle, keeping a respectful distance and standing watch against a wall. "He would not normally attend a ball such as this on his own, though Arthur goes nowhere without him. He is Arthur's everything man. He needs to be watched as well. And then Otis, his father. Well, your grandfather in fact, is there behind him. You can see he is mostly all bluster at this age."

Tessie's mind raced, piecing together the family portrait before her. What a jilted, fractured, strange feeling it was to look upon them. Did she look like him? Were her blue eyes but a replica of his own?

She watched him closely, appearing to be in the midst of a great story with onlookers gathering as the tale gathered steam. Clenching his fists, he was acting something out, ducking, weaving, pretending to hold a pistol. His deep voice rolled above the crowd. "They'll hang him, Dudley, no worries about that."

"Are you so sure that's the right thing? The colonies at least puts these people to good use."

"The public's stomach for an old-fashioned hanging is turning, I know, though maybe that's the problem, old friend. If the colonies aren't a deterrent, a hanging it will have to be. We can't get too civilised for our own good."

A woman grasped at Cynthia's arm. "Must have been frightful."

"Oh, indeed. Just a horrid thing of a man."

They were talking about Finn! Tessie's face flushed red hearing him reduced to a raging tall tale. No. He was more than that. He was more than gossip for the gentry. How dare they!

Arthur turned to survey the crowd and seeing Kyran, held his glass up in a casual greeting, giving him a nod to approach. Kyran saw him but did not respond. His eyes then moved to Ruby, hovering with a detectable tinge of sourness. Ruby reached for Tessie's hand behind her back. Finally, his eyes fell to Tessie and a bolt of panic struck through her. He held his eyes on hers in a drawn-out moment of recognition. It was slow and considered, but it was relish she saw in his expression, and he almost smiled, as if it was she in the honey trap — not he.

Breaking away, Tessie's chest collapsed in on itself. "He saw me," she said, gripping Ruby's arm. "He knows who I am."

Ruby's face flushed but she held hard to Tessie's hand. "Yes. He saw all of us. Good grief, my heart is in my throat."

"I'm going to go now," Kyran said, jumping in quickly. "Let's get this damn thing over with."

Tessie held her breath, willing the thumping in her chest to slow. This was it. This was the moment.

"Go." Tessie pushed Kyran away and he strode toward the Angel.

"Oh, I can't watch." Ruby winced her eyes closed and turned to Tessie. "I'll have a carriage pull out front. It'll be waiting if anything goes awry."

"Yes. Go."

Tessie glanced again as Kyran approached the Angel, then turned away. She had to get into position.

CHAPTER 40

Taking respite from his audience, Arthur picked over the extravagant selection of refreshments and snacks; olives, candied fruits, cold meats and figs. Popping an olive in his mouth, he held out the bowl to Kyran as he approached, "They've brought these in from Spain."

"No, thank you."

"Please help yourself. That seems to be your thing these days."

"Walk with me to the library, please." Kyran tucked his hands behind his back.

"We have a library at home," Arthur posed. "Though you never visit."

Kyran straightened up and breathed deeply.

"Oh. You want to talk?" Arthur frowned, feigning confusion. "Is this to do with your guest? I wonder if the Rochesters realise they're hosting a scrappy pauperess who happens to have borrowed a dress."

"I wonder if they realise they're hosting all manner of men and scoundrels."

Arthur raised an eyebrow and took another olive. "I'd like

nothing more than to talk with Miss O'Shea. If I'd known she'd be here I might have prepared a gift."

Behind him, Arthur offered a slight nod in Castor's direction as he watched from across the room. Castor, attentive as always, kept his dark eyes on Arthur as he moved across the room and away with Kyran.

"Your grandfather's over there if you were planning on saying hello. He's drinking everything in sight so I'd be quick if I were you. He'll cause a scene before the night is out, I'm sure of it. He's having an off night, one of his spells, though he knew enough to still insist on coming. Cranky bugger."

Kyran cleared his throat without answering and led onward down a small corridor off the ballroom. Then, opening the door to the library, he stepped aside for Arthur to enter.

TESSIE STEPPED out of the shadow, her breath stuck in her chest as she clasped her hands in front of her. Stepping into the long narrow room heavy with books and an ominous mood, his eyes flickered, alight with self-assuredness.

"Tessie O'Shea. Or is it Fisher? Or… Crabbe?" He pronounced each word carefully. Yes. He knew her name. His eyes narrowed as his lips pursed. "But it is unmistakable, isn't it? You are Crabbe through and through." He tucked his hands behind him, strolling casually as if to circle her. "And if there's one family trait we have," he mused. "We don't die easy. Though you had some help, did you not?" Arthur looked accusingly at Kyran, who squared his shoulders. "Don't have the appetite for it, do you my son? Your grandfather has a word for that I believe." And he paused for effect. "Was it weak? Or was it cowardly? I can never remember."

"You should show him more respect than that," Tessie cut in, taking another step towards him.

"Respect?"

"He knows everything about you. Enough to bring you down." She bit her lip and swallowed. She hadn't meant to dive in so fast. She'd barely tested the water.

Arthur's blue eyes lit up as he turned them on Kyran. "Enough to bring me down?"

Tessie's jaw locked, willing Kyran to hold tight. *Do not buckle. Do not buckle.* Kyran simply looked him over, his expression calmer than Tessie expected.

"You know it is true." He spoke into the chasm between them, his words echoing up and over the high-rise bookshelves.

Arthur nodded, scrunching up his nose and shaking his head. "Well, that does hurt my feelings, Son. I won't lie about that. After everything I've done—"

"We aren't here to discuss your feelings." *Yes, Kyran!* Tessie cheered. *Hold tight.*

"But I wonder." Arthur smacked his lips and took a step closer to Kyran. "Would you really go through with such a thing?" They were toe-to-toe now. Face-to-face. Arthur looked directly into Kyran's cloudy brown eyes. The muscles in Kyran's jaw clenched as Arthur searched his face. "I think I might actually be impressed if you did. If you could."

Tessie could see the likeness in their profiles, the similar shape of their forehead and nose—though Kyran's eyes sloped with kindness and sincerity where Arthur's were hard-lined and staunch.

"And what do you consider I might do in response?" Arthur's voice dropped an octave, along with his H's. Where just moments earlier his accent was crisp and clear and befitting his company, he was morphing into something else before their very eyes. "What do you think your old pa might do if his very existence were threatened?"

Kyran swallowed, and Tessie could see him fighting to keep the fortitude in his eyes.

"There's no telling." Arthur jabbed his finger into Kyran's chest. "But what I do know, is that right now your Ruby is out there alone. Now, I've put up with this drivel long enough, but you press me, boy, and I'm likely to do something you'll regret. Do not forget who you are talking to."

Now Kyran faltered, and Tessie saw the yellow hue reappear as a shadow on his face.

"You come at me, lad. You come at me with something with a bit more substance than that."

"It's not an empty threat," Tessie said with as much conviction as she could muster, but they were losing ground. Arthur's eyes flashed with aggravation and, taking a large step back from them, he whistled. It was a short and well-practiced burst of tweets. Kyran's expression fell.

Tessie's eyes dashed back and forth between them as a silent standoff took place before her. What did that mean? She was not a part of it and could not intervene, though Arthur's gaze glowered with meaning; an unspoken conversation.

A mixture of fear and anger filled Kyran's eyes and he took a step back. Was he leaving? Breaking away, he moved swiftly for the door without another word.

"Kyran!" Tessie rushed, the sound strangling in her throat. Where was he going! Why was he leaving her here?

Arthur looked back at her as Kyran disappeared from view. "He is just checking on his precious Ruby. It's all about Ruby if you didn't know."

"Why must you treat him like that? You have no idea what you have done or the pain you have caused," she countered.

"Girl, I am not the bringer of pain. I'm not the creator. I did not invent it. Pain is a language. You need to learn how to speak it. How to use it."

"What are you talking about?"

"I learned earlier than most. Some people do. Others fight it all their lives and always lose."

Tessie's eyes wandered. She was losing track of this conversation. "I know why you wanted me. I know about your war with my mother."

"Have you come here to boast, girl? It's unbecoming of a lady, even a fake one."

"No. I have come to warn yer."

"And the warning is what? That Kyran will expose me? Well, girl, he has left you here to fend for yourself. I won't be putting stock in that."

"I don't care," Tessie pushed. "If Kyran won't do it. I will find a way. We'll do it together."

Arthur stepped closer to her now, breathing down on her face so she could smell the faint sourness of olives and champagne. "I put your man in a cell to draw you out, and now you're here. What makes you think I'll crumble at such a threat? You think I can't get to you surrounded by so many people? Think again, darlin'."

The pepperbox revolver pressed against her thigh. Was now the time to reach for it beneath her petticoats and fire at him then and there? She would scream and holler at him, exposing him in the most reckless and brutal way she could think of. The Angel, gunned down at the Arlington Ball, a scandal befitting the most elusive underworld figure in London. Even as the breath caught in her lungs, she thought she may just do it. But her hands did not move. This was about Finn now, and nothing else. Finn.

"Yer will let Finn go. It's me yer want. Not him. Let him

go or we'll tell everyone about yer," she pressed, her cover falling away, her accent cracking.

"You've skulked a long way from the Old Nichol, I'll give you that." And he moved away from her and back towards the door.

"Wait!" Tessie commanded. What was happening? Was it all ending so soon? He had given no answer. No response at all.

"Those are the terms. Release Finn and leave us alone or we will expose yer," she insisted. "We will write letters to everyone imaginable. We'll start a campaign."

He held his hands out, his blue eyes sparkling. "What makes you think they don't already know, girl? And what are you going to do now? Attack me? Go on, scratch my eyes out, bring me down in the Rochester's library and let's hear you sell that story. B-but, b-but he was the Angel? The big scary Angel..." Arthur mocked her. "You came to me here because you thought you'd be safe." He spat the words now. "But you're too bleeding daft and too out of your depth. You are nothing but a charade. It's weak as piss. Full of air. It's not the right setting for a reckoning, darlin'. And the best thing, now I know exactly where to find you."

In a single heartbeat her pretence crumbled, the horror on her face sprawled out for him to see. "No!" This was not the triumphant confrontation she'd fought for. "No, don't leave yet. Come back! I lit those fires. It was me!"

Arthur paused, his back toward her.

"That's right. I followed Moses and burned it all down. I'll do more. We'll burn more."

Arthur swung around, locking down on his jaw, real anger in his eyes now. "I'd check on your friends if I were you." And with that, he left Tessie floundering in the empty library. He was gone. She had not even come close. Not even close.

Gathering her thoughts, she ran after him, peering back out to the ballroom where guests mingled and laughed, oblivious to the terror that coursed through her. "Kyran!" she called, stirring a few onlookers to glance her way though she saw him nowhere. Pushing through the crowd, she wound her way through the string of rooms and the long distance of the grand ballroom, to the entrance hall. Bursting out onto the front steps of the Rochester's grand mansion, there Kyran hovered by a waiting carriage with her cloak. Ruby too was only a step away surrounded by a small group of admirers. Seeing Tessie coming, Ruby tried to break away.

"You're not leaving yet," one of them cried. "The dancing has only just started."

"I'm sorry. I'm not feeling well." She feigned disappointment, though her cheeks flushed with urgency as she rushed around them to meet Tessie. When they were within distance, she ushered her inside the waiting carriage with Kyran.

"What happened?" Ruby gasped as Kyran closed the carriage door and thumped on the ceiling for it to leave. It launched into action, throwing them back in their seats.

"Nothing, nothing happened. He left." Tessie's heart raged, foggy with confusion and failure. "We achieved nothing." She looked to Kyran whose gaze was fixed on the windows, checking back and forth to see if they were followed.

"What was that back there? What was that whistle?"

Kyran flashed a reassuring glance. "Ruby. We shouldn't have left her out there alone and exposed."

Ruby widened her eyes, oblivious. "I was alright. I didn't see anything at all. In fact, Castor left. They all did. I didn't see them at all." Ruby squeezed Kyran's forearm. "We've gotten out of there safely for now. Let's at least be grateful for that."

Tessie nodded in agreement though her chest flooded

with angst. They had failed. She had not known what to expect but surely it was something better than this. What would become of Finn now? How could she possibly save him?

The carriage violently turned a corner, hurling Ruby against the window. Rushing to help her up, Kyran leaned to the window to inspect their route.

"What is it?" Tessie asked at Kyran's concern expression as he turned back and forth.

"We're going the wrong way."

"What?" Ruby gasped. Turning to get the attention of the driver, Kyran thumped insistently with his fist.

"Stop!" he hollered, though it was useless. Opening the speaker window his expression fell away and Tessie leaned forward to see it was Castor at the helm, driving the horses onward.

"Castor! Stop! Let us out!" Kyran hollered but he didn't answer.

"Castor?" Ruby gasped, the colour draining from her face. "But how? I saw the driver..." her voice trailed away as the reality sunk in. Their carriage had been taken over. The night was not over yet.

CHAPTER 41

The carriage rattled on, racing around corners so that Tessie's stomach flipped at the prospect of toppling sideways.

"We're heading towards the park," Kyran said, and Tessie tried to see as they drew to an abrupt stop. Everything went quiet, and with barely a pause the door opened. It was Arthur, his broad shoulders filling the door frame in his thick overcoat.

"Greetings," he said, his eyes alive and searching. He reached for Ruby. Gripping her by the shoulder and dragging her down, he exposed the knife in his hand. Kyran lunged forward as Arthur pierced the knife through her pearly dress. He thrust it upwards as Ruby screamed and then shoved her back against Kyran whose face convulsed in horrified protest. Ruby's eyes welled up, shiny with panic as blood leeched over her dress and her hands clawed and pressed at the wound, panting to breathe. Arthur closed the door again and was gone.

"No! No!" Kyran hollered.

"Oh my god," Tessie panicked. "We need to stop the

bleeding.' All else forgotten she pulled her cloak off, wrapping it over Ruby's trembling body as Kyran pulled her to him, heart-stricken panic straining his every move.

The door opened again, this time a cloth bag was roughly thrown over Tessie's head, dragging her backwards from the cab. Landing with a thud against the snow, she heard the carriage door slam and the horse's hooves beating against the ground as they raced away. She was alone. Footsteps crunched behind her in the snow and then nothing but her heaving breath.

Wrestling the bag from her head, she scrambled to her knees, her dress dampening on the ground. She was in a snowfield, thick mist obscuring all but a towering line of naked trees. "The park," Tessie gasped, seeing a row of lanterns where the path lay buried and the carriage tracks led away. An icy wind howled across the white fields and somewhere out of sight horses shuffled. Her chest thudded with the urge to run, her eyes fighting to find form in the shadows. Then, stepping out of the fog, a silhouette appeared. It was him.

"What have yer done?" Tessie chattered. "She needs a doctor....she's bleeding..." She wrestled in her twisted skirts to find her footing as Arthur's large frame leant down and lifted her to her feet.

"We won't waste time stuttering," he said. "Let's get this over quick and some of us can get back to the party." She could smell his oakmoss cologne as he shoved her face backwards and she stumbled. "Though my wife may disagree, I couldn't think of a better reason to make our exit. "

"Why have yer done this? Why? If yer were warring with my mother, yer should have kept it between yourselves." Tessie's lips were blue, her hands clasped at her chest in a futile attempt to keep warm.

"I like to win. I do win."

"Sending her my body won't stop her. She's as mad as yer are. Faye died in her arms and it's only made her dig in deeper. She doesn't know how to stop. It will do nothing. This was all for nothing. Nothing!"

Arthur held his stance firm and watched her struggle.

"Yer will let Finn out and leave us alone. Let us get on with our lives, and yer can go back to yours doing whatever madness yer do."

"That's not going to happen, girl."

Staggering back she rummaged in her skirts and ripped the revolver from her petticoats. The cold weight of it quivered in her hands as she pointed it at him. "Are yer so stubborn to listen to reason?"

"Yes," Arthur said, savouring the moment. "Now we are getting somewhere." He took a step toward her. "Let's get to the point."

Gripping the revolver tightly, she jabbed it towards him. "Yer will let him out or I'll kill yer."

"If you kill me he'll never get out."

"If I kill yer, I'll find another way."

Arthur smiled and stepped closer. "I will get what I want, girl."

"What? What do yer want?"

"I want Kyran home where he belongs."

"He'll never come back. Not now. Not after Ruby. Not after everything yer have done."

"Then your man will never see the light of day again."

"I want to kill yer! I'll kill yer!" she screamed, tears glistening in her eyes. "It's what yer deserve for everything yer have done."

Suddenly a male figure rushed from the fog. Tackling her in a mighty blow, she tumbled back. His face grimacing close to hers as he wrestled the gun from her. It was Moses, his eyes dark with rage. A bolt of panic shot through her.

Arthur clapped his hands together as his slow chuckle rolled over them. "Well done, Moses. Well done."

Moses ploughed a quick punch to her side, knocking the wind out of her as he dusted himself off.

"Sorry, sir."

Spluttering for air, she struggled to her feet.

"I didn't want her to shoot you." Moses handed him the gun, then turning back to Tessie he jabbed his finger in her chest. "I told you, you'd be got. You'd be got alright."

"I would have killed yer. I would have!" Tessie screamed and her heart raged.

"It's alright, darlin'. I told you, Crabbes do not die easy. Now," he said. "What am I to do with you?" He scratched his sideburns and sighed as if he could not be bothered with the decision.

"Let me have her, sir. You said I could have her. For Johnny. For my boy."

"So I did, Moses," Arthur sighed. "For your boy."

Tessie's eye's darted back and forth between them, Moses dark with intent, and Arthur cool and cocky. He was calculating, always. He raised the pistol, pointing it towards her as a strangled voice sounded from the fog.

"Mr Crabbe!" a panicked female voice called, followed by a low groan. Arthur's focus on Tessie faltered as he peered blindly into the opaque mist. There was a long stretch of silence and another groan. Then the sound of someone tumbling. "Mr Crabbe!" Was that Cynthia? Tessie strained to see. "He's too cold. He's got to get out of the cold, Artie!"

"What's going on?" Arthur called, and Moses disappeared into the mist to investigate. Tessie looked back and forth from Arthur's straining gaze and the place where the voice came from.

"Who is that?"

"Quiet!" Arthur snapped, taking another step towards the

voice but keeping the pistol firmly on Tessie. "Moses! What is it?"

"Your old man, sir, come quickly."

Arthur lowered the pistol as he took strides towards the voice. Tessie stood frozen. What was happening? She was suddenly standing alone in the fog, all she could do was listen.

"Dad?" she heard Arthur cry out.

"He was having trouble breathing and just keeled over." Tessie heard more thuds and shuffling. Then, "Dad! Dad!" It was Arthur with panic in his voice. Tessie's legs wavered beneath her. Why wasn't she running?

Turning in circles around her, she had no idea which way to go and with her legs trembling, she stumbled forward. Arthur's silhouette appeared through the fog crouched over a body in the snow. It was Otis, limp and unmoving, a carriage obscured in the background with Cynthia leaning out. Beside them, the pistol lay discarded only steps away from her.

She ran for it, but a fist struck her in the head, dropping her to the ground. The weight was on top of her. It was Moses. She could smell the stink of him and she scrambled to untangle herself from his maroon coat as she pulled herself from beneath him.

Her legs were trapped. He was wrapped around them like a vice, clawing his way up her until he straddled her. She had one arm pinned at her side, the other ripping at wherever she could grab him.

"Oh I've waited for this. I've waited for this," he crowed, fighting off her arm and ripping at her skirts below. "This is for Johnny!"

"No!" she screamed. It was not going to end this way. She was not going to end this way. "No!"

With her free hand, she lashed her nails at his eyes,

digging her thumb deep and straight into his eye. Hollering, Moses slapped her face and slunk to the side. She twisted again, pulling free and skidding toward the gun, just as Moses too swooped at the snow and she ploughed into him. His weight tumbled over her, burying the pistol again.

Flailing her arms across the ground in front of them, she scrambled to find it, grasping at everything within reach. If he found the gun first it would all be over.

As he held it up triumphantly, desperation strangled in her throat. He waved it in her face and her chest seized.

"Ah huh!" he boasted, and she dived for the protection of the carriage.

Stumbling for traction on the ice, and landing on her belly, she twisted onto her back reaching for the knife in her stockings. Gripping its handle she launched it with all her strength at the angry figure rounding the carriage. It flew fast and straight, striking him in the chest. He made no sound, though stood frozen with his arm raised, pistol in his hand and eyes fixed on hers. It had stabbed him straight through the heart.

His eyes black and raging, a gurgling sound expelled from his mouth. He fell where he stood.

Her heart thundering, she scrambled to her feet, gasping for icy gulps of breath. His body splayed out, limp in the snow, his dark eyes now empty, he stared only ahead. She grabbed the pistol. On the other side of the carriage, Arthur lay still with his father.

Struggling to scoop the old man up in his arms and get to his feet, he headed towards the carriage. "It'll be alright, Dad. It'll be alright." In the background, Cynthia watched on, her face a gasp and pale even in her haughty makeup.

There stood Tessie, the pistol aimed at Arthur. Cynthia moved deeper in the carriage out of view and called to Arthur. "Get us out of here, Artie. Now!"

"Get out of here." He scolded her. But she could not let him go! What about Finn? What about Ruby? What about Faye! Her trigger finger stiffened. Her mind raced. This was the moment. She had imagined it for so long that now standing cold in the night, the scene spun around her.

"Bring Kyran to me and I'll let your man free. Bring him!" Arthur struggled with the weight of the old man.

Tell Kyran to return to the Angel? That would never happen. Not now. Not ever. She struggled forward, keeping the pistol raised as Arthur turned and lifted Otis into the carriage.

Was there hope for Finn? How could she ever ask Kyran for this? Or should she yet shoot Arthur in the back as he tended to his father?

"I'll let your man free if you bring him. Go now. Bring him!"

The decision rushed at her and raising the pistol into the air, the shot rang out. She screamed, loud and gutsy with everything she wished to expel. She couldn't kill him. She couldn't do it. Even here, this vicious man was Finn's only chance.

Dropping to her knees beside the body of Moses, Arthur leant from the carriage. "Get Kyran to me and there is hope for you yet." Then, thumping his fist on the door, he nodded towards Moses' body laying in the snow. "I'd take his coat if I were you. Ride on!" He thumped the carriage and it whisked him into the fog.

The blood on Tessie's dress told the story as Moses' maroon coat billowed around her and dawn's light spilled over the city. Purple with frostbite, she shivered deep into her bones. She'd let the Angel go, Finn remained in his dark cell and Ruby, she prayed was still holding onto life. How could she look Kyran in the eye and tell him what his father asked of him? Why would he sacrifice himself to save a man he doesn't know? But what else could she do? What would Aileen do? Stage a breakout and storm the watch-house, axe in hand? Tessie slumped with it. She was not her mother and never would be.

Her hands still quivered at the memory of flinging her knife at Moses, and her trigger finger jolted at her empty shot into the air. She was returning with nothing.

Frostbitten and wretched, she turned into Albemarle St, the row of houses not yet awake, lifeless and dark in a collective hush. Kyran's door though was open, a harrowing trail of blood leading along the front path and into the entrance hall.

"Kyran? Ruby?" Tessie's voice cracked. Nobody answered,

but checking the other rooms first, she peered into the library, and there was Ruby stretched out on her back across the chaise-de-lounge, her beautiful dress ripped open. Blood pooled on the carpet below her and pressing urgently at her wound stood Kyran, his face drained of everything but yellow panic. A doctor beside him hurriedly arranged his tools.

"Is she...?" Tessie pushed into the room.

"Tessie!" Kyran gasped. "You're alright?"

"I need to get started," the doctor interjected, rolling his sleeves. Kyran returned his attention to Ruby, clasping her hand tightly.

The doctor eyed Tessie's hands. "She has been out in the cold. She has frostbite. She needs to get warm immediately."

Kyran's eyes flooded. It was too much and Martha, who lingered in the background, rushed forward to take over.

"Come on, miss, up to your room."

"No, I'll stay here." Tessie twisted out of her grasp. "I'll get warm here." She pointed at the sofa in the corner behind the door.

Martha wrapped a throw rug around Tessie's shoulders and ushered the other staff to bring basins of hot water. One was placed for each foot and Tessie let them move her into position, her eyes heavy and raw as she stayed focussed on Ruby and the doctor's solemn expression. Hot stones, warmed in the fire were wrapped in blankets and placed about her as Martha swathed her legs in warm towels. The room was quiet and tense as the doctor worked, Kyran's deep furrowed brow never relenting as he squeezed Ruby's hand.

Tessie watched, her stomach in knots and unable to quiet her mind. Here they all were. She had driven them to this point. It was she who pushed them to go to the ball and confront Arthur. It was the only way, she had said. Her own words stung her cheeks. How foolish and naive she had been.

In the quiet after the doctor left, bloody rags lay scattered on the floor and Ruby reclined on a bed of pillows. Kyran sat faithfully close by on the floor, his head resting on the mattress, completely drained of colour. Her hair was still done up but loose and fraying, pearl earrings still pretty on her ears. All this wealth and it was useless now. It gave them nothing.

Tessie looked down at her blood-stained dress, her wrist still bound with lace where beneath it Finn's leather band still endured. She pulled one of her earrings off and held it in her palm, its shiny hue churning an idea in her belly.

"Kyran?" she whispered to see if he was awake. He moved his head only slightly, and she did not call him again.

Instead, she pulled her feet from the bowls of warm water and unwrapped the cooling towels from her legs. Backing out of the room, she padded up the stairs across the hallway rug.

In her bedroom, Madochée lay sleeping on the bed as she carefully opened the door so as not to wake her. She was not yet ready to see the disappointment on her face. The coin bag her mother had given her was tucked into the bedside table and she tiptoed to the drawer and slid it out. Rifling to count her remaining coins, she shook her head. It was not enough. Shoving the coins back in the bag, she scanned the room.

She did not wish to ask Kyran for money, but she needed more. Dropping her necklace also into the bag, her stomach flipped with indecision. She was sure he would say yes if she were to ask him, but she did not want to steal from him. Anxiety drummed through her. Surely they would understand. Surely they would do the same.

Moving out to the hallway, she slipped into Kyran's study and scanned the desk. Nothing. Quickly ransacking the drawers she found a coin purse, but was it enough? Moving back into the hall and into Ruby's room, she shook her head at herself. How could she be doing this! But seeing a bright jewel on the dresser, she shoved it in her coin bag and scooped up a handful of earrings for good measure.

"I'm sorry," she winced, and ran again from the room.

Wrapping a full-bodied cloak about her to cover her bloodstained dress, Tessie absconded with her bag of cash and jewellery. The bells of St. Paul's rang out and Tessie realised it was Sunday. Who would be at the prison on a Sunday? The do-gooders often went to offer charity after mass with prayers and sometimes bread for the wicked and doomed, but would Finn still even be there? Paying the carriage driver an extra shilling to hurry through the streets, Tessie twisted in her seat to give directions as her stomach flipped with every jolt.

If she could buy his way out, maybe they could leave on a ship before anyone realised they were gone. Kyran and Ruby would be free of her. She would not have to face the pain she had brought them. Or perhaps she and Finn could wreak their havoc on the Angel together. As long as they were together. If she had him back she could even the score. This was her last and only chance to free him. She had to get it right, and she had to do it on her own.

The afternoon sky darkened as they flew through the Clerkenwell district. The looming prison walls peeked at the horizon and the carriage quickly drew to a stop. Throwing money at the driver, she ran to the side of the prison and the small grate where she had spoken to Finn only days ago. "Finn!" she called. Again, a mocking call of voices returned to her. "Finn, are yer here?" She lent low to the grate and peered deep inside, seeing only one man curled into the corner and no others. There weren't there!

Moving back to the front, she located the main entrance and strode towards it, her cloak billowing out, showing glimpses of her bloodied skirts. It drove her on, a hidden strength reminding her what was at stake.

Inside, the cold stone walls skirted around a small room, surprisingly dingy for the large prison about them.

"Who are you here to see?" a voice called from a small room off the entrance.

"Ah." Tessie faltered, grappling for the right words. "Ah, who are yer, sir?"

The man, finishing a mouthful, stuck his head just outside the door. "I'm the person what asks you who you are."

"Right. I'm here to see the warden." Tessie moved closer to see he was a small man with a reedy neck and sense of self-importance.

"You don't gets to see the warden," he said simply, resting his forearm on the door frame above his head. "You get to see me. That's how it works." He wiped his hands on his shirt, his black teeth peeking at her as he spoke.

"Well then you're just the person I want to see." Tessie smiled, turning her body to face him.

"Perhaps I am." He moved his eyes over her in a way she didn't like.

"I'm here to see about getting a prisoner released. Two prisoners in fact."

"I don't handle all that. It's Sunday. Everyone's gone home."

"You're still here," Tessie pressed.

"And I'm abouts to go home."

"Is that your office?" Tessie moved closer, peering into the room behind him. "And through there, is that where the prisoners are?"

"I told you. I don't handle all that."

Tessie raised the bag to his line of sight. "I told yer. I'm here to see about two prisoners being released." The man looked back and forth between Tessie and the bag, and with the pause, Tessie pushed into his office, placing the bag on the table.

Eyeing her suspiciously, he followed. Moving around to his side of the table, he inspected the contents, jingling its coins and jewellery.

"What prisoners?"

"Finn O'Shea and Mickey Bell. "

He pulled out one of the jewelled rings Tessie had tossed inside, and a pang of guilt rippled over her thinking of Ruby, though she brushed it aside. He seemed taken with the goodies she'd brought him.

"Can yer fetch them?"

The man sat down, rummaging in the bag and counting the coins. "Fine," he said, rising and pulling a large ring of keys from his pocket. "Follow me." He indicated they would go through the door on the side.

Tessie's heart surged. It was happening! Had it really been this easy all along?

The man clanged about with the keys to pull the door open, and Tessie filed into the dark hallway on the other side. "Come along," the man encouraged. It was a dark line of cells, the air stifled and stale, heavy with excrement and urine. Water rushed at the edges of the walkway and rats pattered across their path as they walked. There were lanterns, but the prisoners in each cell hung back against the wall and out of the light. She could barely make them out and shuddered to think of Finn in this place.

"Where?" Tessie asked, as they pressed deeper into the belly of the prison. "I think yer should lead the way." She paused to let the man come up the rear. Something wasn't right.

"You go on," he encouraged. "You're almost there."

Coughing on the awful smell, Tessie pressed on further, coming to the last cell in the block. Its gate was open and it was empty.

"There you go, in there," the man coaxed.

Tessie stood her ground. "Where are they?"

He started to chuckle, looking her up and down again with a salacious beam in his eyes. "Your mens ain't even here. But thanks for the bonus, love. That's yours now, in you go..." and he moved to shove her in and close the gate. In a burst of panic, Tessie riled back against him, blocking the gate and kicking him in the belly. Surprised by the force, he stumbled into the walkway and struggled to get up again.

He had played her for a fool and the cruelty of it burned, flooding her in a flash of rage. This wasn't happening again! It wasn't going to fall to pieces in her hands—not again! Pulling the knife from her boot, she rushed at him, ramming him towards the far wall with everything she had. "Yer think to play me and take my coins? You're the fool old man. Where is he?"

The man sputtered, his eyes widened from their beady slits at the shock of it. "He's not here, you stupid bitch. Neither of them are." He craned his neck to look around at anyone or anything that could help him though the prisoners in the other cells howled and called out, relishing the drama as Tessie thrust her blade forward against his neck.

"I'm so sick of vultures like yer who think yer can take what yer want! Yer can't! You hear me! Not anymore. I won't have it. It isn't fair!" She had killed one man that night, she would kill another if she had to, and she glared down at him her eyes wild. "Now what do yer mean they're not here? They were here! I saw them."

"Yes," he coughed, trying to squeeze himself some space to breathe. "They move to the Bailey when their trial is up, daft girl. Don't you know anything? That's where they are."

"And the man he was with?"

"Him too."

Tessie's heart sank and she released her grip, letting him slink back away from her. Finn was at the Bailey. She was too late. She looked up at the other prisoners and the dank cavern around her. This was failure.

"You can take me, darlin'," one of the prisoners taunted, and it sunk like a stone in her belly.

She towered over the wretched man, her boots damp with filthy water, the putrid air filling her lungs. She was going to be sick. Doubling over, she retched up in the corner of the cell, the man watched on, his eyes growing beady and defiant again.

"Shame on you." She spat down at him as she wiped her mouth, and jabbing her knife in his face she leant down and snatched back the bag of coins. "Yer will get what's coming to yer one day. So yer will." Then, taking one last look at him, she ran. Pelting down the long dark corridor, ever fearing that weasel of a man might find the gumption to come after her. Disgust riled up in her throat as she drew in fresh air at the front of the prison. Failure. Again. Another dead end. Again. It smacked her in the face, her eyes raw with it.

She travelled home in silence, the world moving around her in a haze. It might have worked if only she had thought of it earlier. They might have avoided the ball entirely. Staring down at her lap she was so sick of maybes. So fed up with 'if only' and twisting and turning her mind at the possibilities of could they? Should they? And how?

She had pushed against every door. They all had. Opposition didn't work. They would never beat the Angel at his own game. He was simply too strong. There would be no justice. No fairness. And how could they have freedom without those things? How could they tolerate a world so off-kilter? Tessie thought of Finn, of Kyran and Ruby, and her heart was broken.

CHAPTER 44

Ready to collapse on the bed and hide from the world, Tessie opened the door and saw Madochée curled beneath the blankets. The image of her sleeping so perfectly untouched by the night's events brought the smallest comfort. She fell back against the door and just watched. She didn't want to break the moment, to spoil it with the reality of everything outside those walls. Whatever she had achieved, this unexpected girl who had attached herself to the man she loved, was safe and sound. Tessie admired her mass of curls against the white pillow, and her cherub cheeks smug in their sleepiness. Laying beside her, she was the blessing she didn't know she needed. If not for her she might have fallen apart at that very moment.

She thought to change her dress and hide the evidence of blood and the horrible story behind it she would have to tell, though somehow she couldn't move her body. Instead, she left her cloak on, ensuring all signs were hidden. She closed her eyes for a moment's respite.

When Madochée stirred beside her, she touched her

fingers to the single delicate earring still hanging from Tessie's ear. "Did you get him? Is he here?"

Tessie opened her eyes and felt the pain in her chest to speak it out loud. "No. He isn't." She couldn't pretend with Madochée. She was but a child and yet seemed to grasp the futility of it all, perhaps better than any of them.

Madochée sat up in the bed, her wild hair spreading in fantastic disarray. "They are still in the prison?"

"Aye."

"And how will we get them out now?" Her small voice rang out in the quiet room and Tessie reached for her hand, trying to clear her expression of all doubt and fear. "We will find another way," she said, though the words felt flimsy and weak. Madochée bounced to the window and looked out at the wintery scene, her oversized nightdress hanging to her ankles.

"Can we take him some biscuits today. He likes biscuits. He will like those ones."

Tessie didn't have the heart to tell her he had been moved to the Old Bailey and instead joined her by the window. "Let's have a big breakfast. And then we'll make a plan, shall we?" Tessie inflected her tone to be cheery, though the stark contrast of it only added to the tragedy she felt.

"At least he has Mickey, even if no you and no me."

"Aye. We are glad for Mickey," Tessie said without thought. She did not know Mickey Bell, but it was true. She could be glad for him. Glad that Finn was not alone in his cell. Not alone in the reality that she couldn't reach him. She couldn't save him.

"He will always lose everyone. That's what he said."

"Finn said that?"

"Yes. He said that. Everyone. Everyone will lose. Be lost."

It sent an ache through Tessie thinking of him speaking those words. She knew his past. She knew what she had meant to him, as he to her. And she knew his story of absent parents and a missing brother. Of young Tadgh lost in the town square. And now this loss, of their life together, of everything they shared. It was another blow from an unfair life.

Having sent for some hot water, Tessie moved to her dressing table and removed the coin purse from her cloak as Madochée moved around the room in playful morning abandon. Running her fingers over the bag on her lap, she felt a single coin shape that had worked its way into the corner seam. Running her fingers over it, she spun it over inside the thick material. Pulling it out, it was the medallion of St. Brigid—the one that had rested on her mother's bedside table in Dublin. She must have tossed it in the bag all those days ago to travel with her from Dublin across the Irish Sea.

She thought of her own medallion, the one she had left by the river, and the small candle she'd left burning to carry her prayers for Finn. Spinning it over in her hand and rubbing its smooth surface into her palm, she thought of St. Brigid, who was born a slave and found her freedom another way, living her life against the grain of cruelty around her. *How had she been so different?* Tessie wondered.

The Angel had spoken of the language of pain, one she needed to learn how to speak — though she could never speak it well enough to compete with him, nor to compete with the torrent of pain gushing through the world around her. Ruby and Kyran had been right. The fight wasn't worth the cost. It would swallow them up if they continued.

St. Brigid spoke a different language. Tessie's fingers traced the surface of her likeness as she thought of the rage that had burned in her chest since the moment Finn had been taken from her. Everything in her wanted to fight and to rage, to make it fair and just and right. It was justice to want the Angel punished. To make him feel the pain he had caused. That was only fair. Though St. Brigid hadn't raged. She hadn't fought against her enslavers and the injustice of it. At least not in the language of the Angel. Not in the same way. Was it surrender to do anything but fight? Was it acceptance of the inevitable? Tessie couldn't make sense of it. How could they find a way through this without being swallowed up by the injustice of it? She had spoken to Kyran about courage. Not all courage looks the same. Not all of it is violence and anger and fighting to the death. Some courage was quiet.

Tessie's head ached with the puzzle before her and she dug hard at her temples with her thumbs. She knew what Arthur wanted. He wanted Kyran back and her mother's surge against him to end. Tessie's body was his weapon of choice. She had been the solution and his plans too had failed. Kyran wanted nothing more than to be free of his father, free to be with Ruby, and yet his father demanded he be close. And Tessie wanted to live, to have Finn freed and yet she was Arthur's final blow against her mother. Were their needs so opposed to each other? Was there no way for everyone to get what they wanted without annihilating each other? Could she even give up the idea of justice to look at it differently?

Tessie swallowed hard, a faint spark of an idea piercing beneath her chest — a niggling idea, timid in the periphery. It was a plan without justice, without triumph or fairness, without punishment, sweet and satisfying. It was a plan that forced her to let go of the burning rage in her belly. But it would give them survival and freedom. And it would give her Finn. It tingled up inside her, unfamiliar and awkward. So many of her ideas had fizzled into failure. She was exhausted, they all were, and in the room below her Ruby still fought for her life. But it was all she had left to try.

~

DOWNSTAIRS IN THE LIBRARY, Tessie stepped into the quiet room. Changed from her bloody clothes, she felt removed and different from Kyran and Ruby who were still in the throws of last night's attack. Kyran crouched by the mantle jostling aimlessly at the fire with the poker as Ruby slept soundly on the bed.

"Yer should rest, Kyran. Change your clothes and wash. Eat something at least."

"No. I won't leave her."

"Is she...?" Tessie didn't know how to ask, as she peered down at Ruby's serene and pretty face. Kyran dusted his hands and moved over to her, adjusting her blankets. "She woke earlier. She is strong. If she makes it through the next few days the doctor said she has a fighting chance."

That was some hope at least, and Tessie stepped forward to take her hand as Ruby's eyes stirred. "Tess?" she whispered, her consciousness failing.

"I'm here." Tessie squeezed her eyes shut, guilt and angst rippling over her.

"Did you get him?" she whispered, and Tessie crouched beside her, clasping her gentle hand and bowing her head. "Did you get your man?"

Tessie opened her mouth to speak, but nothing came out, instead, it choked in her throat and Ruby had her answer. Ruby raised her limp hand and gently cupped Tessie's cheek. "It's alright, Tess."

"It's not alright. None of it is alright. Not yet." And she shuddered. It was too much to bear. "But I'm trying to make it right, Ruby. Really I am." She leant over and kissed Ruby's forehead. "Maybe one day you'll forgive me."

Kyran's eyes were so full of anguish and Tessie clenched hers shut. The world was off-kilter, askew and all wrong. She moved away, feeling her presence somehow insensitive after all that had happened. How could she dare ask more of them?

Padding softly to the door, Kyran followed her. "Tell me what happened?"

"No, Kyran." How could she even get the words out?

"Is my father..."

"No. He's not dead." She thought about Otis and whether she should tell him about the old man collapsing in the snow. But there was so much to say she didn't know where to start.

"And Finn? Will my father release him?"

Tessie held his gaze. "He said..."

"What?"

"He said he'll release him if you return home."

"Oh." His arms hung at his sides, an empty shell of a man, and she held her breath. They both knew it was not an option, though she saw no resentment in him, no anger as he looked at her.

"I have an idea, Kyran." She took a step towards him, testing the water. "But yer will have to hear me out."

Kyran's shoulders heaved with the effort of contemplating another push forward. "I'm done fighting, Tessie. I can't leave Ruby and there is nothing more I can do."

"I know. Yer were right. Yer were both right. I didn't understand what yer already understood and I will always be wrong for that. But I am not wrong for wanting us to be free. We have been fighting him the wrong way. By opposing, by fighting, we play right into his hands. That is his strength. We have been stuck thinking about what we want and didn't think enough about what he wants."

"I don't care what he wants!" Kyran clenched his fists as he tried to keep his voice hushed. "I just want Ruby to be alright and for him to leave us be. That's all I want. For him to leave us be."

"I didn't want to bring this to yer. But I think I have a way. A way for us both to be free of him. He wants yer to come home, and I'll never ask that of yer. But there might be a way to compromise."

"My father won't compromise." Kyran shook his head.

"For yer he might. Only for yer. Yer are the only thing he wants."

"I can't fight anymore."

"I know." Tessie moved closer, searching out his face. "And I have no right to ask for anything after all that has happened. But I know this has a chance, Kyran. This is different. He will not expect it and it will be our way free. Please. Just trust me." Tessie held out her hand, waiting for Kyran's response. "We must go to him together as brother and sister. Let us go."

CHAPTER 45

Tessie gathered close to Kyran in the empty foyer of Arthur's home. Kyran had led her unseen through a back entrance, where the rooms echoed with emptiness and the chill of unlit fires. There now, at the end of the hall, Arthur's study door was open.

Still wearing his unbuttoned coat from the ball, Arthur flung his tie across the room. He finished the whisky in his glass and set it down. It was quiet. Unbearably so.

Rummaging in his drawers, he placed a bowl of oddly shaped clay marbles on the desk and rolled one, letting it topple onto the hardwood floor. He didn't see them.

"What are you doing?" Kyran finally spoke. He stood neatly dressed, though his complexion was washed out and pale. Tessie stood beside him, her arms folded in a guarded brace. This was her final stand, less grand and extravagant than anything she could have imagined.

"What's it look like?" Arthur rolled another marble and watched it bounce past Kyran and strike Tessie's boot. "Should have run while you had the chance, bloody stupid girl."

"I'm not running without Finn. That's the whole point of this." She heard her Irish lilt roll across the expanse between them, and he pursed his lips as if he was going to respond. Instead, he stood and moved to the window, his frame bulky and heavy. Tessie tried to imagine this place as Kyran's home. This long empty study of Arthur's, a horrible echo chamber. It made Arthur looked small.

"Aren't you going to ask about her?" Kyran shot at Arthur.

Arthur raised his eyebrow in a long pause, seeming to have genuinely forgotten about Ruby. "Yes. How is she?"

"She's not dead if that's what you were hoping."

"Well my pa is. Your grandfather is. She saw him flailing around in the snow, didn't she tell you?"

"She told me."

"He was only out there to deal with you." He narrowed his eyes. "My dad, frail old man—"

"I didn't tell yer to drag him out there," she shot back. "I didn't want to be out there either."

Kyran looked over his father, assessing the statement for truth. "I'm sorry."

"Sorry for me? Or sorry he is dead?"

Kyran seemed unsure himself. "He barely gave me the time of day. I won't miss him."

"He gave no one the time of day. But he was your grandfather."

"And he was your father."

"I know who he was." Arthur stared at his feet and spoke slowly. "My back is covered with the scars to prove it. Scars thicker than fingers." He held his hand up to Tessie as if bragging at the size of them, impressed by the extent of his suffering.

"I know, you've shown me a hundred times."

"Clearly I didn't show you enough, my boy, because you still don't know how good you had it."

Kyran took a deep breath and turned to the window.

"Know what his last words were? Do you?" Arthur gritted his teeth. "Mind my marbles. That from a man who would have died in the snow 20 years ago if it weren't for me. I dragged him up from the cesspool he raised me in when I should have left him in it to drown. I should have left him there in the rot and the rats but I didn't. Because I'm Arthur Crabbe. I'm the Angel of fucking Bishopsgate and my dad doesn't eat with the rats. My dad eats like a bleeding king. A king!" He was talking to himself now, his face flushing red, swinging his arm in front of him with his fists clenched. "And all he bloody cared about were some worthless clay marbles he made himself."

Tessie stepped forward, "This isn't why we're here."

Arthur's cloudy eyes re-focussed, honing in on her. He was drunk. She could see that now. He was heavy with liquor so that his eyes were foggy. But it was not his undoing. He could and would hold his own. He breathed deeply, returning his focus to Kyran, his rant dissipating into the vacuous space. "I know I need to make room — more room, for your set of talents." His voice dropped an octave, returning to business. "Your kind of attributes. I have to learn to diversify—"

"You're never going to stop!" Kyran shouted.

"Stop what?"

"Being you. Being vicious and cruel and..."

"You think I am the one who is vicious and cruel? That is the world, boy. That is not me. That is the way of it."

"Oh my God." Kyran threw his hands to his face in exasperation. "You just can't get it. You'll never get it."

"Life is ugly. Every step of it. Ugly and dark and we stick pretty houses on it." He ripped at his own collar. "We cover our scars with tailor-made suits. But underneath it is all the same. That is not me, boy. That is life!"

Kyran's face flushed. "It doesn't have to be! It doesn't have to be. It can be full of other things. Things that are meaningful and full of life. Full of people. Warmth. What you do is not life. It is not living."

Arthur thumped his fist on the desk. "I did not make the rules!"

"You hurt people. Ruby. You hurt Ruby. My Ruby, gutted like a pig!"

"She put this family at risk, boy. That is my job."

"You made thousands with the information she brought you. For years she did what you asked. Flirting and skirting and weaselling her way into secrets and—"

"She made the decision to go against me. Against us!"

"She warned a friend. Someone she'd come to care about. Is that so punishable?"

"She let herself get too close. That was her mistake."

"It was her job to get close."

"No. It was her job to protect us. That's why she was there. I don't care if she became fond of a Mrs-sister-in-law-and-fucking-such-a-such who cares. She was there for one reason, and one reason only. To protect our interests and she did the opposite."

"I love her! Do you understand? I love her."

Arthur ground his jaw and tossed his fist up in dismissal. "Love isn't real. Blood connects us. Blood! Blood is stronger than love."

"Blood is not enough. It's not enough. It is nothing. Blood connects you too." Kyran pointed towards Tessie. "And yet you have tried to obliterate her. All of this because you and Aileen are stuck in a stranglehold about money."

"It's not about money. It's about control. It's about respect. It's about people Goddamn knowing who you are! Who I am! And I will never let that go."

Kyran pressed his temples and Tessie knew it was

pointless. He was not going to change. "I'm not coming back," he said. "I'm not coming home. You need to let me go."

"I don't know how to do that." Arthur settled back in his chair.

"You need to let me go."

"You are my son."

"Tessie is your daughter." He pointed again.

"I chose you. Do you wish I'd left you with your mother, cowering in a stable? You're my son. My only son."

"I wish I wasn't. All of this. Look at it. Ruby and Tessie and Finn and God knows who else, all of it to get me back and you push me further away. And you can't even see it, can you?"

"I know what is best for you, even if you reject it. Even if you hate it. Even if you despise me for it. I'll not let you go."

Kyran heaved his breath in deep, his chest sunk with it. "Tessie thinks there is another way. It is the only reason I've come here. She has a proposal and you will listen or you will not. But that is what's on the table."

Tessie cleared her throat, stepping into the space thick with family history. It was now or never. She had to make this good.

"Kyran and Ruby..." her voice faded.

"Speak up, darlin!"

"They want their own lives. They want to be free."

"So he keeps saying." Arthur cut his eyes.

"And you want to expand your business. The legitimate side of it."

"I love a girl who tells me what I want." He leaned forward on the desk, a wry expression inviting the challenge.

"Kyran is perfect for this. He and Ruby will go to America. To Boston, to establish another branch of your shipping company."

Arthur stood up abruptly, knocking another marble

rolling from the bowl onto the floor as he moved to the front of the desk and perched on its corner. He folded his arms and stared hard at Tessie.

"They'll be independent. They'll run it as they please. But they'll still be attached to your business, under your umbrella company. You will know where they are. They'll—"

Arthur raised his arm up to stop her talking more. "Enough." He stepped towards Kyran who had turned away and faced the garden. Tessie watched Arthur's sharp blue eyes searching him out. How different they were, these men of the same blood. Their dispositions and outlook, and what beat within their chests.

Tessie stood back, afraid to breathe lest she nudge Arthur in the wrong direction. What was he thinking? Why was he taking so long to answer? His brow lowered and a slow nod rocked him back and forth as he tucked his hands into his waistcoat.

"You'll agree to this?" he asked plainly, eyes still locked intently on Kyran. Tessie thought she saw something in Arthur's eyes. It wasn't admiration. Perhaps too faint and shadowed to have the name of love. But it was there, a spark of yearning. Something from a father to his son. Tessie blinked as if it couldn't be true. Kyran was the chink in Arthur's armour.

Clearing his throat, Kyran nodded. "If Ruby pulls through, and you should pray that she does, she will never be in the same room as you again. She will never look upon your face. But you'll know where I am. You can write to me. We will stay in communication."

"I can write to you." The sarcasm rippled over Arthur's expression though he swallowed it down, prickly and hard. "Fine. You will go to Boston." He slit his eyes, though nodded in agreement and stretched. "If that's what you want, that's what we'll do."

Kyran squared his shoulders. "This is real. This is what's on offer."

"I say go. Good luck to you there."

Tessie breathed out a hefty sigh of relief as Kyran glanced back at her and they shared a moment of appeasement. He had agreed!

Arthur returned to his place behind the desk and turned his eyes on Tessie. "And what about your mother?"

Tessie shook her head, startled. "What about her?"

"If I let you go, what do I have left to throw at her?" Arthur tucked his hands behind his back, watching the challenge wash over her.

"You said if I brought Kyran to you, you would have Finn released."

Kyran glared at his father, daring him to retract his word as Arthur scratched his goatee, his blue eyes shining.

"And still I might. Though I never said anything about you, girl."

"You will stop this!" Kyran boomed. Though Arthur held his hand up to silence him.

"Your mother remains a problem. Letting you and Finn go gives me nothing. I need her gone. Dead. Dealt with. My father for your mother. That's a fair swap is it not?"

Tessie's eyes searched the room, struggling for an answer. "My mother fights her own battles. She can take care of herself."

"You're not listening. I'm laying her life on you, girl. Your choice. Yours. You tell me what to do about it. What is her life worth to you?"

Tessie looked back and forth between him and Kyran trying to understand. What was he looking for? What was he after? Kyran looked to the ceiling, and she could see he understood what she did not. This was what he did. It was how he kept them drawn in. Tangled, never quite free of him.

"He's tried to kill her but he can't. It's dragging out too long. Costing time and money. You can get close to her. He wants you to take care of it for him."

She threw her arms up. "I'm not going to kill her!"

"He wants you to stop her. Get her out of his way." Kyran stuffed his hands in his pockets and hung his head, thinking hard on it.

"See, I tell you it's a world of violence and pain and you say it can be different. If she can find another way to do it, I'm right fucking ears." Arthur plucked his goatee and rolled his knuckles. "She's in the midst of her death rattle. The last dying breaths of the late and great Aileen Fisher, a woman who was once something to shudder at. The Black Bonnet of Dublin. Something to behold. And I'll get to her if it don't take a minute. But the woman doesn't know when to walk."

"And I'm to convince her to walk away? She'll never do it!" Tessie's nerves thundered through her. Her mother, stubborn and staunch, fighter to the end. Her Dublin, she'd called it. Her streets. How was she to save a woman who didn't want to be saved? A woman who had thrust her away, again and again. Was it even her place to try?

"It'll be done, girl, one way or another. I'll push on the bloody way, my way, the way that works, with knives and hatchets, and she'll be strung up and gutted, hacked to pieces. An end befitting a woman like her. Unless you find another way. The choice is yours, darlin'."

Tessie's eyes flared, her mind reeling. "But releasing Finn now is the deal." She moved forward. "Say you'll release him and the rest will come."

essie and Madochée furiously paced the parlour on Albemarle Street. She had set out a platter of candied fruits and custards to occupy Madochée, though they both sat glued to the windows, their insides a burst of flutters and tingles.

"Why are they taking so long?" Madochée cried.

Tessie mirrored her agonising impatience. "I don't know." It had been hours now since she had left Kyran with Arthur as they moved to the Old Bailey. She had demanded to go with them, though Arthur insisted on taking care of his business affairs without a flighty female overseeing him in public. She had reluctantly acquiesced, allowing Kyran the role of bringing Finn and Mickey back to Albemarle Street. Though now her suspicions had roused. Madochée was right. It was taking too long. Had Arthur double-crossed them already? Had he done something to Kyran? Whatever could be blocking them now?

She and Madochée had paced the span of that parlour more than a hundred times, their feet weary with tapping and nervous fidgeting. They could barely sit down to save the butterflies in their stomachs. Tessie couldn't bear it another moment, and taking up her cloak, she made for the door. "Something must have happened. I'm going to the Bailey to find them."

"There they are!" Madochée squealed and surely enough as Tessie ripped open the door, Kyran's carriage drew by the gate. She saw Finn's loping frame lean out of the cab before it even drew to a stop and her feet ran without her into the cold. Flinging herself against him, his long arms wrapped around her and pulled her tight, locking them in the warmest of embraces.

"I'm here, *mo chara*. I'm here." Dropping to their knees in the snow, Finn held her face out in front of him, his eyes shiny with emotion and his face still puffy with bruises. His lopsided grin peered out from under his long fringe, in the way it had always done.

Tears sprung in Tessie's eyes as she pressed against him, ignoring the grime and stench that filled his clothes. "I must be dreaming. I must," she cried. He was here! He was real! She could scream with the perfect ache of it all. How she had longed to hold him, to wrap herself around him, to have them both safe and sound.

Beside her Madochée danced about them, wrapping her arms around Finn's neck. Mickey whisked her up high on his shoulders. It was a celebration surging with relief, an outpouring of all their pent-up angst and grief, of all their days apart.

"What have they done to yer?" Tessie said pulling back to see the sight of him dark with grime.

"Nothing a bath won't fix." He smiled and pressed his lips to her forehead. "Yer gonna need one too because I can't let yer go."

Madochée held her nose though her grin was ear to ear. "Pew, you both stink!"

TESSIE SAT DRAPED over the side of the tub wearing only her petticoat as Finn lay back in the now murky brown water. Playfully splashing his chest, he relaxed, staring up at the ceiling. They were quiet, basking in each others company, their eyes warm and alight with affection and joy.

A bang sounded at the door. "Are you finished? Hurry up." It was Madochée, kicking her boots impatiently. "Mickey wants to play whist."

Tessie laughed and covered her mouth.

"I'll be out soon, Mado. Yer two go ahead." They waited as her reluctant footsteps moved away.

"Yer have a dedicated little admirer there."

"Aye." He ran his hand over his wet hair. "I'm glad she's alright."

Seeing the dark purple scar at the base of Tessie's neck, he traced his finger over it. "Does it hurt?"

"Not that one no, but this one." She pointed to her side. "This one aches sometimes, or feels weird if I bend a certain way, that's all. It's not those scars I'm worried about."

"You've been through so much." He touched her chin and then, as if stolen away in his thoughts, he turned back to the water and splashed it over his face and hair. She could see something of a shadow on him. "I wanted to be the one to make this right. I wanted to be the one to save yer. That night..." he spoke of the Nichol. "That night I should have been stronger. I should have never let us go back to the room."

"That is nonsense." Tessie tried to tease away the seriousness of it, though it stuck in his eyes. "It was I who stopped us from running in the night, remember." Though Finn shook his head and held his large hands out in front of him.

"These hands can't keep no one safe. I can't hold yer tight enough, or long enough to guard yer from the world. Just like Tadhg, I might turn around and yer will be gone to me forever."

"Tadhg were not yer fault. Neither was this. And I'd do what I did to get yer back a million times over if it meant we'd be here together."

"I should have done better, Tess. I left yer to fight all on yer own."

"And I left yer to fight on yer own. And we did it. We both did. We both fought to get back to each other."

Finn lifted his eyes and her heart ached at the weight she could see upon him. "Yer can't carry that, Finn. Yer mustn't. Yer can't fight the world all on yer own. If I've learnt anything it's that. Yer can't guard against every possible wild it's gonna throw at us. It's being here that counts. Being here when it hits. Because it will hit and it will hit again. And we'll both be here to take the blows and we will always find each other." Tessie reached into the water and took his hand, pulling it to her chest. "Promise me that and that is enough."

He pulled her close, kissing her tenderly. They were together in this moment, against all the odds. Here and now. The warmth of it surged through them, all their time apart, their moments of grief, shuddering heartbreak and terror, and the longing to go back to the beginning, to when it was simple, to when it was just them.

Stepping out of the tub, Finn lifted Tessie to his chest. "You're all wet," she cried, as he splashed water over her petticoats and collapsed with her on the bed.

"I don't care."

He kissed her again, and breath upon breath, they reached for each other. They were home.

CHAPTER 47

In the library, Kyran crouched by the mantle jostling at the fire as Ruby behind him slept with a book open on her chest.

Tessie moved quietly into the room. "How is she?"

"She was awake earlier. She is doing better."

"Have yer told her about America?"

"Not yet. But she will be happy enough to be away from this place. To have a fresh start. And to never have to see or think of him again. The rest I will deal with."

Kyran dusted his hands and moved over to Ruby, adjusting her blankets and moving her book to the side table. Tessie looked guiltily at her hands. "I owe yer both so much."

"No. You don't. All of this happened because of my father. It was him, Tessie. And if I had been stronger to end this earlier, to do something, anything, things might have been different for all of us."

"Yer did do something, Kyran. Yer stepped in and saved Ruby. Yer stepped in to help me when yer didn't have to. Yer showed great courage. I'm the one who pushed it this far. I insisted on going to the ball. And there is something else."

She stepped forward and held out the small coin purse she had taken from his study and the jewellery from Ruby's bedroom.

"What is that?"

Blushing, she tugged at her sleeves. "While yer were here with Ruby, I returned to the prison to bribe the jailers for his release. I didn't have enough and I didn't wish to involve yer so I took some cash and a ring. We didn't use it and I'm so very sorry. After yer opened your home to me. It's all I could think of—"

Kyran held his hand up and shook his head. "None of that matters now. We all do things when we're backed into a corner. We defend ourselves any way we can, trying to feel safe. To protect what and who we love. I understand. I hold none of it against you. It was not your doing."

Tessie looked him over affectionately, his blonde hair and brown eyes striking in the firelight as he watched over Ruby. He was a stronger man than he realised. Not everyone could arise so unscathed and without bitterness from such an ordeal.

"I hope yer know what yer mean to me, Kyran. What yer have meant to us in this."

From the front parlour, Mickey and Madochée's jovial tones floated into the room as they played their card games. "It's good to have voices in the house." Kyran shoved his hands in his pockets. "It's good for her to hear laughter."

"Aye. It is good for us all."

"And Finn. How is Finn?"

Tessie's blue eyes sparkled as she answered. "He's well. He's fine." Even spoken from her own mouth, the words were a wash of warmth and relief. It was the truth. He was upstairs this very moment, and he was alright. They both were.

"And you have another venture in front of you. To

Dublin. Have you told him?" He spoke of her deal with the Angel and Tessie turned back to the fire.

"I haven't. That can wait a little longer." There was no room for that yet. She wanted to hold this moment for as long as she could, untouched and perfect.

Ascending the staircase in the foyer, the chatter of Madochée and Mickey enveloped her, soft laughter and her small Haitian accent rising through the quiet house. Looking upward to the landing, Finn's tall frame leant over the dresser in her room. Smelling the array of perfume bottles, he scrunched his nose at the pungent smell before moving on to sample the next.

Her chest swelled for the jumbled band of strangers gathered in this terrace home on Albemarle Street. They had survived, carrying the scars of the Angel and of life and loss, though somehow persisting in warmth and safety. Perhaps it was only relief. A moment of respite. Or perhaps it was hope that after everything they might make something of it all together. They had made it this far. They had linked arms, woven their strengths and their struggles into one hearth. What would become of them now?

Taking a deep breath, she ran her hand up the bannister, her feet scuffing the tufted teal rug as she joined Finn on the landing.

Charged with the impossible task of convincing her mother, the Black Bonnet, to step aside or accept her fate, Tessie and Finn are drawn into the battle raging for Dublin's underground.

While Tessie tries to force her mother's hand, Finn and Mickey confront their past, as a deadly showdown between the Angel of Bishopsgate and the Black Bonnet brews on the horizon.

Can Tessie and Finn survive the inevitable clash of foes, or will Dublin's murky clutches drag them ever deeper and further from their dream?

Available Now!

THANK YOU!

The greatest gift you can give an author - is a review!

If you enjoyed this book, please leave a review for fellow readers wherever you made your purchase.